HO HO HOMICIDE

"What's going on?" Stan asked.

Tony shook his head, his face grim. "Something's wrong with Santa."

They both looked at the sleigh. Stan caught a glimpse of the bright red coat from the Santa costume, but Santa himself wasn't budging.

"Is that why you did the lighting so fast?" Stan asked.

Tony nodded. "Amara jumped out and let us know there was a problem. We didn't want to call attention to it in front of all the children." He looked at the crowd still dispersing. There were a few people hanging around, still hoping for a glimpse of the elusive Santa Claus. "So we got him out of everyone's line of sight and lit the tree."

Stan looked at the unmoving red blob in the sleigh, then her eyes traveled to where Amara stood a few feet away from the crowd, looking ill. Ted Brahm spoke quietly to her. "Are you sure something's wrong and this isn't some kind of joke? I mean, doesn't Seamus like pranks?" She'd heard all about Seamus McGee's unique sense of humor. His family enjoyed telling the tales.

"If this is a prank, it's a really good one," Tony said. "Because when I felt for a pulse, I couldn't find one . . ."

Books by Liz Mugavero

KNEADING TO DIE

A BISCUIT, A CASKET

THE ICING ON THE CORPSE

MURDER MOST FINICKY

CUSTOM BAKED MURDER

PURRING AROUND THE CHRISTMAS TREE

Published by Kensington Publishing Corporation

PURRING AROUND THE CHRISTMAS TREE

LIZ MUGAVERO

KENSINGTON PUBLISHING
www.kensingtonbooks.com

KENSINGTON BOOKS are published by

Kensington Publishing Corp.
119 West 40th Street
New York, NY 10018

All Kensington titles, imprints, and distributed lines are available at special quantity discounts for bulk purchases for sales promotion, premiums, fund-raising, educational, or institutional use.

Special book excerpts or customized printings can also be created to fit specific needs. For details, write or phone the office of the Kensington Sales Manager: Attn.: Sales Department. Kensington Publishing Corp., 119 West 40th Street, New York, NY 10018. Phone: 1-800-221-2647.

First Printing: October 2017
ISBN-13: 978-1-4967-0021-6
ISBN-10: 1-4967-0021-X

eISBN-13: 978-1-4967-0022-3
eISBN-10: 1-4967-002-8

10 9 8 7 6 5 4 3 2 1

Printed in the United States of America

For the Wicked Cozy Authors—my partners in crime, sisters and the best friends a girl could ask for.

Chapter One

The whole night could've been straight from a Norman Rockwell painting, if only Santa hadn't dropped dead in his sleigh as he rode up to light the Frog Ledge Christmas tree.

Before that happened, it had been almost magical. The kind of holiday scene from a movie or TV show. A few inches of snow set the scene for the picturesque Connecticut town, adding just enough atmosphere without making it difficult to get around. White holiday lights framed the green and continued down Main Street, illuminating the Christmas wreaths perched atop the streetlights. Children and dogs scrambled through the snow joyously as they often did in the special days preceding Christmas, when snow seemed miraculous rather than a burden.

Townspeople packed the streets, the town green, and the area in front of the library where the town Christmas tree stood, adorned with lights, proudly waiting for the switch to flip. Good cheer permeated the air. The festive mood was contagious, and how could it not be? Christmas carols played from the speakers outside of town hall, and red bows adorned the town center landmarks.

Stan Connor watched the scene with a smile on her nearly-frozen face. It was way too cold to be outdoors—so cold she had her warmest wool pom-pom hat covering her long blond hair and a scarf wrapped around her face—but she still wouldn't miss this night. In years past, the Christmas season had buzzed by her almost without notice as she went about her busy life. She didn't even know if her old town *had* a Christmas celebration like this one, never mind attended one herself and been happy about it.

But in her new town—her new life—everything was different. In Frog Ledge, population barely anyone, residents had an obligation to partake in festivities. And that didn't mean simply Christmas or Halloween. It encompassed lesser-known events like National Dance Like a Chicken Day, and old favorites like Groundhog Day. It was . . . quaint. And usually enjoyable. Stan had moved fairly quickly from thinking it was all weird to jumping in with both feet in the year and a half she'd lived here.

"This is very exciting," the woman next to her said, leaning over so Stan caught a whiff of some fruity perfume. "Isn't it? I'm so proud of my Seamus for doing this every year." Vivian O'Sullivan, affectionately known as Miss Viv around town, had been Seamus McGee's seasonal love interest since the two were in high school some forty-five years ago. Part of the Frog Ledge McGee family—which included Stan's boyfriend, Jake—Seamus only came to town a few times a year, but always at Christmas to take on the starring role as Santa. He spent the rest of his time in Ireland, and quite possibly elsewhere. No one seemed really sure.

Miss Viv adjusted her faux-fur wrap and beamed, squeezing Stan's hand. "Christmas is my favorite time of year."

"It's wonderful," Stan agreed.

Miss Viv nodded, stealing a glance at the woman on the other side of her before sliding a hand through her arm. "Come on, Victoria," she said. "You have to admit this is fun." When she got no response, she winked at Stan. "My sister is such an uptight Yankee."

Victoria O'Sullivan didn't look as enamored as her sister with the scene of small-town Christmas bliss. Maybe she was simply cold, but she seemed incredibly stiff. Her jaw had a set quality to it that conveyed a lack of interest in participating in the obligatory small talk that filled a night like this. She had brown hair—clearly a dye job—cut into a severe bob that landed at her chin line. Her short bangs barely touched the middle of her forehead, giving her a stern, substitute teacher look. The wire-rimmed glasses she kept pushing higher on her nose added to the look. Her face was devoid of any makeup.

"It's wonderful," she said, but her tone suggested she'd rather be strung up by her hair on the town green. "I'm going to go get a cup of coffee in the library." She slipped away into the crowd.

Miss Viv—seemingly the polar opposite of her sister with her long, flowing, silver hair, glittery green eyeliner and way too much mascara—shook her head affectionately, watching Victoria carefully make her way across the parking lot. "My poor sister. She's never been one to let herself have much fun. She hates the cold, for one thing. And she's been so down lately. I wish I could help her more."

Stan only knew Miss Viv through small talk, and she didn't know Victoria at all to comment. But since she was basically part of Jake's family, they'd all ended up standing out here together with a front-row view of Santa's arrival—Jake's parents, sisters, cousins, and a gaggle of aunts and uncles who were in town for the annual McGee holiday festivities. Everyone except for Jake, who'd been part of the crew hanging the lights earlier in the day and was now at his pub, McSwigg's, preparing for the onslaught of revelers who'd want a hot Irish coffee to warm their bones after being out in the cold.

And there would be an onslaught, both at the pub and all the local businesses. It was one reason why this tree lighting and holiday stroll was so important, especially as the town had grown and evolved and new businesses had taken root. Folks from neighboring towns who didn't have a holiday celebration like Frog Ledge's would come over to enjoy the evening. The shops in town were open all evening with specials and refreshments. Some, like Stan's new Pawsitively Organic Pet Patisserie, were having extra special activities. She'd timed the grand opening of her new pet bakery to coincide with this weekend. Tonight was her soft opening, and tomorrow was the all-day main event. She couldn't wait.

Stan had asked Santa to come and have his photo taken with the town pets once he was done with his tree lighting duties, and Seamus jovially agreed. Stan had taken full advantage of the advertising opportunities, and she knew many townspeople, including her new-to-town sister, Caitlyn, and her fiancé, were looking forward to bringing their dogs.

But before they could get to that portion of the evening the tree had to be lit, the signature activity signifying the official start of the holiday season. This year, the new planning committee—which included Stan, against her better judgment—wanted to make a splash with Santa's entrance. In the past, he'd arrived on a fire truck.

"*Booooring*." Betty Meany, the executive director of the Frog Ledge Library and new head of the committee, had yawned at the first meeting. "We need to shake things up this year."

So "shaking things up" ultimately translated to creating a custom sleigh for Santa to ride in on. Emmalee Hoffman, a local dairy farmer, came up with the idea. The committee jumped on it. One of Jake's bartenders, who dabbled in woodworking, offered to make the sleigh. Emmalee's new husband, Ted Brahm, volunteered to tow it behind one of his snowmobiles. The plan was to pull the sleigh containing Santa and his elf across the town green as people lined up to watch its arrival, then coast across the street to the town hall and land in front of the tree, where Mayor Tony Falco and Santa would flip the switch together while the Frog Ledge Elementary School choir sang Christmas carols.

But, like most things in life, it didn't go as planned.

Stan missed the first cue, despite her position at the front of the crowd. She'd been busy fixing Scruffy's elf collar, an adornment her schnoodle didn't especially love, but tolerated. So Stan didn't see the exact moment Ted's snowmobile skidded to a stop, perfectly positioning his gorgeous sleigh right next to the mayor so Santa could disembark gracefully and flip the switch. Which meant she didn't see Santa's elf—Amara Leonard, Stan's neighbor and the owner of Frog Ledge's specialty veterinary practice—leap from the sleigh in a panic.

The next thing she saw was the sleigh moving again, this time to a position behind the tree. Then the Christmas carols stopped abruptly and Tony Falco's voice rang out over the intercom system. "Okay, everyone! Three, two, one! Merry Christmas!" Then the tree bloomed bright with white lights, before anyone had even properly prepared for it.

There was a moment's pause while everyone tried to catch up, then a few people cheered, which started a trend. Stan joined in the clapping, but something felt strange.

"Now go walk around town, visit the stores, and get some hot cider to warm up," Tony's voice continued. "We know how cold it is out here. Thanks for celebrating with all of us in Frog Ledge!" The intercom crackled and went silent.

Next to her, Miss Viv frowned. "What's going on? Why didn't Santa come out and greet everyone?"

"I have no idea. That did seem kind of fast." Stan pulled her scarf away from her face and tried to see what was going on with the small crowd around the sleigh, but she couldn't see past the newly lit tree. A couple of people in the crowd were calling for Santa, but their chant wasn't picking up steam. Everyone else had already moved on to the next thing—food and warm beverages, most likely—and were flocking toward the stores and food establishments on Main Street.

Just as Stan started to walk toward the crowd, she saw Tony step away from the group. His cell phone was pressed to his ear. She clearly heard him say, "We need an ambulance at the town hall. For Santa."

Every hair on the back of her neck stood up. She glanced at Miss Viv to see if she'd heard. She hadn't. Her hands nervously tugged on her wrap, eyes scanning the scene in front of her, but she gave no indication she knew anything was wrong.

"I'll be right back," Stan murmured, squeezing her hand, and started toward Tony. Miss Viv nodded anxiously.

She and Scruffy reached Tony just as he'd ended the call. "What's going on?"

He shook his head, his face grim. "Something's wrong with Santa."

They both looked at the sleigh. Stan caught a glimpse of the bright red coat from the Santa costume, but Santa himself wasn't budging.

"Is that why you did the lighting so fast?" Stan asked.

Tony nodded. "Amara jumped out and let us know there was a problem. We didn't want to call attention to it in front of all the children." He looked at the crowd still dispersing. There were a few people hanging around, still hoping for a glimpse of the elusive Santa Claus. "So we got him out of everyone's line of sight and lit the tree."

Stan looked at the unmoving red blob in the sleigh, then her eyes traveled to where Amara stood a few feet away from the crowd, looking ill. Ted Brahm spoke quietly to her. "Are you sure something's wrong and this isn't some kind of joke? I mean, doesn't Seamus like pranks?" She'd heard all about Seamus McGee's unique sense of humor. His family enjoyed telling the tales.

"If this is a prank, it's a really good one," Tony said. "Because when I felt for a pulse, I couldn't find one."

Stan gaped at him. "You mean . . ."

"What the heck is going on?"

They both turned as Sergeant Jessie Pasquale, Jake's sister and the town's resident state trooper, rushed up. It had been her night off, so she was dressed in jeans, UGGs and a puffy black parka. Her long red hair was stuffed under a hat. She'd obviously been alerted either by the 911 call, or simply the odd nature of the celebration.

Tony waved helplessly in the direction of the sleigh. Jessie marched over, looking for all the world like she was about to give her uncle a good talking to. Stan held her breath as she watched the scene unfold in slow motion: Jessie reaching in to grab Santa and haul him up by the arm. Amara and Ted watching from a distance, Amara's hands covering her mouth. Everyone held their breath, waiting for his eyes to pop open, shining with amusement. But when Jessie loosened her grasp, Santa simply slid back into the curve of the sleigh, his head flopping forward.

He didn't move at all.

Chapter Two

Stan hadn't realized Miss Viv was next to her until she began to scream, a loud, keening sound that jolted anyone within hearing distance into a state of panic.

"What's wrong with my Seamus?" she cried, grabbing Stan's arm, her long fingernails penetrating Stan's coat to dig into her flesh.

Stan looked around for help before Miss Viv alerted the whole town that there was a serious problem. Liam, Seamus's older son, noticed the commotion and came over. "What's going on? Is everything okay?" He huddled inside a leather jacket that barely looked warm enough for the cold night.

"Can you take her to sit down somewhere?" Stan pointed to a row of folding chairs that had been set up for anyone who couldn't stand for the celebration.

"Viv, come on." Liam slipped his arm around the distraught woman, still looking at Stan with a question. She shook her head. He'd just begun to lead her away when Victoria O'Sullivan appeared, two steaming paper cups in hand. She squinted at them, then looked at her sobbing sister.

"What on earth is going on?" she asked.

"Something's wrong with Seamus," Miss Viv wailed, flinging her arms around her sister. The coffees went flying. Stan felt one batch of the liquid splash down her jeans, luckily not hitting Scruffy in the process. She bent to scoop up her dog while Liam tried to wrangle the two women, his eyes searching Stan's questioningly. She shrugged helplessly.

Jessie waited, lips pressed together, until Liam had gotten them out of sight. Then, cursing under her breath, she reached into the sleigh and yanked the unruly white beard away from Santa's face.

And stopped and stared. "What the . . . ?"

Stan moved to her side and looked down. Her mouth dropped open. She and Jessie looked at each other.

It wasn't Seamus McGee. The man looked vaguely familiar, but Stan couldn't place him. She was also distracted by his black eye, which looked quite fresh. His ashen face and slitted eyes were a sharp contrast to his bright red, jolly Santa suit. There didn't seem to be any life left in him, and he looked even worse against the backdrop of the handcrafted sleigh, such a beautiful work of art. The bench where Santa and his elf, Amara, had sat looked like cherrywood. It still smelled of fresh wood shavings. Brightly wrapped Christmas boxes were scattered on the floor, a stark contrast to the still figure. Stan's stomach turned and she looked away.

Jessie's face went through the range of confusion to relief then back to blank. Trooper Lou Sturgis raced up, speaking into the radio sitting on his shoulder. "Have the ambulance pull up in front of the town hall," he instructed.

Seconds later the ambulance roared to a stop in the street. Members of the crowd began to notice something wasn't right and drifted back to the area, curious. The paramedics unloaded a stretcher. They pushed it up through the snow piles, through the crowd of holiday revelers-turned-gawkers and over to the waiting sleigh. They took over as Jessie stepped back to let them do their job.

"Is this for real? Santa keeled over?" the female EMT asked no one in particular.

"I don't know why anyone would lie about that." Her partner, a bearded guy who looked like he hadn't slept in days, yawned. "That's a big bummer for the holiday season."

Stan's entire body felt chilled, and she knew it didn't have anything to do with the cold weather. She hugged Scruffy tighter against her. Had Santa really died on his way to light the tree? How awful. What a Christmas memory. At least Tony's fast thinking had saved the entire town's children from being completely traumatized.

Jessie came over to Stan. "Did you see that?" she asked. "It wasn't my uncle!"

"Thank God," Stan said. "Cause this guy's not looking too good."

"Yeah, but, what the heck's going on?" Jessie dropped her voice. "My uncle is supposed to be Santa. Not this guy. And how the hell did he end up . . . in this condition, anyway?" She looked at the paramedics bent over the unresponsive man again and shook her head. "Shoot, Harold. I'm sorry."

"Heart attack, maybe?" Stan suggested helpfully. "Harold who?"

"Harold Dewey," said Trooper Lou, coming over to them, his face grim. "And he looks dead."

Jessie didn't respond. The EMTs would be the ones to make that call, but all the evidence pointed to that outcome.

"You think he finally did it?" Lou asked. "Drank himself to death?"

"I heard he was getting sober," Jessie said. "Either way, it's a darn shame. He could be a pain in the rear, but he had a hard life." She watched the paramedics wrestle Harold's body onto the stretcher, then walked over to confer with them.

Stan watched her go, then turned to Tony, who had come up next to her. He looked at her, his lips pressed together, jaw set in a serious line. "I don't know what happened," he said in response to her unasked question. "He . . . was just slumped over. I wish I could've helped him." He looked sad. And in shock. Stan felt sorry for him. She and Tony hadn't gotten off to the best start when he'd come to town. The fact that he'd started dating her mother, and was now engaged to her, hadn't helped much either. But they'd recently come to a new understanding of each other, as well as a mutual respect. He'd certainly had his share of challenges to deal with since taking this job. Challenges one might not expect from such a small town.

Behind them, Trooper Garrett Colby and his K-9, Rosie, slipped into place, a human and canine barrier against the gawkers who were starting to gather. It all seemed surreal— the joy that only a few moments ago had filled the air had now faded into a blanket of sorrow covering the town.

Stan didn't know Harold Dewey, although he looked familiar enough that she must've seen him around. It made her sad, thinking of how he must've been excited to play Santa and make the town happy, and now he wouldn't even be around to see Christmas. She wondered how he'd come to be doing Seamus's job, and getting dead while attempting it.

Jessie came back to stand beside Stan. "You should really stand back with the other civilians," she said, but her voice held no conviction.

"Sure," Stan agreed. "I'll go in a second." She watched as the EMTs wheeled the stretcher away, and sighed before setting Scruffy down. "Is he dead? For sure?"

"For sure," Jessie said.

"What a way to end the evening."

"Tell me about it." Jessie sighed. "You know, this was supposed to be a fun night. My kid was looking forward to this. Heck, Marty was looking forward to this." Marty Thompson, Jessie's boyfriend, was used to their evenings being interrupted by unfortunate events that called Jessie away to work. But Marty's enthusiasm for Jessie's police work kept him from becoming too bothered by it all. "Leave it to this town to have a disaster at Christmas."

Stan, for once, wholeheartedly agreed. How could a night so magical have turned so sour?

"Hey, Jess," Lou called. "Ted wants to know if he should take the sleigh away."

Jessie walked over to join Lou. They conferred briefly. Jessie glanced into the sleigh, then Stan saw her look again. She said something to Lou. He reached into his belt and handed her a glove and a flashlight. She pulled on the glove and shined the flashlight into the sleigh before bending over it. When she stood up, she held a Styrofoam cup in her hand.

Stan frowned, watching carefully. Lou cocked his head, then called to Colby, who came over with a kit. Stan inched closer, hoping to overhear what was going on. Jessie sniffed the cup, then held it out. Colby dropped it into a bag and sealed it.

"I want a test run on that," Stan heard Jessie say. "Just to be safe." Jessie looked up and saw Stan watching her. She broke eye contact and turned back to Lou. "And I need all civilians out of here. Stan, that means you. Go make sure Liam gets Miss Viv out of here. This is an unattended death and we have a job to do."

Chapter Three

Unattended death. It certainly sounded ominous, and a shift in tone from a moment ago. Before Stan could try to get any more info out of Jessie, she heard a shout behind her.

"What in blazes is going on over here?" Char Mackey pushed past Trooper Colby, completely ignoring his attempts to hold her back. She had bulk on her side—she merely brushed him aside like a fly. She'd attempted to tame her big orange hair with a purple scarf, but it had slipped out of place and curls stuck out every which way.

Trooper Lou immediately stepped into her path. "Ms. Mackey. I'm afraid you can't be over here," he said. "Please wait across the street. Stan, can you go with her?"

"Char. Come on," Stan said, reaching for her friend's hand.

"What on earth happened?" Char peered over Trooper Lou's shoulder, which wasn't difficult considering the four-inch platform boots she wore despite the winter weather. "What did y'all do with Santa? I heard he got taken away in an ambulance?" She looked at Stan. "Is Seamus alright?"

"Seamus is fine, as far as I know. He wasn't in the Santa suit." Stan tugged her arm to pull her away. "It was someone else. He got sick. Come on. I'll explain."

"Wait. What do you mean?" Char dug her heels in, refusing to move, her eyes wild. "How could it not be Seamus? Have you seen him?" She spun in a circle, eyes wildly searching the crowd as if he'd pop out at any minute, laughing.

"I haven't seen him," Stan said. "Char, you need to calm down. People are staring." She took Char's arm and turned her away from the curious crowd members who'd heard her outburst and were wondering what the second half of this macabre show would entail.

"I don't care. Have you seen Ray?" There was a frantic note to her voice that Stan had never heard from Char before. Fear started to work its way up her body, chilling her.

"I haven't seen Ray *or* Seamus," Stan said. "Do you need to sit down?"

"No, I do not need to sit down," Char snapped. "I need to find my mysterious vanishing husband!"

"Char." Stan was starting to get worried about her friend's mental state. "What are you talking about? Ray? Vanish? He's the most dependable person I've ever met. I'm sure he's just over at the pub or something."

It was true. In contrast to his gregarious, outgoing wife who hailed from New Orleans, Ray was a simple New Englander who'd lived in Connecticut all his life. He enjoyed spending time with the alpacas on the grounds of their bed-and-breakfast in town, and fixing things around the house for their guests while Char cooked genuine Southern meals and made drinks that would make her ancestors proud. As far as Stan knew, Ray rarely left his wife's side. Stan had bonded with the couple her first weekend in town, and they'd been friends ever since. Ray had quickly become her go-to person too. She'd be surprised if he'd ever let anyone down in his life.

But Char was adamant. "He's not at the pub. He's not anywhere. And his phone is off. He was with Seamus. They went to Boston together last night for their annual poker game and I haven't seen him since."

Stan let that sink in for a moment. Ray was supposed to be with Seamus. Seamus was supposed to be in the Santa suit. The guy in the Santa suit was dead. She looked at her friend carefully. "You're sure his phone is off?"

"Baby doll. It goes straight to voicemail. Trust me, it's off."

Stan pondered that. "Was he supposed to meet you here?"

"Meet me here?" Char snorted. "He was supposed to be home earlier today. Well before it was time for Seamus to dress up as Santa. But they never showed."

And someone else ended up in the Santa suit. Dead. Stan tried to keep her best blank face on. She failed miserably.

"See?" Char said triumphantly. "*You* even think that's odd."

"Kristan! Char! My God, what's happened?"

They both turned to see Stan's mother shoving through the crowd to get to them. Patricia Connor looked shaken, something one didn't see often. Especially her daughters. When she reached Stan, she grabbed her hand. "Have you seen Tony? I was a few minutes late getting here because I was with the caterer. But I heard something terrible happened and I couldn't reach him."

Tony and Patricia were getting married on Christmas Eve. Which was another reason why Stan hoped this was all simply a misunderstanding. Their engagement party had been marred by a murder. Stan didn't think her mother could handle her actual wedding falling to the same fate.

"Tony's right there, Mom." She pointed to where Tony and Trooper Lou huddled together. Probably giving a statement. "Santa . . . got sick in transit," she said.

"You never told me who was in the Santa suit," Char said.

"Harold Dewey," Stan said. "Did you know him?"

Char's eyes widened. "Harold? My goodness, are you sure?"

Stan nodded.

Patricia frowned. "I don't know who that is, but it's terrible, regardless." She turned to Stan. "Please tell me you weren't involved."

"Mom! Jeez. What do you mean, involved? I was here to watch the lighting."

"Don't be defensive. You have a history with these things," Patricia said.

Thanks for reminding me, Stan thought. She gritted her teeth and didn't say anything.

Tony spotted them from where he'd been talking with Trooper Lou and made his way over. "Darling. I'm sorry I couldn't pick up when you called," he said to Patricia, bending down to kiss her cheek. "What a terrible tragedy."

"I just heard. What will happen now?"

"We're trying to keep people from panicking and finding out Santa's fate. The shops are still open, so hopefully most people are preoccupied." He looked at Stan. "I'm sorry. I know you were looking forward to tonight."

Shop. Jeez. Stan had forgotten about her own shop needing to be open. She hoped Brenna had made her way back over there before the commotion began. Brenna McGee, Jake's other sister, worked with her. "You shouldn't be sorry. I feel terrible about Harold. Are you guys going to go home?"

"I think so," Tony said. "If we leave, hopefully the crowd will start to disperse. Plus it's getting cold."

"I'll make us a coffee brandy at home," Patricia said to Tony.

Stan watched them walk away, still amazed at how much her mother had changed over the past few months. She still had moments when she wanted to wring her mother's neck—almost thirty-eight years of not seeing eye-to-eye could hardly be reversed in a few weeks—but this was definitely a kinder, gentler Patricia. She wasn't even minding so much having her in town.

Stan's cell rang as she picked up Scruffy and retreated far enough away from Jessie and her team that she wouldn't be in the way. She fumbled with her glove and finally answered, puzzled when she saw Amara's number. Inadvertently, she glanced over at the spot where Amara had stood a few minutes ago, but she was gone.

"Amara? Are you okay? Where are you?"

"I'm at my house. I asked Jessie to come take my statement here when she's ready. Can you come over? The front door is unlocked." Amara's voice shook. It unnerved Stan. Her Zen-like neighbor had an unshakeable inner peace that Stan had envied from the moment she'd met her. Amara was the quirky neighbor who did yoga out on the green in the summer and invited people over for sage-burning parties to help reinvigorate their chi. She always had a wise outlook and a calming presence. But tonight she sounded absolutely distraught.

Which was even more unsettling.

Chapter Four

"I'll be right there," Stan said, recognizing the urgency in her friend's voice. She turned back to Char. "Listen. Why don't you go to my shop and wait for me. There's coffee and food there. And it's warm. Brenna's there." She tugged her scarf tighter around her neck, realizing for the first time how stinking cold it was to be standing outside. Even Scruffy was starting to shiver under her new wool sweater.

"Fine," Char said. "I'll go in a minute. I want to talk to Jessica first."

Ouch. Using Jessie's full name meant Char wasn't happy with her. And Jessie would be just as unhappy if Char actually called her that.

"Good. I'll see you over there."

"Where are you going?" Char wanted to know.

"To call Jake," Stan lied. She waited until Char had walked away, back toward where Jessie and her team stood, then scurried across the parking lot, past the throngs of people clustered together talking a million miles an hour about what happened—speculation included Santa had gone on a drunken binge before he reported for duty and that he'd died of alcohol poisoning—and wondering out loud if this would ruin the entire holiday season for everyone. Stan shook her head. People never ceased to amaze her.

On her way, she texted Brenna.

Are you at the shop?

Brenna responded immediately.

Yup. Open for business.
Be there soon, Stan texted back.

She hurried down the sidewalk, Scruffy trotting next to her, and crossed the street into Amara's driveway. Before she could ring the bell, the door opened. Vincent, Amara's fiancé, motioned her inside. Gratefully, she stepped into the warm house. They had the heat blasting, which was a relief after being out in the cold for so long. Their golden retriever, Beau, lumbered over to sniff Scruffy, whose tail vibrated with excitement at the potential play-mate. Stan took off her leash and let her enjoy her time with her friend, then turned to Vincent.

"Hey," she said. "What's going on?"

"I'll let Amara tell you." Vince motioned toward the kitchen, where Amara huddled at the table over a mug of tea.

Stan hurried over and sat down across from her friend. "Are you okay?" She squeezed Amara's hand.

"No. Maybe. I have no idea." Amara shook her head. She twisted the mug in a circle on the table, leaving a ring of moisture from the heat. "Stan. Before Jessie comes, I have to tell you something."

"Okay," Stan said, glancing at Vincent. His face was white, his mouth set in a grim line, but he said nothing.

"Santa . . . he was fine until he had the refreshments that were in the headquarters. I swear to God. I know it sounds crazy."

Another chill raced up Stan's spine, despite the cozy temperature in here. She sat back on her heels, her mind racing. She remembered Jessie reaching into the sleigh and picking up the Styrofoam cup, realizing for the first time what had escaped her earlier. Izzy, Stan's good friend and the owner of Izzy Sweet's Sweets, had supplied those refreshments. If something was wrong with them, was Izzy at fault?

"What are you saying?" Stan asked. "Izzy did the refreshments, Amara. Harold could've been feeling sick to begin with and just didn't say anything. I mean, if he had a heart attack or something, you don't get a lot of warning, right?" She looked at Vincent again, encouraging him to agree with her, but he said nothing.

"He seemed fine," Amara said. "He came in wearing his costume and nodded at me. He didn't say much, but there was nothing about him that suggested he wasn't feeling well. We didn't have time to chat. But he was eating the cookies and drinking the cider and lifting things. He seemed perfectly healthy."

"So why would you think it had something to do with the food or the drinks?"

"Because he had a lot of them. Like, two cups of cider before we got in the sleigh, and he brought one with him."

"Did he eat anything?"

"He ate like five cookies. Almost like he hadn't eaten all day or something. And . . . I don't know, it just seemed to hit him all of a sudden when we were driving. And he grabbed his stomach, not his chest. Like he suddenly got massive pains." She sighed and looked at Vincent. "He's more of an expert on this than me."

Stan glanced at him. "You are?"

Vincent shrugged modestly. "I studied a lot of science. Worked in a research lab." He hesitated. "We researched poisons and how fast they would kill certain mammals."

"Sounds like a fun job. But . . ." Stan sat back, trying to process this. "This sounds a little crazy, Amara. Weren't there other people eating and drinking the refreshments too?"

Amara shook her head slowly. "Santa has special refreshments. Don't you remember the committee talking about that from the meetings? They wanted to make sure Izzy did it right this year. I guess he—Seamus—has some weird thing about sharing food with strangers." Stan had a vague memory of an incredibly long conversation about a special carafe of coffee or cider for Santa and some personalized cookies. At some point she'd tuned out.

"He gets his own plate of cookies and his own Crock-Pot of whatever he likes to drink," Amara went on. "Just like the kids would leave him special milk and cookies on Christmas Eve. They had some bottles of water and a small tray of cookies for the elves."

"And you're sure no one else touched his food or drink?" Stan asked.

Amara shrugged. "I can only be sure no one did while I was there. But there was no one from the committee in the room when I got there, so who knows?"

"Are you going to tell Jessie?" Stan asked.

Amara rubbed her temples. "I have to, don't I? But then it looks bad for Izzy. Especially since I haven't seen her at all. She was supposed to meet me there with the refreshments, not just leave them. It was one of the stipulations the museum staff had. You're on the committee, you know this. They wanted someone there at all times while they were letting us use the room, so it wasn't sitting there unlocked to anyone who happened to wander in."

Stan felt her heart sink a little. It was true. The museum people had been adamant about not leaving the room unattended. Why would Izzy blow off her duties like that? It was her food—her reputation—at stake. "We should just ask her, before she hears about this from someone else. You know how fast news travels around here." She pulled out her phone, noticed a text message from Jake she hadn't heard come through. She'd have to get back to him later. "Maybe she got the apples for the cider from a new farm. Maybe they were bad?" She noticed her hands shaking as she hit buttons and knew she was babbling. "And maybe something came up and she had to drop the stuff off early and just forgot to tell you?"

"I guess," Amara said, sounding unconvinced. "But that's not like her."

It wasn't. Izzy took her food very seriously. She'd worked hard to build up her reputation in town and never took for granted any event that got her coffee, chocolates, and pastries in front of a broader audience. Plus, she loved Christmas. It was unlike her to not be in the midst of all the activity. And come to think of it, Stan hadn't caught a glimpse of her friend all night. Earlier she'd been too caught up in the McGee crowd to notice, but now it became painfully obvious.

"I'm calling her." She pressed speed dial two on her phone and waited. Izzy's mobile rang four times on the other end before it went to voicemail. Stan disconnected and tried the café. Jana, one of Izzy's baristas, answered.

"Hey. It's Stan. Izzy around?"

"Hi, Stan." Jana sounded distracted. "She's not. And a ton of people just came in here and they're saying Santa died? What the heck is going on?"

Stan groaned inwardly. Of course the Frog Ledge gossip mill would be out in full force. "Have Izzy call me if you see her?" Without waiting for an answer, she ended the call and looked at Amara. "I have no idea where she would be."

"Maybe the bookstore?" Vincent suggested. "She was distracted with all that, getting ready for her own opening."

"Good thought." Stan nodded, encouraged. "I bet that's where she is. And why she's not picking up." *But still, it's the town Christmas celebration*, a little voice nagged at her. *She wouldn't miss that.*

The doorbell rang. They all looked at each other like it was the Grim Reaper calling. Finally Vince went to open it. Seconds later, he reappeared with Jessie on his heels. Jessie took one look at Stan and shook her head.

"Don't you have a store to run?" she asked.

"It's open," Stan said. "Brenna's there."

Jessie turned to Amara. "Can we talk? Alone," she added.

"Sure," Amara said with as much enthusiasm as if she was going to a root canal. "We can go to my office."

"Great, lead the way," Jessie said.

Amara sent Stan and Vincent a pleading look, then turned and led Jessie out of the room.

Stan watched them go, then turned to Vincent. "What do you think? Is everyone just a little murder crazy lately with . . . all the things that have happened recently?"

Vincent chewed on his lower lip, one hand absently stroking the stubble on his chin. Lately he'd been growing just enough beard to have a perpetual five o'clock shadow. Amara said he thought it made him look more dangerous. "I don't know," he said finally. "I mean, the guy could've died from a heart attack, you're right. Or some other kind of attack. But . . ." He lowered his voice and looked around. "During my research years, I saw some sudden onslaught deaths . . . in the lab animals." He hesitated, watching Stan for a reaction. He knew she hated any kind of research that involved hurting animals. But right now she just wanted to hear his reasoning. "Deaths like what Amara described. And they were usually the result of some fast-acting poison."

Chapter Five

Stan scooped up Scruffy and headed out with a promise to check in on Amara in the morning. She wanted to go by Izzy's bookstore and see if she could track her friend down. She also needed to get to her shop. It was her opening night and she was missing it. She'd waited a long time to get her shop open, and she'd like to actually be there to experience the first night.

She remembered that Izzy had also delivered all the refreshments intended for Stan's soft opening this evening, and was seized by panic. Not that she thought Izzy had done anything, but what if someone had tampered with her food?

She shuddered a bit, thinking of what could be ahead for her friend if Amara was right about the cider. And she needed to talk to Jake. She had no idea if he'd heard yet, but suspected he would have. If people were at Izzy's talking about it, the stories at McSwigg's had to be even more wild given the accompanying alcohol. She felt a headache coming on just thinking about it. Plus, he was looking for her and would worry if he didn't hear from her.

On her way, she called Brenna. "Hey. I'll be there soon."

"Okay. Have you heard anything else? This is crazy!"

"I haven't. But can you put the pastries and drinks Izzy brought out in the kitchen? Don't give them to anyone. And don't have any."

"I couldn't eat anyway. But oh my God. Why?"

"I'll tell you later. Don't worry. Hey, is Izzy there by any chance?"

"Haven't seen her."

Stan hung up and hurried along down the sidewalk. Despite Tony's efforts to make the situation as unnoticeable as possible, the town was in a bit of an uproar. She could feel the hum of energy in the air as people tried to piece together the events of the night and Santa's mistaken identity. Plus the terribly disturbing fact that Santa had died. And there would be the added speculation about Ray Mackey's disappearance, since Char sure as heck wouldn't be quiet about it.

She turned onto Main Street, setting Scruffy down to walk beside her. Of course she felt terrible for Harold, but this had really put a kink in things.

"Stan!"

She turned at the sound of her name, sighing when she saw Cyril Pierce jogging toward her. Frog Ledge's quirky newspaperman was on the story, from the looks of things. Scruffy sat and *woo wooed* at Cyril until he reached them. He bent down to awkwardly pat her head. Cyril wasn't much of a dog person.

"Hey, Cyril. I'm kind of in a hurry."

"I hear you. I'm on a deadline too. Were you there when the sleigh pulled up? Did you see what happened to Harold? Did you know it was Harold instead of Seamus McGee?" Cyril whipped a steno pad out of the pocket of his long black winter coat. Cyril owned two coats—a black trench coat for summer and a warmer, black wool version for winter. It was part of his brand. Tonight, he looked absolutely jazzed. Reporters, Stan had found over the years, were a different kind of animal. They had a strange balance of frenzy for news, no matter how sad or disturbing it was, and empathy for the people affected.

"I didn't know it was Harold until everyone else did. And no, I was there but I didn't see anything."

He looked disappointed. "You didn't? You always have great seats for unattended deaths."

"Thanks for reminding me. Between you and my mother I'm going to get a complex." Stan turned and started walking. Scruffy trotted along beside her, tail wagging.

Cyril fell into step next to them. "Big news week this week, between this, all the controversy around the new restaurant, and the breaking news out of Ireland. I'm going to have to hire more staff soon. Are you interested?"

"No. Thanks. New restaurant? Ireland? What are you talking about, Cyril?"

He looked offended. "You haven't been reading the paper? This is your town, Stan. You of all people, as a freelancer, have a duty to be up on the news."

"Cyril. I wrote one story for you. I'm hardly a regular."

"Well, the offer's always open. And since it's your almost brother-in-law's restaurant proposal causing all the controversy, that would be an even better reason to know. At least about that story."

"Kyle?" Stan stopped and turned to him. Her sister Caitlyn's fiancé, Kyle McLeod, had mentioned wanting to open a vegetarian restaurant in Frog Ledge once they were settled. They'd moved in only a month ago after Caitlyn had fallen in love with the tiny town—much to Stan's surprise—and he was apparently moving full steam ahead. But Stan'd been so busy getting her own shop ready that she hadn't been paying attention to any progress he'd made.

Cyril nodded. "Yep. He filed an application and the zoning board is giving him a hard time. Apparently the owners of the farmland next door don't want a restaurant there. Since they're already getting a bunch of condos, they want nothing to do with it. Of course, you know who the owners are, don't you?" He waggled his bushy, untamed eyebrows at her.

She sighed. "No, Cyril. Since I didn't even know there was a restaurant, I don't know who the owners of the proposed land are."

"The O'Sullivan sisters."

She blanked for a second, then realized who he meant. "Miss Viv and Victoria?"

He nodded. "The very same."

"Really?"

"I wouldn't lie to you. I'm a journalist. We look for the truth." He puffed out his chest a little bit. "Now. Maybe this will cause a rift between the Connors and the McGees?"

"Why on earth would that happen?" Stan asked, exasperated. At the same time, she was also overcome with a sudden urge to giggle at the image of a modern-day Hatfield and McCoy small-town feud.

"Well, you know. You're almost a McGee, and so's Miss Viv. You're also a Connor. There could be problems."

"Cyril. I think we all have bigger problems tonight," Stan said.

"You're right about that. There's way bigger news, at least for a fellow Irish. Have you heard about the Book of Kells?"

Stan frowned. She was familiar with the treasured religious artifact featuring the four gospels of the New Testament—had even seen them once on a trip to Ireland with her dad—but couldn't fathom what they had to do with Cyril. "What about it?"

Cyril face-palmed his forehead. "I expected more from you, Stan Connor."

"Cyril." Stan was slowly losing her patience. "I don't have time for this."

"Someone stole the Book of Kells last week."

"*What?*" It seemed far-fetched. The book was housed at the Trinity College Library in Dublin, which would be hard to break into. Also, the book was really four large volumes, only two of which were on display at a time, which would make it difficult, should a thief get that far. "How is that even possible? And why are you reporting on that? You only do local news."

"I've been picking up Associated Press stories that matter to us out here," he said defensively. "I happen to have personal ties to the Book of Kells."

"You do?"

"My father was a scholar of Irish artifacts. He did a whole series of articles about the book. And, he got to interview the last guy who tried to steal it. While he was in jail. I'm planning to republish his pieces next week."

"Wow. I had no idea. How is your dad doing?"

Cyril's dad, Arthur, had even more newsprint running through his blood than his son, if that were possible. He'd run the *Frog Ledge Holler* for nearly sixty years. Over the past year, he'd been ill and was in an assisted living community.

"You know, this has given him some new life," Cyril said. "He's actually engaged and following the news. I'm wondering if I should ask him to try writing a piece. He thought it could never happen, after the botched theft."

"Well, that's really interesting. I'll look for the articles. I have to run, Cyril."

"I'll walk with you." Cyril was not one to be deterred. "We're going in the same direction."

"I was hoping to find Izzy at the bookstore," Stan said.

Cyril raised an eyebrow. "Ah. Wasn't she supposed to be serving refreshments for the event tonight?" His tone told her he knew exactly that she was supposed to be doing that.

"Yup," Stan said.

He let it go. For the moment. "So any idea where Seamus is?" he asked as they picked up the pace down the street.

Stan sighed. And here was the real reason he wanted to talk to her. "Nope."

"Weren't you with the family?"

Stan sent him a sideways look. "I was. But clearly he wasn't."

"Char is freaking out about Ray being with him," Cyril said. "Have you talked to her?"

"I saw her over at the green. She's upset, but I'm sure there's a good explanation for where those two are," she said, praying it was true. "Cyril, I really have to go. I need to find Izzy and go deal with some stuff at my store."

"Okay." He continued to walk with her.

"Cyril!"

"What?" he asked, offended. "I'm going to my office to file a story."

"Oh." She felt silly now. His office was in the same newly remodeled building as Izzy's bookstore, a building in which Jake and Izzy were business partners. Which meant she and Cyril were heading to the same place.

They walked in silence the rest of the way. When they got there, Cyril unlocked the front door and they stepped into the hallway. One door led to Izzy's bookstore, while a staircase led down to the basement where the *Holler*'s operations were.

Cyril paused in the foyer before heading down to his cave, and nodded at her. "I'll see you soon."

It sounded, unfortunately, like a promise. "See you," Stan said, and tried the door to the bookstore. It was locked, and all was quiet inside. Stan knocked on the door just for kicks, but heard only silence.

Great. Where on earth was her friend?

She turned to leave, almost bumping into Tyler Hoffman rushing in from the street.

"Sorry, Stan! Got to upload my photos," he said, racing by her.

"Hey, Tyler. What photos?"

He paused on the stairs and turned back to her. "You know. From tonight." He had the grace to look sheepish. "I got some shots of Santa in the sleigh. Cyril wants them online pronto."

Tyler, Emmalee Hoffman's son and Ted Brahm's stepson, had taken the job with Cyril over the summer when he returned to Frog Ledge from a stint at a faraway college. He'd been running away from his hometown after the untimely death of his father last year, but had missed it more than he realized. He'd started out photographing council meetings and happy town events, but apparently Cyril had brought him over to the dark side of the news.

"I'm sorry you had to see that," Stan said.

"Yeah." Tyler's face fell. "Harold wasn't a bad guy. When he was drunk he could be kind of a jerk, you know? But when he wasn't drunk he was okay. I felt bad for him. My mom used to let him help out at the farm sometimes."

"Really? So you knew him?"

Tyler nodded. "He was only in town for the fall and winter. Those were the months he could stay at Lester Crookshank's. He had some other gig in the spring and summer."

"Lester? The guy who owns the tree farm?"

Tyler nodded.

Stan knew Lester from last summer, when he'd needed help with some feral cats that were living on his property. She'd helped him trap the cats and get them fixed, then set him up with food and some places where they could sleep. As far as she knew, Lester and the cats were enjoying coexisting. And he'd forever endeared himself to her by caring about them. "So Harold was kind of a seasonal resident. Did he get along with most people?" Stan asked, hoping her questions sounded casual.

"Eh, depends. Not when he was drunk, like I said. And he was kind of drunk a lot. My dad tore into him once when he came to the farm to push cows and was completely plastered."

Stan suddenly felt a strange camaraderie with Harold Dewey. She'd had some experience pushing cows for the Hoffmans too, and in retrospect, being drunk might've made it a better experience. But she'd also known Hal Hoffman, Tyler's dad, a bit before he was killed a year ago, and he'd had his own anger issues.

"Only reason he got to come back was my mom felt sorry for him," Tyler went on. "Anyway, I gotta go post my pictures. See ya, Stan." He clattered the rest of the way down the stairs and into the newspaper offices. The door clicked shut behind him, leaving Stan to wonder if Jessie's and Amara's theories about Harold were true after all. Had Harold made a fatal enemy during one of his drunken binges?

Chapter Six

Stan and Scruffy left the bookstore and hurried a few doors down to McSwigg's. A light snow still flew, glittering in the air as it caught the holiday lights lining the lampposts all along the downtown area. It was wild, really, how welcoming and innocent the town would look to someone just passing through. Someone who had no idea of the fate that had just befallen Santa Claus.

Stan scooped up Scruffy, shoved open the heavy wooden front door, and stepped inside, taking in the familiar smell of beer and comfort food. McSwigg's was jam-packed. Apparently everyone whose plans included holiday strolling had decided to shift that to holiday drinking instead. Especially with the promise of some gossip and a big story. Every table and bar stool was occupied, and people who had no place to sit stood around in small groups holding drinks and talking. Stan scanned the bar area until she spotted Jake. His back was to the door as he searched for a bottle of something on his wall of liquor. She made her way over.

He turned as she reached the bar, his face lighting up when he saw her. "There you are. I tried texting you. Hey,

Scruff." He ruffled the little dog's ears. "What's going on out there? I've been hearing some wild stories."

As usual, she felt better simply looking at him. Despite the long workday, he still looked as good as he had that morning when he'd left the house, aside from the usual wear and tear of the day. He'd tried to tuck his longish hair into a short ponytail, but strands of it escaped. Five o'clock shadow darkened his jawline, and it looked like he'd had a fight with some mustard. His T-shirt had lost.

"Sorry. I know, that's why I came by. There's a lot going on. Can you talk?"

"Let me make this drink. Two minutes. You doing okay?" He deftly mixed up a whiskey sour, added a cherry and lime wedge.

Stan shrugged. "As okay as anyone at the tree lighting, I guess."

Jake finished the drink and presented it to a grateful patron. Then he leaned over and said something to one of his bartenders before motioning Stan to come with. He slung an arm around her shoulders and led her upstairs to his old apartment, where Brenna lived now with her boyfriend, Scott. The place was empty.

"Is Brenna at your shop?" Jake asked, pulling out a chair for Stan at the kitchen table.

She set Scruffy down on the floor and sank into the chair gratefully, realizing how exhausted she was. "She is. I haven't been back there yet. What are you hearing?"

"First of all, tell me what happened."

Stan debriefed him on the events of the night, from the time the sleigh pulled up with an unresponsive Santa, to the surprise unveiling of not-Seamus, to Jessie's suspicions about the cup, and finally Amara's observation about the cider and its effects on Harold. Jake listened to the entire story without a word. When Stan finished, he was silent for nearly a full minute.

"Harold Dewey," he said, his face grim. "I'd hoped it wasn't true."

"You . . . were fond of him?" Stan asked. Given Tyler Hoffman's assessment of the man, she wondered what it was about him Jake had found endearing.

Jake let out a long *whoosh* of air. "Yeah. I was. He wasn't everyone's cup of tea, but I felt bad for him. He worked for me at the pub sometimes, when he was in town. I paid him in drinks, and I threw him a few bucks here and there."

Which Stan figured meant he'd basically been taking care of the guy when he was in town. Same as Emmalee Hoffman, according to Tyler. "I'm sorry," she said softly.

He shrugged. "Me too. He wasn't a bad guy. Just a little adrift, you know? Sort of homeless, just down on his luck." He paused. "Does my sister really buy into this idea that his death was anything other than natural causes?"

"You know your sister, Jake. She's a good cop. I'm sure she'll explore every angle." When had she started to sound like a cop show? "Like I said, she took the cup before Amara said anything. But it could be nothing."

Jake stood up and went to the fridge. He pulled out two bottles of water and handed one to Stan. "So that leaves the big question. Where's my uncle?"

"That's what everyone wants to know," Stan said. "And wherever he is, Ray Mackey is with him. Which is why Char is freaking out. She hasn't heard from him."

Jake's hand stopped halfway to his mouth with the water bottle. "Oh man. I forgot all about Ray."

"Yep. Char was hysterical. Said she hasn't heard from Ray at all and they were supposed to be back this afternoon."

Jake leaned against the counter. "I don't like that."

"Me neither. Do you think . . ." She didn't want to finish the sentence, but it was the natural next question: Did something happen to them that would make them unable to call home? "Although, if Seamus made arrangements for Harold to take his place, he had to have known he'd be tied up, right? But then I wonder why Ray didn't call."

"Ray's not exactly a technology guru. I'd be surprised if the guy knows how to use his cell phone," Jake said.

"That's not a good excuse. I don't know, Jake. It seems irresponsible. And unusual."

"I'm sure there's a good reason. We just have to figure out what it is. Have you seen Liam or Declan?"

Jake's cousins were staying with them for the annual McGee holiday festivities. Jake's parents' house was full of other relatives, and the rest of the crew was at Char's B and B. Jake had figured they were the most normal of the clan to foist on Stan for a few weeks—at least, that's how he'd positioned it to Stan. She thought they were both delightful. And they had those adorable Irish accents, thanks to Seamus moving them to Ireland when they were very young after their mum died.

"I saw Liam. Luckily he was there when Miss Viv realized what was going on. Although we didn't know it wasn't Seamus then. I lost track of them after that."

"Poor Miss Viv." Jake shook his head. "She's such a nice lady."

Stan thought about what Cyril had just told her about Miss Viv and her sister blocking Kyle's restaurant application, but decided not to mention it to Jake right now.

"Listen, you better get over to the shop and get it closed up," Jake said. "I don't want you walking home too late. I'm getting out of here as soon as I can."

Chapter Seven

But when Stan and Scruffy got to the patisserie, they found a full house. Brenna was indeed keeping the shop running. As Stan watched, she presented a doggie cannoli to a Boston terrier, who grunted in anticipation of the treat. In honor of tonight's celebration, she wore her long brown hair in two pigtails garnished with red ribbons. Blinking Christmas lights dangled from her ears. Despite her festive holiday garb, she looked troubled. Scott, her boyfriend, rearranged pet pastries in the case to fill empty spots. He looked even more troubled. Then again, he was the sensitive type, so he often looked troubled. A social worker by trade, Scott was taking a hiatus from his work after a difficult situation with one of his clients a few months back. He hadn't seemed to have recovered yet, either. He'd lost weight, and he looked a bit pale—a switch from his usual outdoorsy, tanned, healthy appearance. Char and Jessie sat at a back table on the human side of the store, deep in conversation. Marty Thompson sat at a nearby table in the pet area with Jessie's daughter, Lily, helping her color a picture. Stan sighed a little at the sight of all this company. Why did Jessie need her place as a command center? She really just wanted to go home.

But she pasted on a smile, pushed open the door, and set Scruffy down. The sweet, spicy scent of hot apple cider filled the room. Normally the smell would make Stan's mouth water, but tonight it made her feel a bit sick. She scanned the counter area anxiously, but Brenna had removed everything. Thank goodness.

"Hey there," she said, lifting her hand in a wave when all eyes turned to her. Scruffy made an excited beeline to all the guests, eager to say hi to everyone.

"I hope you don't mind we're using your shop to talk for a bit," Jessie said, in a tone that indicated she didn't much care if Stan minded.

"Not at all," Stan said. "Talk away. How are you doing, Char?"

Char sniffed and dabbed at her eyes. "My husband's missing and no one will put in a missing persons report." She glared a little at Jessie before her eyes drifted to the cell phone clenched in her hand, probably checking to see if she'd missed a call or message from Ray.

Stan's heart ached for her friend. She'd barely ever seen Char without Ray, even around town.

Jessie, however, looked unfazed. "Char. I told you to stop panicking. You know my uncle as well as I do. They're out carousing."

Now Char stood up, nearly upending the table with her bulk. She thrust her hands on her generous hips. "My Raymond does *not* carouse!"

"Hey, can I get anyone anything? Tea? Coffee?" Stan broke in. Then she remembered refreshments were a no-no tonight. Jessie and Char both looked at her like she'd lost her mind. She threw up her hands. "Fine. Jessie, can I talk to you for a second out back?"

Jessie looked like she was about to argue, but instead

she got up and stalked to the kitchen without a word. Stan raised her eyes to heaven, squeezed Char's arm, and followed, sharing a pained glance with Brenna as she passed the counter.

"What?" Jessie snapped once they'd reached Stan's brand-new kitchen and shut the door. Scott, who'd come into the kitchen and was carefully boxing the specialty doggie Christmas cookies slated for the grand opening, froze. He took one look at Jessie's face, then mumbled something and fled to the café area. He was still a little unsure of how to deal with his girlfriend's fiery sister.

Stan waited until the door closed behind Scott, then turned to Jessie, who looked like she was about to jump out of her skin. "Take it easy on Char. She's worried about her husband."

"Her husband is with my crazy uncle. Anything can happen when Seamus is running the show. Char should know that. Ray's been friends with him forever. Can I go back to my investigation now?"

"What are you investigating if you think they're just out carousing?" Stan pressed.

"Gee, I didn't realize you'd been promoted to lieutenant," Jessie said. When Stan didn't react, she sighed. "I need to know when my uncle commissioned Harold to do his job. So I can figure out who else knew about Harold being in that suit. In case he didn't just die of old age or hard living. You see? Am I done answering questions now?" She started out of the room, then her gaze fell on the tray of pastries Brenna had removed from out front. "Are those from Izzy's?"

Stan nodded.

"Don't touch them. Did anyone eat any of these tonight?"

"I asked Brenna to put them back here."

Jessie reached for her phone. "Lou. Come to Stan's shop. I want the food and drink—the human stuff—tested."

Stan watched her in disbelief. "You can't be serious."

"I'm dead serious. And Harold's just dead. Is there anything else she made?"

Stan shook her head. "I got the main dishes from the new Italian place."

"Make sure Lou gets everything she brought." Without waiting for a response, she pushed through the door and disappeared.

Stan watched her go, then headed back to the café, stopping at the counter. "Thanks for helping, you guys," she said to Scott and Brenna.

"No problem," Brenna said. "What a mess, huh? And I'm so worried about Uncle Seamus."

Scott squeezed her hand. "I'm sure he's fine, Bren."

Brenna watched Char and Jessie resume their conversation. "I hope so."

Across the room, Char started to cry. Stan hurried over and squeezed her friend's hand. "Listen. Ray is okay. I'm sure of it. There's just been some kind of communication breakdown. Right, Jessie?"

Jessie ignored her and focused on Char, waiting for her to gain some control. "So you were about to tell me their plan when we were interrupted."

A fat, fresh tear ran down Char's cheek. "I thought I knew the plan. And Raymond. But apparently I was mistaken."

Jessie's face said she had no time for the added drama, but she maintained her calm. "Let's take it step by step. When did they leave?" she asked.

"Yesterday afternoon."

"And Ray told you where they were going."

"Yes. They were going to their annual Christmas poker game with the group Seamus knows."

"Do you have names of the other players? Or a location?" Jessie asked.

Char shook her head. "It's top secret."

"Okay. Were they doing anything else? Dinner first?" Jessie asked.

"They usually go to the North End for cannoli. It's not an Irish thing, but they'll eat anything. Especially sweets," Char said.

"Cannoli?" Marty's ears perked up from across the room.

"Sorry," Jessie said. "The food's going to the lab."

Marty sat back, deflated.

Jessie ignored him. "What time was the poker game? Did they make it there? Did you hear from Ray after that?"

Char shook her head. "Those games usually go on for so long. I tell him, you go out once a year. Don't spend all your time calling home. Usually he calls once or twice," she added. "But it's not like I was expecting it."

"So did he call?"

"Once. When they were finishing up with dinner last night. He said he'd see me t-today," she said, dissolving into tears again. "If he didn't talk to me again."

"And you haven't heard from them since."

"No." She dabbed at her eyes. "He set up for someone to come in and take care of the alpacas this morning. And I was busy cooking for my guests—the B and B is full, you know, all these people wanting to come for the festivities tonight, and the McGees—and then I went to the library to help Betty set up for the Christmas craft show, and before I knew it, it was time to leave for the tree lighting. And then I realized Raymond hadn't come back. He always came back from these outings in the early afternoon the next day."

"Where were they staying?" Jessie asked.

Char looked blank. "I don't know."

Jessie bit back whatever impatient reply threatened to burst off her tongue and tried for a softer tone. "Well, they had to be staying somewhere, right? Did they stay

with a friend of my uncle's? A hotel? Where do they usually stay?"

Char thought. "I . . . I think last year they stayed at the
Marriott. You know, the fancy one by the water? I remember that because Ray talked about how he wanted to
go to the aquarium, but they never made it." She brightened. "Should we call there?"

Jessie scribbled a note in her pad. "I'll call the Boston
PD and see if they can make an inquiry. So when you
talked to Ray, did he mention Seamus finding a replacement for the Santa gig?"

Char shook her head. "Not a word."

She looked so despondent. Stan wished with all her
heart she knew the right words to help her friend through
this situation. After all the times Char had helped her,
comforted her, Stan felt grossly inadequate.

"Do you think something . . . bad happened to them?"
Char asked, her voice breaking.

Jessie said nothing, so Stan felt compelled to answer.

"Don't worry," she said. "I promise we'll figure it
out."

Chapter Eight

Stan's cell phone chimed in her pocket. She excused herself and rose to check her text messages. Scruffy followed her down the hall into the kitchen. She closed the door behind her and checked her phone, almost swooning with relief when she saw Izzy's name.

Don't want to walk into that crowd. Can you let me in the back?

Stan opened the door a crack and peeked into the hallway. Jessie was still occupied with Char—she could see them at the table. She quietly shut the door again before she unlocked the back exit. Izzy slipped inside, pulling her slouchy hat off her head and shaking her long braids free. In her all-black garb, she reminded Stan of a cat burglar from some trendy Hollywood movie. Izzy Sweet could've been a model without even trying. Her caramel colored skin and trademark head of braids gave her an exotic look. Especially in Frog Ledge, an old, rural farming town where diversity was not the norm. But she'd always held her head high, even with the people who'd been less than welcoming.

"Are you okay? The entire town's looking for you," Stan said, throwing her arms around her friend.

Izzy squeezed her back. "I'm fine. I just had a couple of things to take care of. What the heck is going on, though? What happened to Santa? And why do I have two messages from our esteemed state trooper about my cider?"

Stan glanced over her shoulder at the door, hoping Jessie hadn't realized yet that she'd vanished. "Didn't you hear—Harold's dead?"

Izzy looked blank. "Harold? Who the heck is Harold?"

"Harold Dewey. That's who was in the Santa suit, not Seamus."

Something dark passed over Izzy's face before it cleared again. "Wow. Okay. Haven't seen him in a while. So what happened to him?"

Stan shook her head. "That's the big question. He keeled over during the sleigh ride."

Izzy sucked in a breath. "That's terrible. A heart attack?"

"They don't know how he died yet. Here's the thing, Izzy." She took a deep breath. "Jessie wants to talk to you because Amara was worried about the way Harold died. She saw him drink a couple cups of the cider and almost immediately get sick. And you know Jessie. She's going to look into it."

Izzy's mouth formed an O of surprise. She leaned back against the counter, clearly trying to get her bearings. "What . . . what are you saying, Stan? That my cider was bad and it made him sick?"

"I'm not saying anything. They're worried something like that happened. And when no one could reach you . . ."

"My God." Izzy walked slowly around the kitchen,

tugging at her braids. "That's not possible. It's just not.
I—"

"Izzy. Did you not get my messages?"

They both turned to find Jessie in the doorway, arms
crossed, one foot tapping in annoyance. She'd been
stealth opening that door, for sure.

"I just got them. I was on my way over here anyway,"
Izzy said coolly. "Stan was filling me in."

"I bet," Jessie said, frowning at Stan. "Look, I need to
ask you a few questions about tonight. Do you want to
talk here?"

"If you're asking if Stan can stay, yeah, she can. We
can talk here."

"Fine. You were in charge of refreshments for tonight?"

Izzy nodded.

"What did you provide and where?"

"The main refreshments at my café. Hot cider. A carafe
of hot water for tea. Coffee. And some pastries. Cookies,
mostly. Here, for Stan's place. And at Santa's headquarters.
He gets his own small Crock-Pot of cider and his own
plate. A tradition. There were cookies and bottles of water
for anyone else in there helping him."

Jessie made a couple of notes. "When did you get
everything ready?"

"This afternoon. I like my orders fresh."

"Okay. You made the cider?"

Izzy gave her a strange look. "I poured it into a Crock-
Pot and added mulling spices. I didn't actually make the
cider. I bought it from the Cloverleigh Farm."

"And the coffee?"

"I made the coffee."

The door opened and Lou stuck his head in. "All the
edibles you want bagged—they're all back here?"

"Bagged?" Izzy looked from Jessie to Stan and back
again. "You're taking my food? What on earth for?"

Jessie ignored her. "Yeah. Right there." She pointed at

the counter. Lou nodded and started packing up the food. Jessie turned back to Izzy. "Did you deliver Santa's food to the museum conference room?"

Izzy shook her head slowly. "I couldn't. I sent Jana."

"You gave her the key? Or was the museum staff unlocking the door for you?"

"The staff was supposed to open it for Jana, and then she was supposed to lock it back up until Santa got there."

"Did that happen?"

Izzy lifted her shoulders in a listless shrug. "I wasn't there."

"So the room could've been left unattended."

"It's likely."

"Why didn't you bring the goods? Don't you usually?"

"I had some other things going on," Izzy said evenly, tossing her braids.

"You were at the café the whole time?"

"I was back and forth between the café and the bookstore all day. And I was up in my apartment some. Junior's been sick." Junior was the elderly dog Izzy had adopted last year. Izzy lived above her café in a two-bedroom apartment with Junior and her two other dogs, Baxter and Elvira.

Jessie looked like she wanted to say something else, but she didn't. "Okay. Do you have a number for Jana? I need to talk to her too, since she delivered the food. And I may need to circle back with you."

Izzy frowned. "Hold on a second. Grilling me is one thing, but why do you need to bother Jana?"

"Because it's my job to know everything that happened tonight," Jessie said. "Don't make this difficult, Izzy."

Izzy looked like she might fire back. Stan held her breath. This might not end well.

But Izzy apparently decided to play her cards differently. She folded her arms against her chest and recited a number. Jessie wrote it down.

"You think my food or drinks killed Harold," Izzy said. "Do you know how crazy that is?"

"I'll be in touch," Jessie said, slapping her notebook shut.

"Great. Something to look forward to," Izzy said under her breath.

Jessie shot her a look. "Actually, I do have one more question."

"Hey, why not," Izzy said.

"Did you see Harold since he's been back to town? Before he turned up dead, that is."

Izzy shook her head. "Nope."

"He didn't show up at your café?"

"Not while I was there."

"You didn't speak at all?"

"Not once."

Jessie watched her for what seemed like a long time, then nodded again. "Okay. Thanks." She headed back out to the main room.

Once she was gone, Izzy looked at Stan. "I don't believe this. Do you think they're overreacting? Or do you think something really made him sick?"

"I have no idea," Stan said grimly. "And why did she want to know if you'd seen Harold since he came back to town?"

"Who knows. You know her." Izzy waved it off.

"I guess. And on top of all this, the real Santa is apparently missing. With Ray."

Izzy gaped at her. "Seamus? Missing how?"

"Well, as far as everyone knew, he was supposed to be Santa. Finding out it was Harold was a huge surprise. No one's heard from him. And then Char said Ray was due back from the poker game he and Seamus had gone to, up in Boston, but he never showed and hasn't been in touch."

Izzy leaned against the counter. "That's not like Ray. You can set your clock by Ray. Do you think they're okay?"

"That," Stan said, "is the million-dollar question. Second only to, did Harold Dewey die for some reason other than an illness, and if so, what?"

Chapter Nine

Izzy slipped out the back door the same way she'd come in. Stan didn't feel like going back out into the mix, so she tidied up her kitchen a bit. It was probably wrong to be disappointed about her soft opening night getting derailed, given the fact that someone had lost his life, however it had happened, but she'd be lying to herself if she said she wasn't. She and Brenna had spent a ton of time over the past month planning for this weekend. They'd set up an area within the café where Santa could have his picture taken with the animals. Tyler Hoffman had been on board for the gig, since he was always looking to supplement his meager *Frog Ledge Holler* income. Although he seemed to be swept up in the excitement of a big story instead.

And then tomorrow, they'd planned a whole spread—a catered buffet for customers provided by the new Italian restaurant in town, and special signature Christmas treats for the pets. They'd held a contest in the weeks leading up to the grand opening. Residents who submitted Christmas photos of their animals for the patisserie's new website would have their pets' names entered for a chance to win a signature treat named after them. Miss Viv's little Pomeranian, Chuckie, had been chosen for this round of dog treats, while Betty Meany's cat, Houdini, won on the cat side. Stan still planned to open tomorrow and feature Chuckie's Christmas Cookies and Houdini's Holly Jolly Catnolis, since she and Brenna had made them all today, but it wasn't the same. She couldn't in good conscience, out of respect for the dead man, hold an official grand opening celebration. She'd just have to reschedule.

Which meant more work and double the bills. With a big sigh, she leaned against the counter and looked around. For just a moment, she allowed her pride in the shop to bubble up, despite the drama playing out around her. Though it pained her to admit it, her mother's recommendations had all been right on. The marble countertops, the double oven, the extra counter space, had all turned what could have been a lackluster room into a place in which Stan loved to spend time on her creations. She wished tonight had been spent baking and planning recipes rather than running around in the middle of this chaos.

If this was a murder, she might need to heed her best friend Nikki's warning from a few months ago and go see a psychic or someone who could clear her energy. Seemed like these days, every time a momentous occasion was on track to occur in her life, someone was killed.

She was starting to get a complex.

Brenna stuck her head in. "Hey. Need help back here?"

"Hey, Bren. No, just trying to stay out of Jessie's way. What's going on out there?"

"Jessie just left and took Char home." Brenna came all the way in and closed the door behind her. "Marty and Lily went home, and Scott's waiting for me." She twisted a chunk of long brown hair around her finger. Her eyes were dark with worry. "I can't even wrap my head around this night. Why did Jessie take the food? And I've been calling my uncle's phone nonstop. He's not answering."

"I'm sorry, Bren. We'll figure this out. Jessie's just being cautious, I think. As for your uncle, there has to be a good explanation. Maybe the game just ran long. Doesn't that happen sometimes with these really serious card people?" It sounded lame to her own ears. Plus, despite Seamus's propensity to be flighty, Ray didn't strike her as the type who would forget everything if a card game got too intense.

The kitchen door swung open again. This time it was Jake. Thank goodness. Stan always felt better when he was around. He crossed the room and gave her a big hug, then did the same to his sister. "I heard you didn't make it home yet," he said to Stan. "How are you guys doing?"

"Bad," Brenna blurted out. "I'm so worried about Uncle Seamus!"

"I know. But let's not worry yet," Jake said. "He may waltz back into town any minute and have no idea what all the fuss was about." He looked at Stan. "Holding up?"

"I am. Just trying to put this place in order. I have no idea what I'm going to do with all the food for tomorrow." Stan blew out a breath and shoved at the hair falling out of her ponytail. "Maybe I'll just put it out anyway. Otherwise it will go to waste."

"Good idea. Keep things as normal as possible. Look. It's been a really long day. Why don't we all go home?"

"Will you call me if you hear anything?" Brenna asked.

"Of course."

Once she'd gone, Jake turned to Stan. "Actually, let's bring some of the food you ordered back to the house for Liam and Declan. I'm not sure if anyone will feel like eating, but if they do it'll be there."

"Okay. They took all the pastries. Everything Izzy made."

Jake arched an eyebrow. "Really."

"Jessie's got this crazy notion that Izzy's cider killed Harold." She pulled a tray of pasta and another one of salad out of the fridge. Jake grabbed another one of some kind of chicken. They loaded the food, along with Scruffy, into Jake's truck and headed home. But when they drove past the Frog Ledge Museum, Stan sat up straight. Two police cars were parked out front.

"Can you pull over?" she asked Jake.

"Stan. You know Jessie won't want anyone here."

"No, I'm on the committee," Stan said. "She probably needs someone who can walk her through how this was supposed to work. Please?"

Reluctantly, he pulled into the parking lot. "Fine, but I'm not responsible when she tosses you out."

They walked around to the back conference room where Santa's headquarters had been set up earlier in the night. Jessie, Lou, and Colby were inside. Stan rapped on the door. They all turned. Jessie said something, and Colby came to the door.

"Hey," he said, somewhat apologetically. "Jessie—uh, Sergeant Pasquale doesn't think—"

"It's okay," Stan said, pushing past him. The room had been transformed from a conference room with a large table and chairs to a Christmas scene, with multicolored lights strung around the perimeter of the room, a Christmas tree in the corner with presents stacked underneath, and ornaments hanging strategically from the ceiling. Santa would've spent time back here after the ceremony, meeting kids and noting Christmas wishes. "Jess. I figured you needed someone from the committee to walk you through how this night was supposed to work. Right? I bet you forgot I was on the committee."

"Hey, that's perfect," Lou said to Jessie. "You were just saying you needed to talk to Betty and couldn't find her."

Jessie shot him a look. He turned away and pulled out his fingerprint kit. Stan felt a knot form in her belly. Fingerprints. Serious stuff.

Meanwhile, Jessie looked unhappy to admit that Stan was right. "It would be helpful to speak to someone who set this up, sure. And Lou's right. I couldn't track Betty down, so I guess I'll have to go with you."

Jake chuckled. "Jess. You have such a way with people."

Jessie ignored her brother. "So tell me how you guys ended up having this here. This was the first time, right? Santa's headquarters used to be in the library."

Stan thought back to the last committee meeting on the tree lighting. She hadn't been too involved in that part of the evening—her piece had more to do with the actual stroll and working with the other merchants—but she vaguely remembered Betty gleefully cooking up the sleigh ride with Ted and his snowmobile, and determining that they needed a new place for Santa to wait in order to create that dramatic effect they were after. She nodded. "This was the first year of the sleigh ride. They needed a place where Santa could hang out before the sleigh ride, but it had to be close enough that they could load him up and go when it was time. So Ginny Featherstone offered up this room." Ginny ran the programs and events department at the museum. "They gave us full access but wanted someone from the committee here at all times."

"But that sounds like it didn't happen. Because Izzy had things to do," Jessie said, using air quotes. "So she sent the other girl."

"She told you she had a good reason," Stan defended her. "Junior was sick. She's been trying to run a business, be on this committee, and get another business ready to open. Cut her a break, Jessie."

"Mm-hmm. So anyone who knew the room was going to be used could've figured out that it was open and un-monitored if they were in the area. Which is basically the whole committee."

"Pretty much, yes." Stan sighed. "Not helpful, huh?"

"Not even a little. Remind me again who was on the committee?"

"Me. Betty. Izzy." Stan listed the rest of the names that she could remember—twelve in all—then thought for a minute. "I think that's it."

They watched Lou dust the two Crock-Pots of cider. One was clearly marked *For Santa* with a smiley face and a little Christmas tree drawn on the note.

Stan was silent for a minute. "Hey, Jess?"

"What?"

"You really think someone poisoned Harold?"

"We'll see what the toxicology reports say." Jessie turned back to her work, dismissing Stan.

"Tell me you don't really think it was Izzy, just because it was her cider. I mean, you just said anyone could have access to the room."

Jessie ignored her not-so-subtle question. Stan expected it. She had to know, though.

"Are you sure about this?" Stan pressed. "I mean, this whole thing is a little crazy. Why would anyone want to poison Santa, for God's sakes?"

"Someone who got coal in their stocking?" Lou asked, trying for levity.

Jessie shot him a death glare. Once again, he turned away with a long-suffering sigh, but Stan could see a tiny smile playing on his lips.

"I want us to talk to everyone on the committee, anyone related to anyone on the committee, and anyone from the museum who was around tonight," Jessie said, addressing Lou and Colby. "I also heard Harold had a girlfriend. Anyone know anything about that?"

"Nope," Lou said.

"No idea," Colby said.

They all looked at Jake.

"Why are you looking at me?" he asked.

"I figured he'd tell you about her. Over a drink or something."

"I haven't seen Harold since he came back to town," Jake said. "But I do know he had been getting friendly with Helen Hayes last year."

"Helen? Really?" Jessie shook her head.

"Who's that?" Stan asked.

"She used to work at town hall. In the voter registration office. Her husband died a few years ago. I thought she had better taste than that. Lou, make sure you talk to her. I should have the tox report back Sunday or Monday. I asked for overtime at the lab to get it done, and miraculously, I got it. So I want to be able to move on any information if and when it comes in. Also, we need to find out where Harold got that shiner. It looked pretty fresh. Colby, go see Lester Crookshank. That's where Harold stays when he's in town."

Colby nodded. "On it."

It all sounded so official. Stan shivered a little. They hadn't turned the heat up in the room at all, and it had gotten colder outside.

"Stan," Jake said quietly. "We better go."

"Amara too," Jessie said, still thinking out loud. "I have to circle back with Amara. She said there were some extra elves. I wonder if she's still up?"

"Can't you talk to her tomorrow?" Stan asked. "She was pretty shaken up tonight."

"I can imagine." Lou shook his head. "Imagine being in a sleigh with Santa and the guy keels over and dies?"

When he put it that way . . .

Jessie checked her watch. "You're right. I'll catch her in the morning. Thanks, Stan."

Stan let Jake lead her out into the night, thinking that death had become way too common an event in her life since moving here.

Chapter Ten

Stan and Jake drove the short distance home in silence. Jake pulled into their driveway and opened his door, but Stan paused with her hand on the door handle and turned to him.

"Do you think someone hated Harold enough to kill him? Or do you think Jessie's way off base here?"

"I honestly don't know," Jake said. "Jessie said he had a black eye?"

Stan nodded. "Is it weird that you haven't seen Harold since he got back to town?"

"Not terribly," Jake said. "He wasn't super dependable. Depends on how much money he needed, or where he was at with his drinking. He's usually back early December, and I think he was a bit late this year. I remember Lester saying he'd had to hire some extra hands because his usual help wasn't around."

Scruffy squirmed in Stan's grasp, anxious to get inside. "Come on," he said, gazing at the brightly lit house. "We better go in. Maybe somebody's heard from my uncle by now."

"I hope so," Stan said. "I don't want to think they're in trouble."

"Me either," Jake said.

Stan got out of the car with Scruffy while Jake gathered the food. "But what I don't get is, Seamus had to be in touch with Harold to ask him to take over Santa duties. So why didn't Ray call Char, or why didn't Seamus tell anyone else what he was doing?"

Jake shook his head. "I don't have a good answer for you. Maybe my cousins have some thoughts."

Stan followed him to the door while Scruffy strained at her leash, looking forward to seeing her new relatives. Jake balanced the trays of food on his knee so he could use a hand to unlock the door, but it swung open before he could insert the key. Liam stood there, with the rest of the dogs gathered around him. Duncan, Jake's Weimaraner, launched himself at both of them, barking excitedly. Liam easily intercepted him so he didn't knock the food to the floor.

"Thanks, man," Jake said gratefully.

"Anytime." Liam stepped aside to let him pass, still holding Dunc's collar, then reached over to ruffle Scruffy's ears. "Hey, Stan." Liam—in Stan's opinion—was the more handsome of Jake's two cousins, with dark hair, blue eyes, and that brooding Irish personality. He was the creative brother too, living in New York and working as a writer. Declan, the younger brother, was the Serious Banker. He had red hair, brown eyes, and looked more Irish than anyone in the family. He lived in the Boston suburbs with his wife and two children and worked in the financial district. He had little patience for his father's shenanigans, according to Jake. Actually, neither of them did, but they demonstrated it differently. Declan constantly tried to get his father to see the error of his ways and do things differently, while Liam mostly ignored him.

"Hi, Liam." Stan unhooked Scruffy's leash. The little dog stood up on Liam's leg, batting her eyelashes, until he petted her. Then she sauntered over to see Henry the pit bull and Gaston the Australian shepherd, both of whom were behaving a lot better than Duncan. "How are you doing?"

He shrugged. "I'm fine." He peered out into the night beyond her, then closed and locked the door.

"Have you heard from your dad?"

Liam shook his head. "Want me to heat these up?" He indicated the trays of food. "Declan's making tea." He headed for the kitchen. She guessed that meant he didn't want to talk about it.

She'd let Jake bring it up.

"I'll be right there," she called after him, then hurried upstairs. She desperately wanted to put her jammies on and get warm—even though she'd been inside for the latter part of the evening, she felt like the cold had seeped into her bones. Some tea would be nice.

She changed and pulled on a pair of fuzzy slippers, then broke into a smile as Benedict, her orange tabby cat, sauntered into the room. He looked like he'd just woken up. "Hey, Benny," she said, reaching down to stroke his back. "What are you up to? Where's Nutty?"

He meowed plaintively at her, suggesting that he had no idea where his adoptive brother was and quite possibly didn't care.

"Okay, I'll look for him myself. I'm guessing he's down in the kitchen scrounging for treats. Come on." She scooped up the round ball of fluff and carried him downstairs to join the rest of the gang.

Liam and Jake were at the table, heads together, talking in low voices. Declan was pouring hot water over tea bags. He offered a mug to Stan when she walked into the room. "I'm sure you need this," he said in a low voice. "What a crazy night, yeah?"

"It really was," she said, releasing Benny and accepting the tea. "Thanks, Declan."

He nodded, then carried two mugs to the table and handed them to Jake and Liam, pulling Stan's chair out for her after he'd set them down. Then he carefully wiped down the counter and brought his own drink over.

Jake and Liam let their conversation trail off, then Jake turned to Declan. "Do you think your dad would've gone to your house for some reason? Have you talked to Grace?"

Declan looked horrified. "My house? No. He wouldn't . . ." Abruptly he rose, patting his pockets for his phone, and left the room.

"Why would that be bad?" Stan asked, looking from Jake to Liam.

Liam shook his head, an amused look on his face as he scooped some salad onto a plate. "Declan thinks Dad would corrupt his kids and lure his wife into a life of debauchery. Which he might try, but I doubt he'd succeed."

"Really?" Stan thought back to the one time she'd met Uncle Seamus during last year's holiday season. He'd been at the pub, and a wee bit drunk. The impression she'd gotten was one of a happy man, maybe a tad too carefree, but charming and lovable. Then again, people's public faces often differed from their private ones, and his immediate family knew him best.

"Everyone's stressing out over nothing," Liam was saying around a mouthful of chocolate fudge. "I bet he found a lady friend. Don't tell Viv."

"No." Jake shook his head. "Ray wouldn't go along with that. Why wouldn't he just come back, then? Plus, I know Uncle Seamus really looks forward to this time with Ray. I don't think he'd do that."

"Then you, my favorite cousin, have a lot to learn about my dad," Liam said. "Because he's got a way of getting people to agree to things they wouldn't normally agree to."

Jake looked like he wanted to argue, but Declan came back in the room waving his phone triumphantly.

"He's not there," he said, returning to his seat. "Grace thought it was silly I'd even ask. Dad never comes to my house," he explained to Jake and Stan. "Says we're too uptight. I tell him we're just responsible adults with a family."

"Ah, you're hard on the guy," Jake said.

"I knew he wouldn't be there," Liam said. "Doesn't exactly solve the problem though, does it?"

Declan pressed his lips together. "You know it's all a joke. Dad's out somewhere being Dad. I don't know why we're even bothering to discuss it. He'll turn up when he turns up. And he'll laugh about it and say we were all overreacting. His usual line, eh, Liam?"

Liam nodded. "Or, we may just not see him until next Christmas."

"Or else," Declan went on, "maybe he ticked someone off good enough this time and they got sick and tired of letting him off the hook."

Liam raised his mug in a salute. "Could've happened."

Stan's antennae went up. She wanted to ask Declan what he meant by that, but Declan was already moving on.

He yawned. "I'm going to bed."

Liam nodded, swallowing the last of his tea. "Me too. Night."

The two brothers got up and left the room. Henry, always looking for someone to go to bed with, lumbered out after them. After they'd gone, Stan looked at Jake. "Wow. They really aren't forgiving of their dad, huh?"

"No," Jake said. "I'll admit Seamus isn't perfect, but he's not that bad. He deserves at least a little concern from his sons. I'm kind of disappointed in them. Come on, dogs, let's go outside." He led the remaining three dogs out into the backyard.

Stan watched him from the window for a few minutes as he leaned against the fence, lost in thought, before she went upstairs to bed.

Chapter Eleven

Stan tossed and turned all night. Jake was awake too—she could feel it, but he didn't seem to want to talk, so she let him be. She had her own thoughts churning through her brain. Like, why would Declan think his dad had made someone angry enough that they *wouldn't let him off the hook this time*? What did that mean, exactly? She wondered again if anyone had even known Harold was in that Santa suit. Jessie was trying to figure out the same thing, but in her mind it was because, if there had been a murder, she would work it under the assumption that Harold was the target. At least at the beginning.

But what if it had been Seamus all along? If he could encourage such strong negative emotions from his own sons, who knew how many other people felt that way about him?

Then she spent some time chiding herself for getting way ahead. This could end up that Harold had been sick and hadn't known it, and all this speculation would be for nothing.

After a couple hours of broken sleep and crazy dreams, she gave up around six and went downstairs. Despite having houseguests and six animals, the house was silent. None of the dogs had even stirred when she'd gotten up. She took advantage of the quiet and went to the kitchen to start coffee. It might take more than one pot, given the number of coffee drinkers staying here. Once the beans were grinding, she sat at the table and thought about last night. Specifically, about Char and Miss Viv. The two of them had to be so anxious. At least Miss Viv had her sister to help her. Char only had the guests at the B and B, and she was supposed to be taking care of them, not the other way around.

Stan took out her phone and dialed Char's number. Her friend was always up early cooking. But today, the phone rang and rang, unanswered.

That wasn't a good sign.

She needed to do something, though. So she went to the porch to see if the *Holler* had arrived.

It had, of course. Cyril had been up all night, most likely. But Stan had to admit that the paper had taken on a whole new level of quality in recent months. It was even more than four pages long these days.

After he'd broken the story of a sixty-year-old murder case being solved last winter, the recognition he'd received both in town and around the state had generated interest in his tiny paper. Coupled with the "renaissance of Frog Ledge," as dubbed by *Connecticut Magazine* because of the redevelopment efforts and new boutique stores opening, the synergy had resulted in advertising dollars for the *Holler*—something previously unheard of. And frankly, something to which Cyril had never given a second thought. He published the paper because it was in his blood, a tradition handed down through his family. Stan often thought that he approached this task with a fervor born not only of his passion for journalism, but also out of a sense of guilt that he might not extend the family to keep the tradition going. A bit of an odd duck, Cyril had never dated anyone, as far as Stan knew. He certainly didn't leave himself enough time to look for a date. And while he seemed happy enough, Stan guessed it must weigh on him. He'd looked up to his father and grandfather and wouldn't have wanted to disappoint.

She bent to pick the paper up off the porch, shaking a dusting of snow off the wrapper. As she turned to go back inside, her gaze automatically went next door to Amara's quiet house. She should stop by on her way out and make sure her friend was doing okay. It had to have been an unbelievably rough night for her.

Pulling the paper out of the plastic, Stan scanned the headlines as she walked back to the kitchen and sat at the table. Above the fold, of course, blared news of the botched holiday celebration, as well as an article about Harold Dewey. As much as she didn't want to look at Tyler's photo, her eyes were drawn to it. Cyril must be proud. Tyler had captured the scene, and its unease, well. His photo wasn't super close-up, but you could just make out the red of Santa's suit puddled in the sleigh. She shivered a little and turned her attention to the articles.

DOA Santa Dims Holiday Activities
by Cyril Pierce

The article didn't mention any hint of murder. Jessie had probably threatened him with a lawsuit if it had. Instead, he'd relayed the details of Santa's dramatic, fatal entrance to the holiday celebration while still managing to capture the magic of the night before all the bad. He really was a good writer.

Next she skimmed the piece about Harold, which was accompanied by a photo. It looked to have been taken for some kind of ID card, because he wasn't smiling and the photo looked sparse and bleached. His graying hair was cut short but unevenly. Despite a despondence that glinted in his eyes, Stan could see a handsome man lurking underneath the hard living he'd done. She felt sad all over again.

The article said Harold had "died unexpectedly" while playing the role of town Santa Claus. It then went into some basic facts about the dead man. Most of which she already knew from the conversations last night—no official address, spent part of his year living and working at Lester's tree farm, a fixture around town. She did note with interest a quote from Helen Hayes, the lady friend Jessie had referred to last night.

"Harold was a kind man. Misunderstood, sadly," Helen said in the article. "He'll be dearly missed."

How had Cyril found her darn near in the middle of the night? Silly question, she reminded herself. Cyril might not look it, but he was resourceful. And he'd do anything for the scoop.

The next headline was Cyril's international story, and apparent personal crusade:

Theft of Ireland's National Treasure Baffles Authorities, No Strong Leads

And the subhead:

Trinity College heist planned for years, Interpol says.

He'd borrowed the AP news update, but also added his own take on the events. The article opened with a note about his father's connection to the Book of Kells, the series he'd written, and the interview with the unsuccessful thief. He went on to say the series would be reprinted over the coming week, and updates on the search for the prized religious artifact would be printed as they were made available.

It was shocking, Stan had to admit after reading both stories. For someone to pull off such a grand theft screamed professional. But then what did one do with such a thing, even if you did pull off the job? Surely you couldn't sell it without getting busted. Not her problem, certainly, but it provided a moment of distraction from everything else.

She flipped to the inside pages. There was a notice for a zoning board meeting Wednesday night to discuss a proposal for a restaurant. Had to be Kyle's place. She tore the notice out of the paper and stuck it on the fridge as a reminder to go, for moral support if nothing else.

The coffeepot beeped. Stan rose to pour a cup. The coffee was delicious—it was from Izzy's shop. Which reminded her, she needed to check in on her too. She fished her cell phone out of her coat pocket and sent her friend a text.

How are you holding up?

While she waited for a response, she surveyed the contents of her refrigerator. Aside from the remains of the grand opening food she'd brought home—most of which she intended to bring next door—it wasn't promising. She'd better go buy some food soon or Liam and Declan would have to go eat at McSwigg's for every meal.

She settled on boiling herself an egg. By the time she'd cooked it, peeled it, and eaten it, she still hadn't heard from Izzy. Maybe she'd stop by the café on her way to the shop. She had a feeling people would be out in full force today. Nothing like gossip and death to drive people to a sense of community.

Chapter Twelve

Jake got up a few minutes later. Stan had a cup of coffee with him, then rose to go.

"Hey, do you have Miss Viv's number?" she asked, pulling her coat on. "I wanted to check in with her. She was so distraught last night and I didn't get to see her again."

"Sure. That's nice of you." Jake scrolled through his contacts and recited it. "I'm going to go shower." He kissed her and headed upstairs.

Stan dialed the number, then packed up some of the leftover food to bring to Amara's while waiting for someone to answer. Liam had eaten a few bites of pasta last night, but other than that it had gone untouched. She and Vincent could both use some prepared food on a day like this, she suspected.

On the other end of the line, the phone rang and rang. She was about to hang up when a woman's voice picked up.

"Hi, Miss Viv? It's Stan Connor."

"No, this is Victoria. I'm sorry, Vivian isn't home."

"I'm sorry if I woke you," Stan said. "I was just wondering how she's doing. I don't suppose Seamus returned?"

"I'm afraid he didn't. But I think my sister understands that's par for the course with him. She'll be fine."

"What do you mean?" Stan asked.

Stan could almost see Victoria pushing those glasses up on her nose before she answered.

"My poor sister. She's been cutting that man slack the majority of his life, and he's disappointed her over and over. Still, she makes excuses for him. So if he doesn't show up to do what he promised today, he'll be back next week and he'll somehow make it up to her."

Stan didn't know what to say to that. "Oh," she managed finally. "Well. I'm sorry, Victoria. Miss Viv is lucky she has you."

"To pick up the pieces? Why, yes, I suppose she is." Victoria sounded amused. "I've been doing it as long as she has, so I guess at some point you just get used to it. But you're a dear to call. I'll let her know."

"Thanks." Stan hung up, feeling sorry for Miss Viv. Why had she never moved on? As soon as she asked herself the question, she scoffed at it. Love did crazy things to people.

She loaded Scruffy and Henry into the car. They were coming to the patisserie for the day, while Duncan and Gaston went to the pub with Jake.

She parked in Amara's driveway and hurried to the porch. It might be too early to ring the bell. But as she pondered, the inside door swung open and Amara stood there. She looked like she hadn't slept all night. Her usually sleek, styled bob was lackluster and looked like she'd been running her fingers through it. She wore fleece sweats and a sweatshirt so large it must've been Vincent's.

"Hi! I'm sorry. I didn't mean to wake you," Stan said.

"I just wanted to leave you some food. It's from my not-happening grand opening." She held up the tray.

"You didn't wake me at all. I thought you were Vince and Beau coming back from their walk." She swung the door wider. "Can you come in for a minute?"

"A quick minute. Scruffy and Henry are in the car. But I can make us a quick coffee."

Amara smiled a little and swung the door wider. "Thank God. I don't have the energy." She closed and locked the door behind Stan and shuffled into the kitchen.

"How are you holding up?" Stan asked, slipping out of her jacket.

Amara shrugged. "Fine."

"That doesn't sound convincing. Where do you hide your coffee?"

Amara pointed to a cabinet. Stan opened it and perused the contents before selecting an Ethiopian blend she recognized as one of Izzy's most popular brands. She set to work grinding and brewing.

"So what else have you heard?" Amara asked. "About . . . last night?"

"I haven't heard much," Stan said, keeping her back to her friend.

Amara frowned. "Not even from Jessie?"

"No. I mean, I know she's pursuing this as something more than natural causes. I think if she waited for results and it was something . . . else, she'd never forgive herself for sitting on it. But who knows," Stan said. "It *could* be natural causes, and then this would all be just a big misunderstanding." She turned to look at Amara. "She wants to talk to everyone on the committee, and basically everyone involved somehow in the celebration. She wants to circle back with you. About extra elves or something."

"I figured," Amara said. "Although the extra elves didn't

show up. I told her everything I knew last night. Well . . ."
She trailed off.

"What? There's more?"

Amara sat down heavily at the kitchen table and adjusted her glasses. "I have no idea if it means anything at all. I guess I'm just wondering—you know, if someone really did kill him—if they thought it was Seamus."

Stan's hand stilled on the way to get coffee mugs. "What makes you say that?" she asked casually. She didn't mention that her own train of thought had gone to the same station. "I keep hearing Harold had the potential to make a few enemies. He was a bit of a loose cannon, right? Plenty of opportunity to rile people up when you're as unstable as he sounded."

Amara looked skeptical. "Maybe. But then . . ." She trailed off again.

"But then what?" Stan asked.

Amara hesitated so long Stan thought she might not answer. She was about to find another way to ask when Amara blurted out, "I saw Seamus's son outside the museum. Outside the headquarters, actually. The cute one." She hesitated. "He was kind of . . . looking like he didn't want to be seen."

"Liam?" Stan asked. "The one with the dark hair and blue eyes?"

Amara nodded.

"When?"

"Early. Before people would've started coming around." Amara thought. "Around four?"

Stan hit the button on the coffee machine and leaned on the counter, her mind racing. Why would Liam have been at the museum? Unless he'd been looking for his dad. Or . . . no way. Stan shook her head to clear it. Seamus's own son? Admittedly the man had his flaws, and likely hadn't been in the running for father of the year, but would his own son try to poison him? She thought back to the conversation last night, the blatant disdain both sons had shown, in their own way. The thought was chilling.

Amara watched Stan, the question obvious on her face.

"Are you asking if he would try to kill his own father? Come on. That's absurd." Stan laughed it off. "Liam is a decent guy. Jake's closest to him out of any of his cousins. He wouldn't have him staying with us if he thought he . . . could do something like that. It's crazy, Amara. I bet there were a lot of people around the museum that day. It was open, right? And besides," she went on, not waiting for an answer, "there could've been a ton of reasons he'd be out there."

"Like he suddenly wanted to know the history of Frog Ledge and couldn't find the front door?" Amara snorted. "I don't know, Stan. Maybe you're right, but it looked weird to me. That's all I'm saying."

"Look." Stan poured coffee into two mugs. "Jessie doesn't even know for sure yet what happened. Until she does, let's not jump to crazy conclusions, okay?"

"You're right. You're so right. God, I don't know what I'm saying." Amara grasped her hair in both her fists. "I just can't believe that poor man died right in front of me."

"I know," Stan said quietly. Amara sank into a chair at the kitchen table. The refrigerator hummed on. Somewhere outside, a horn honked.

"That was a crazy thing to say. Forget I even mentioned it," Amara said finally. "And please don't tell Jake I said anything, okay?"

"I won't," Stan promised. She definitely wouldn't say anything to Jake. But she might find a way to casually ask Liam what he'd been doing there. Just to see how he reacted.

Chapter Thirteen

Stan had already had too many cups of coffee, but she needed more. A dull headache had started pounding behind her eyes after she left Amara's, and by the time she got to Izzy's it had increased in intensity. Logic told her that something healthy, like a green juice, would be a better choice. But today wasn't a day for logic. It was a day for one of Izzy's lattes and something sweet, hot, and gooey from her pastry case. So she detoured into the café, telling herself it was as much for her own caffeine intake as it was to check on Izzy—who still hadn't responded to her message.

"Guys, I promise I'll be right back," she said to the dogs. At least it wasn't too cold out today—she didn't feel as guilty leaving them in the car again for a few minutes.

As usual, the place was packed. She was relieved to see Izzy and two other baristas working the counter, fluidly moving around each other to steam milk, pour coffee, and warm pastries. Stan took a moment to appreciate the fact that more locals than ever before now took advantage of the café, something that had taken a while, given the New England-y nature of this area—resistant to change and anything new and scary. She joined the long line waiting for their morning fix, and realized she stood behind Tony Falco.

He wore running clothes and had a hat pulled low over his forehead, clearly hoping for incognito status, but that hadn't stopped the woman in line yammering on at him about how terrible it was about poor Harold, and how awful for the town to have this stain on such a (usually) lovely Christmas celebration! And by the way, had they given any thought to having a do-over tree lighting ceremony?

Stan took pity on Tony, something she wouldn't have thought possible a few months ago. "Excuse me," she broke in smoothly, smiling widely at the woman. "I actually need to discuss Christmas activities with Tony. I'm on the committee."

"Oh! How wonderful." The nosy woman looked pleased. "I'll let you talk, then." She turned back to the bored-looking man standing beside her. Husband, probably, who was used to this sort of thing.

Tony shot Stan a grateful look. "Thank you," he muttered.

"No problem. Have time to sit for a minute?"

He looked a bit surprised at the invitation, but nodded. They stood in silence until they reached the counter. Izzy greeted them with her usual smile, but today it looked forced. Her long braids were swept up in a ponytail. Her normally glowing caramel skin had a pallor to it.

"Hey," Stan said. "I messaged you earlier."

"Yeah, sorry. I've been running around since I got up. What can I get for you?" she asked.

Stan wanted to ask how she was, but Izzy didn't seem to want to talk. So they ordered coffees—a regular black coffee for Tony and a mocha latte for Stan. Tony declined a pastry. His obvious morning exercise and low-calorie coffee choice had her feeling guilty, so she reluctantly skipped the muffin she'd been ogling. Izzy called their order to one of the girls, and then she was on to the next customer before Stan had a chance to say anything else. Odd, but it was super busy in here. They collected their drinks and went to Stan's favorite table in the back, which a group of women had miraculously just vacated. A copy of the *Frog Ledge Holler* sat discarded on the table, Tyler's picture front and center. Stan pushed the paper aside.

Tony took the seat across from her and took a sip of his coffee, his eyes troubled.

"Are you doing okay?" Stan asked finally, once the silence had stretched far enough into the uncomfortable zone.

Tony nodded, but his face was a grimace. "I feel terrible for Harold."

"Did you know him well?"

He shrugged. "About as well as most people knew him. I'd actually worked with him once at the museum. He was helping put together an exhibit on farming during the Revolutionary War. The equipment we were displaying was quite heavy and we needed extra hands. He was a good worker."

He looked distraught. Stan got the sense that he wasn't simply repeating a party line, but was truly saddened by the death of a member of his community. Stan actually thought she'd started to like him—something she'd never anticipated when they'd first met.

"I'm sorry," she said softly. "It's a shame." She hesitated a minute. "Have you talked to Jessie since last night?"

His eyes dropped to his coffee cup, which he tipped back and forth, watching the liquid slosh around in his cup. He'd barely sipped yet. "No. But I suspect I'll see her when I go into the office. She likely won't have news for me, but probably more questions."

"Yeah." Stan sipped her latte, wishing she could derive more enjoyment from it. "So where's Mom this morning?" she asked, changing the subject.

"Your mother is home. She's meeting with the wedding planner. We're getting close now." He smiled for the first time since last night. "I can't wait. And I won't let anything ruin the day for her," he added, as if anticipating Stan's thought.

"Hopefully it won't even be a question," Stan said. "Maybe this will all end up being a mistake. Poor Harold could've just gotten sick." She felt like she kept saying that in hopes of making it true. It would still be awful for poor Harold, but some of the other awfulness could be alleviated.

"One can only hope. Any word from Ray?" Tony asked.

"I haven't talked to Char. She didn't answer when I called her this morning. She's pretty upset."

He nodded. "I'm sure she is. Who wouldn't be? So what do you think she'll do?"

Stan lifted her shoulders in a helpless shrug. "I'm not sure. I suppose if he doesn't show up soon she'll file a police report, once the window for waiting has passed. I know Jessie has already been in touch with the Boston police to at least give them a heads-up."

"So she's certain that's where they are?"

"That's where they were headed."

Tony absorbed that information. When he spoke, he did so with hesitation. "What do you know about Seamus McGee? I only met him once."

Something in his voice gave Stan pause. She searched his face, but he wouldn't meet her eyes. She thought about the question. Truth was, she didn't really know much about Seamus, other than what she'd heard from the family. "Not much," she admitted. "Jake is fond of him. He's got sons. I don't think they're overly fond of him. They're staying with us. Liam and Declan."

"What do you know about his relationship with Vivian O'Sullivan?"

"Just that they've been seeing each other for years. Since they were kids, really, aside from the time Seamus was married. But it's a seasonal thing. He lives in Ireland mostly."

"What's he do for a living?"

"I have no idea." Stan regarded him curiously. "Why?"

Tony shrugged. "Curious, is all. Listen, I need to get ready to go to the office. If you hear anything, let me know." He pushed his chair back and stood, picking up his coffee cup.

As he strode away, Stan couldn't help but think there was a reason he was asking so many questions about Seamus. She wondered what it was.

Chapter Fourteen

When she arrived at the bakery with Scruffy and Henry, the lights were on and a car was parked in the front lot. Her sister's car. What was Caitlyn doing here so early? Stan parked around back to leave spaces open for customers and let herself in via the back door. Her nostrils perked up at the heavenly smells. If she didn't know this was a dog bakery, she'd have no trouble believing these were people goodies in the oven. Which, technically, they could be. All the ingredients were natural, organic, and real food—the only difference would be the level of sweetness, since she used items like honey to sweeten the doggie treats instead of the typical sugar one would use in a human pastry.

Kyle was bent over, peering into the oven. When he heard the door, he stood and smiled. "Hey there. Good morning." He'd let his blond hair grow a bit longer than when she'd met him over the summer, and it had darkened a bit since he'd been out of the Florida sun. He still had his trademark stubble. Kyle was a cutie, no doubt about it. And her sister was smitten.

Caitlyn waved a spoon coated with batter from her station at the counter. "Hi! We figured you weren't going to want to come in so early. With all your company and everything. And Brenna is probably with her family, sick with worry about her uncle." She glanced at Kyle, the adoration apparent in her eyes. "Kyle suggested we come in and get everything up and running for you."

"Wow. You guys are the best," Stan said, suddenly feeling a little weepy. It was a strange feeling to want to cry tears of happiness over her younger sister instead of tears of frustration, but she welcomed the change. She'd had a third baker for a little while over the summer, but now that the position was open again, she and Brenna had scrambled to keep up. Having Kyle around was a life-saver, she had to admit. And the fact that he had Caitlyn baking, well, that said it all. Her sister had gone from having a full household staff to being a hands-on, involved girlfriend, mother, and sister. In Frog Ledge, no less. What had started as a visit to avoid the daily divorce drama infiltrating Caitlyn's and her daughter Eva's lives had led to her deciding to move here. She'd simultaneously reconciled with Kyle, whom she'd left her husband for in the first place but then split with after some misunderstandings. She'd refused to see him when he first came to town to woo her back, but had since given in. Now they were getting married and had just bought a house in town—which was surreal to Stan.

"I told you he was fantastic," Caitlyn said with a big grin.

Stan resisted the urge to point out to her sister that only a few months ago, she was trying to convince Jessie to throw Kyle out of town. "You sure did," she agreed. "Where's Eva?"

"She slept over at Jessie's last night," Caitlyn said, returning her attention to her dough, which she now laid out on a cookie sheet and began cutting into shapes.

"At *Jessie's*? Why?"

Caitlyn looked at her like she'd lost her mind. "Because she's friends with Lily?"

"But Jessie's working a—she's working," Stan finished lamely. She didn't want to let on anything about the suspicions of murder yet.

"Sure. Marty's there too. They'd already said the girls could have a sleepover and didn't want to disappoint them. So we took advantage of the opportunity to help you. Babe, can you slide my tray in?" She handed her tray of Santa Claus heads to Kyle, who rearranged a couple of things in the oven before sliding them onto the top rack.

"You got it," he said, setting the timer and grabbing two trays of cooled cookies. "I'm going to go load the case. Stan, I took your list of pastries off the fridge. I'm hoping that was the right thing to do?"

"It's perfect," Stan said. "I owe you, Kyle."

He waved her off. "Don't be silly. We're family now." He winked at her and headed out into the main room.

Caitlyn watched him go, a lovesick expression on her face. Stan had to smile.

"I love him tons," her sister said, glancing at Stan. "I really do. And I love this town. Which is so crazy, right? I mean, you thought I would hate it. Heck, *I* thought I would hate it. But I don't. Eva loves it too, which makes me happy. Even though her dad is going to try to convince her otherwise when she goes to visit him. But he won't. Especially now that she's got a dog."

In another un-Caitlyn-like move, her sister had adopted a dog who had recently lost his owner. Cooper, a golden retriever, had bonded with the whole family, but he and Eva had become instant best buds.

"I'm glad," Stan said. "And I'm even more glad today. Really, Caitlyn, I'm so grateful to you guys. I never would've caught up."

Caitlyn waved her off. "So how is Jake? And his family?" she asked. "They holding up okay?"

"They are. I think Char is more of a mess, honestly." Stan shook her head. "This is so not like Ray. That's what keeps bringing me back to this idea that they're in trouble."

Caitlyn measured out blueberries and added them to her mixture. "I can't believe any of this is happening. I mean, that poor man dying like that. After what happened over the summer . . . God, it seems surreal."

"Well, we don't know that this is anything like that," Stan warned.

Caitlyn shot her a *How dumb do you think I am?* look. "I've heard the rumors."

"Great, there are rumors? And how have *you* heard?"

"Hey, I have friends here," Caitlyn said indignantly. "And people saw the cops over at the museum last night. At Santa's headquarters. But you're right. We can't speculate until they say more." She leaned forward conspiratorially. "You have an in. What's she saying?"

Stan narrowed her eyes and folded her arms across her chest.

Caitlyn sighed. "Fine."

"Fine," Stan agreed. She looked around. "So what do I need to do?"

"You should go check out the case. Make sure it's got enough stuff in it and that Kyle's setting it up the way you want."

"Good idea." Stan went out into the main room. Kyle had done a remarkable job with the case, masterfully balancing colors and sizes of treats to create an enticing, but not overwhelming, selection.

"You've got a good eye," Stan said, admiring his work. The pastry cases themselves were stunning. One was shaped like a dog, the other like a cat, and their tails entwined in the middle, connecting them. Her mother had been right, pushing her to have a professional do these. They were way too important to leave to chance.

"Thanks." Kyle beamed. "This is fun. I can't wait to have my own place."

His own place. She'd nearly forgotten the conversation with Cyril. "That's right! I heard you have a prospect. Tell me about it. And I'm sorry I haven't asked. I've been so wrapped up in trying to get this place ready." Stan took out her phone and jotted down a few notes for things to add to the bakery selection while she waited for him to talk.

"No worries. I get it, believe me. I found a storefront down by the town line heading that way," he said, pointing east. "There's an empty spot that I think will be perfect."

"That's wonderful!" She gave him a hug.

"Don't get too excited." Kyle laughed. "I have to jump through all the town hoops. Some people don't like the idea. And the zoning people are, well, you know. Then if it goes through I have to create my experience, hire staff, decide on a menu . . ."

"Tell me about it," Stan said. "I agonized over the way I wanted to set this place up, how I wanted to work the menu, what I wanted to offer. But you're a pro, Kyle. It will be great." She hesitated. "Just don't let Sheldon catch wind of it."

Sheldon Allyn, the formerly much-revered pastry chef of the New England area, had introduced Stan and Kyle during an ill-fated chef's weekend. Allyn had been intent on getting the best and brightest chefs on board for a new project he was working on. Unfortunately, the whole thing backfired when one of his prized chefs was murdered. Allyn had since lost some of his stature in the community and was making grabs for anything that might propel him back to the top. Stan had washed her hands of him once and for all when Jake and her mother stepped in as investors in her pet patisserie, but Kyle had held on for a lot longer due to his own financial circumstances.

Now he grimaced. "Yeah. That parting didn't go so well. But it's fine. We're all adults here. Sheldon will find some newbie to latch onto. Someone he can mold into thinking just like him. Now," he said, glancing at his watch, "we better get the rest of the goodies in the oven before it's time to open."

Stan followed him into the kitchen, thinking again about how lucky she was to have her family here—a thought that, one year ago, would never have crossed her mind. Which made her think of Char, and how sad her friend likely was today. She watched the dogs get settled on the beds she'd set up for them. They knew if they waited patiently and stayed out of the way, they'd get some treats as soon as the goodies came out of the ovens and cooled. "Can you give me a couple minutes before I jump in?" she asked. "I have to make a quick call."

"Of course. Take your time." Kyle waved her off.

Stan pulled out her cell and dialed Char's number. She was caught off guard when her mother answered the phone. "Mom?"

"Kristan? Hello. Are you looking for Char?"

"Yeah. How is she?"

Patricia blew out a breath and lowered her voice. "Not good. She's still in bed."

"In *bed*?" Char was never in bed past six a.m. Especially when she had an inn full of guests.

"Yes. I'm afraid so. I came over to help with breakfast."

"Wait." Stan shook her head, trying to process both these facts. Char still in bed, and her mother helping with breakfast. Add in Caitlyn's newfound baking prowess and she may as well have entered the twilight zone. "You're helping with breakfast?"

"Well, yes. I called and one of the guests—Jake's aunt,

I think—said Char was still in bed. So I brought my cook over."

That was more like her mother. The fact that she had a cook was both disturbing and familiar to Stan.

"I'm not sure what to do about the farm," Patricia went on. "Doesn't Ray have any helpers?"

"I know he hired someone for the morning he was supposed to be gone, but I'm not sure who it was. I thought he had a couple of regular people, at least part-time. Can you ask Char?"

"I'll try. Did you need her for something?"

"No. Just checking in. I wish there was something I could do for her."

"I wish there was too." Patricia sounded troubled. "At the very least, I wish someone could just tell her that Ray's okay."

Chapter Fifteen

After Stan hung up with her mother, she worked mostly in silence with Caitlyn and Kyle for the next hour until they had enough treats to fill the pastry cases. Once they were done with that, Stan set to work heating up the rest of the hot food they'd ordered for the grand opening, while Caitlyn set up the salads. The new Italian place she'd ordered it from had gotten fabulous reviews. Too bad no one had gotten to eat any of it properly yet.

"Should I get some coffee from Izzy's?" she asked her sister.

"Yeah. I can go get it," Caitlyn said. "I'll get two to-gos of regular, one decaf, and one hot cider." She jotted down a note. "Anything else?"

"That sounds perfect. Thanks."

"I'll be right back." She grabbed her coat and slipped out the back door. When Stan went out front, Kyle was still admiring the pastry cases, rearranging trays based on treat color and shape until he had them just right.

"You're hilarious," Stan said, watching him.

"No way. The setup is important," he insisted. "People's eyes are drawn based on certain things. I'm telling you. This stuff will sell out today."

"I hope so." Stan clasped her hands together and looked around. The doggie beds she'd set up strategically around the room were in place. Water bowls were full, and menus were out on each of the café tables, listing all today's special doggie and kitty treats. She'd had them made specially for the grand opening, and wondered if she'd have to come up with a whole new idea for the "real" grand opening once it was rescheduled.

"Stan. The place looks amazing. Quit worrying." Kyle squeezed her hand. "You're going to be an amazing success. Truly."

"Thanks, Kyle. Really. I don't know what I'd have done without you and Caitlyn these last few months."

"That's what family's for. Now. Should I flip the sign?" He motioned to her closed sign. Outside the door, she could see a few people and pups gathered on the sidewalk. Betty Meany was one of them. She'd taken up a position right next to the door and kept peering in, cupping her hands around her eyes to see.

"Are they waiting to come in here? God, I'm nervous!" Stan took a couple of deep breaths. "Okay. Go."

Kyle went to the door and unlocked it, then flipped the sign to open.

"Thank goodness!" Betty swept in, tugging her friend Gail behind her. Gail held tight to her black Labrador retriever, Louie, who strained his leash, nose going a mile a minute. "We've been waiting so patiently!"

"Hey, Betty. I hope it's worth it. Hi, Gail."

"Hello," Gail said, looking around with barely concealed glee. "This is so lovely! What a treat for the dogs."

"Yes! We wanted to be the first ones on the official opening day," Betty announced, hugging Stan. "I love what you've done! It's gorgeous!"

Stan looked around proudly. It *was* gorgeous. Her mother, for all her faults, had great decorating taste. She'd gone with a moss green for the walls, and had stenciled paw prints along the tops and bottoms. Jake had made the red, bone-shaped sign she'd designed proclaiming STAN'S, which hung above the counter, a prominent position for everyone to see when they walked in. The mix of doggie and people furniture gave the place a living room feel. And of course, it smelled delightful—like a real bakery.

Caitlyn had actually been here most of last week decorating for Christmas. She'd strung the café area with multicolored lights, a mini (real!) tree from Lester Crookshank's tree farm that they'd decorated with all cat and dog ornaments, and numerous themed tchotchkes around the café. Amazingly, she'd made it look homey without clutter.

"It does look good, right? Thanks for being here." Stan motioned them in. "Have a seat. Hi, Louie." She bent to the dog, who licked her nose. "Fresh treats in the case. Go ahead and pick some out. Hello, come on in, get comfortable," she said, greeting the other patrons who'd filed in after Betty and Gail. One of them being Victoria O'Sullivan, Miss Viv's sister, holding a little Pomeranian wearing a jeweled collar and a (hopefully fake) fur coat. Despite the well-dressed dog, Victoria wore a pair of jeans, snow boots, and a parka that had seen better days. She walked in, hesitating when she saw Kyle.

Curious, Stan looked at him. His face hadn't changed. Instead, he nodded at her. "Ms. O'Sullivan," he said, but Stan could hear strain in his voice.

Brenna rushed in behind them. "I'm so sorry I'm late," she exclaimed, breathless. "I totally overslept and I swear I'll bake fast—oh wow, the cases are full! Hi, Victoria! Hi, Betty! What happened?" she asked Stan, all in one whoosh of air.

Stan laughed. "Caitlyn and Kyle came over early and did a ton of the baking. They figured you and I were both exhausted."

"That's so sweet of them, and it looks amazing in here." Brenna swept her knit cap off her head and went over to admire the treats. "Everything just seems to flow so well! Want me to take the counter? That way you can greet your customers and chat. And play with dogs," Brenna added. "What do you think?"

"That sounds perfect. Thanks. Caitlyn ran over to Izzy's to get coffees and cider. I think she and Kyle will head out when she gets back and it'll just be us. But we shouldn't need to do any baking for a while."

"Great. I'm excited, Stan! It's almost like your grand opening is happening after all, even if we're not calling it that." Brenna hurried out back to put her things away as the door banged open again and Caitlyn came in, juggling three boxes of coffee and a carafe of cider.

"Let me help you." Stan hurried over and took a couple of the beverages. "Let's set them up here." She pointed to one of the tables housing the hot food. "Thanks for going to get this. Really."

"No problem. I'm so glad this day came for you. Even though it isn't official." Caitlyn hugged her sister. "Now we have to go and do some things before the zoning board meeting. And plan out our Christmas decorations." She grinned. "I want to win the contest, so we're going all out."

Stan laughed. "Good luck. There's stiff competition out here."

"I'm ready for it." She looked at Kyle, who was making one last adjustment to a tray in the dog pastry case, and sighed. "I really hope Kyle can get his restaurant. He so wants to open something out here. Look at him. He's dying to have his own place again." Kyle had sold his restaurant in Florida when he'd moved up here full time.

"I hope so too. Let me know if I can do anything. Like talk to Tony," Stan said. "I heard the O'Sullivans are giving him some trouble."

Caitlyn wrinkled her nose. "They're trying to block him. But they really don't have a legal right to stop it. They sold the land. They're just being contrary. So talking to Tony might be just what we need to happen."

Stan started to ask another question, but turned when Betty called to her. "Stan. Can Gail and I get coffees? And can you come sit with us?"

Caitlyn gave her a little shove. "Go. We'll talk later." She winked at her, then went over to Kyle. He slipped an arm around her waist and the two of them went out to the kitchen.

"Sure," Stan said, forcing a smile. She poured two coffees and carried them over, then returned and poured one for herself. She loaded a plate with a doggie cannoli for Louie, then headed over to humor her friends. On her way, she passed Victoria, who was playing with the dog, pointing things out to her from the menu.

"Hello!" she called. "I'll be over to see you in a moment."

Victoria waved. "We're still deciding on a pastry," she said.

"So how are you holding up with all the excitement?" Gail asked, breaking off a piece of Louie's treat and handing it to him. He snarfed it down and waited expectantly for more.

"I'm okay," Stan said. "I feel terrible about Harold, as I'm sure everyone does."

"Is it true? What everyone's saying?" Gail leaned closer. "That he was *murdered*?"

"I have no idea," Stan lied. "You'd have to ask Jessie that."

Betty tsked at her. "Come on, Stan. You're practically

Jessie's *family*. I'm sure she's told you what's happening, especially given the scare that it was their own *uncle* who died? By the way, I had to recruit your boyfriend to go do some cleanup from last night. I hope you don't mind."

"Of course not. And you know Jessie," Stan said. "She keeps things close to the vest."

Betty narrowed her eyes. Stan could tell she didn't believe one word of it. "So has anyone heard anything about Seamus? Or Raymond?"

Stan shook her head slowly. "No. Not that I know of, anyway."

Gail shook her head sadly. "You know what they say about situations like these."

"What do they say?"

"That when men of a certain age pull a vanishing act like this, it's a crisis. I think this would be considered more of a late-life crisis than a midlife crisis, but still."

"Oh, nonsense," Betty said, waving aside Gail's comment. "Ray Mackey is about the last person on earth who would have any kind of crisis, never mind that kind."

"I don't know," Gail said. "It's awfully strange. Anyway, if Harold *was* murdered, who do you think did it?" She propped her chin in her hand and looked at Stan, her eyes shining with anticipation. Louie nudged her leg with his chin, eyes still on the remaining cookie. "You know, he was married to my friend Mary many years ago. She went through hell with him. I can't believe he lived this long, quite frankly. But about seven years ago he really went downhill. Lost his house. Went begging her to help him, can you believe the nerve? They'd been divorced for twenty-five years! She's a kindhearted person so she did what she could, but he never wanted to help himself."

Betty nodded. "So many people had problems with him. Starting with Lester."

"Lester Crookshank?" Stan asked. "But he's such a sweetheart."

"Lester's got a temper. Especially when his livelihood is in jeopardy. And having someone like Harold on the payroll, well, let's just say he wasn't the most dependable of workers. I could see him messing something up and invoking Lester's wrath," Betty said knowingly, draining her coffee cup. "This is delightful, Stan. Is there more?"

"Yes, I'll get it," Stan said, grateful to have a distraction from this conversation.

"I did hear," Gail said, leaning in again, "that there was a fight out on Lester's farm the other day. That Harold ended up with a black eye." She leaned back, clicking her tongue against her teeth. "I wonder if they had another run-in, and this time Lester finished the job."

Chapter Sixteen

Stan rose and went to fill up Betty's coffee. After delivering it back to the table, she excused herself to check on her other customers. Which was true, but really she didn't want to hear any more speculation from the townsfolk.

She knew from personal experience how easy it was to be blacklisted once rumors like this started flying. She felt sorry for Lester Crookshank, who would now be under scrutiny from not only the police, but the townspeople too. This time of year was critical for Lester's business, and this kind of thing could have significant negative effects on his livelihood.

She pushed it out of her mind for the moment and focused on her customers, starting with Victoria O'Sullivan. "Who do we have here?" she asked, sliding into the empty chair at their table and holding out her hand so the Pom could sniff her.

"This is Daisy," Victoria said. "It's my sister's dog. She's supposed to be joining us here any minute." Her lips tightened as she glanced at her watch. "Well, that was a while ago now, wasn't it?"

"Oh. Do you think she's okay?" Stan glanced at the door, as if she could conjure Miss Viv out of thin air.

"I hope so," Victoria said. "She has been gone quite a while." She nervously pushed her glasses up.

"Maybe she forgot you were coming here," Stan suggested. "Should you call her?"

"I'll give her a bit longer," Victoria decided. "Sometimes she goes off and loses track of time."

"Okay. What can we get Daisy in the meantime?" Stan asked.

"How about an apple puff?" Victoria said, carefully reading the menu. "Those are made with gluten-free flour, right?"

Stan nodded. "I try to make just as many gluten-free items as I do regular items," she said. "I know a lot of animals don't react well to it. Just like people."

Victoria nodded. "Daisy has a sensitive tummy. Sometimes Vivian forgets that," she said. "So I try to make sure the dog has the right types of foods."

"Of course. Let me go get that for you." Stan went behind the counter and got an apple puff for Daisy. She put it on a special pink doggie plate and brought it over. Victoria carefully broke it into pieces and fed it to the dog, who daintily ate it.

Smiling, Stan left them to it. She walked around greeting people and their dogs, making sure each pup had what they liked. The wagging tails made it all worthwhile. People and dogs passed through in an endless stream, some to stay and sip coffee, chat, and let their dogs play together, and others to pick up treats on their way home to their babies. She'd seen it happen before during collective trauma—people looking for solace in the normal, in each other, in familiar places. On this cold winter morning, instead of choosing to stay in their beds and hide from the tragedy of last evening, they were out and about and looking for ways to make themselves smile.

She couldn't deny that hearing the praise of the townspeople felt wonderful. As she and Brenna made their way around the café checking in with people, meeting new pets, and collecting dishes, she heard comments like *What a lovely place! Such a fabulous idea . . . who knew Frog Ledge was so trendy? What did my Coco ever do without this place?*

"Looks like we're a hit," Brenna said at one point.

"Looks like," Stan agreed. "It's a great feeling, isn't it?" Still, she couldn't help feeling a little . . . off. Worrying about Char, wondering what had happened to Ray and Uncle Seamus, thinking about poor Harold Dewey—all of it was enough to take away the Christmas cheer and happy feelings about her new store. And the worry for Char topped her list. For as independent as her friend was, she'd be lost without Ray. And Stan couldn't deny that the longer Ray was out of touch, the worse she felt. The worse they all felt.

"This is so lovely," one woman said to her. "What a great idea. I've never heard of such a place before, but I knew my Bruno would love it."

They both looked at Bruno, a little Maltese whose big name belied his fluffy, tiny appearance. He gnawed on a stocking-shaped cookie, watching them out of the corner of his eye. Stan smiled. "I'm so glad. Help yourself to some food. And come again, okay?"

After she'd said hello to everyone, she grabbed a couple of empty doggie water bowls and retreated behind the counter where Brenna was filling holes in trays.

"People love these new apple ones Kyle made," Brenna said, pointing to the Christmas tree–shaped cookies. "Or I guess I should say the dogs love them. But everyone wants to try those."

"Good," Stan said, refilling the bowls. "I think he added something special to the recipe. I'm going to have to get it from him."

"Excuse me, Stan?"

She turned to find Julius Akin, an elderly gentleman who walked everywhere around town with his cocker spaniel, Rufus, holding an empty cream container. "Hi, Julius. What can I do for you?"

"You're out of cream," he said with a touch of sorrow. "I love my half-and-half. Milk just won't do it."

"Gosh, I'm sorry. Let me run out back and get you some—" She stopped when Brenna shook her head.

"We're out," she whispered. "I'm sorry, I forgot all about it."

"Shoot. I can run over to the general store," Stan said.

"Are you sure? I can go."

"No, you man the counter. You're better at it." Stan winked. "Can you hang on for ten minutes, Julius? I need to go grab some. We've had a run on half-and-half, I guess."

Julius shrugged. "I guess. Don't really have anywhere to be, and Rufus is playing." They both looked over to where Rufus and Louie each held the end of a rope toy. Despite his smaller size, Rufus was winning.

"Great. I'll be right back." Stan hurried out back, grabbed her coat, and hurried to her car, intent on being gone the least amount of time possible.

Chapter Seventeen

When Stan pushed open the door of the general store, Abby glanced up from behind the counter. Her face lit up when she saw Stan.

"Morning," Stan said, making a beeline for the refrigerator section.

"Good morning! Hey, wait a second." Abby rose and motioned her closer.

Defeated, Stan slowed and turned back to the counter. "Yeah? I'm in a hurry, Abby. I have customers waiting."

Abby waved her off. "The grand opening was postponed. I heard all about it. You can relax a bit today."

"Actually, I'm open. And pretty busy—"

"So what's the real story about what happened last night? I heard someone murdered that poor schmuck Harold Dewey," Abby said, as if Stan hadn't even spoken.

Stan sucked in a breath. "Abby. There's been no confirmation of that. If it is true—and it's still very much an *if*—the police will confirm it."

"It's just too bad the wrong guy was in the suit," Abby continued. At this rate, she may as well be having the conversation with herself, for all that she was listening to

Stan. "That no-good Seamus McGee deserved it more than Harold, if you ask me." She shot a sly glance at Stan and leaned forward over the counter. "Sorry, dear. I know you're almost part of that family, but it's true. Seamus is not their best asset."

Stan raised an eyebrow. Abby could be rough on people, but this was a bit much, even for her. "That's harsh, no?"

Abby barked out a laugh. "Harsh? Seamus is an irresponsible train wreck of a man. At least with Harold, you knew what you were getting. But with Seamus, it's all blarney. Nothing underneath." Her eyes flashed with something Stan couldn't quite read. "He's been a menace since the day he was born." She stood to her full height again and straightened her Christmas vest. "Anyway, I'm guessing no one's heard from him? I heard he and Ray apparently went MIA."

"I haven't heard anything today," Stan said, noncommittal. She moved down the aisle again and found the creamer section. Grabbing her usual quart of half-and-half, she frowned at the price. Almost five dollars. She wondered if Abby had mislabeled the shelf.

When she returned to the counter, Abby continued as if there'd never been a break in the conversation.

"So someone would've had to poison him, right? Harold, that is. I mean, that's the only way this would've happened. My goodness. What's this world coming to?" She shook her head.

"I don't know," Stan said. "But did your half-and-half prices go up?"

Abby nodded. "All my prices went up, unfortunately."

"They did? How come?"

Abby shrugged. "Food is expensive these days. We all have to live, you know. I heard poor Izzy is being questioned about her lovely beverages. That must've given her a scare, especially after what happened last year."

Stan never ceased to be amazed at how fast word traveled around this town. The fact that Abby knew all of this left her bewildered. Plus, she still wanted to get more clarity on why all of Abby's prices had risen, but she was distracted by whatever else Abby was talking about in reference to Izzy. Which was probably what Abby wanted. She sighed and gave in, handing over the money. "What happened last year?"

"You never heard that story?" Abby got a glint in her eye that Stan recognized. She loved to be the one to share news for the first time, even if it was old news. "Well, Harold did odd jobs around town when he was here. He wasn't here all the time, mind you. He went down to New York every spring to work with his friends. Something with cars, I don't know. But here, he took odd jobs. And he got Izzy to let him do some handyman duties at the café. Then she caught him with his hand in the till." Pursing her lips, she nodded. "Fired him on the spot. Harold swore up and down that he'd had a relapse with the drink, needed a quick fix, and that he'd never done it before. She didn't care. Frankly, I'd have done the same. He was angry. And since he'd fallen off the alleged wagon he was on, things went south. He even slurred her around town. *Racially.*" Abby wiggled her eyebrows at Stan to make sure she understood.

Stan did, and a wave of dislike for the deceased Harold Dewey washed over her. Bigots made her angry. And it ratcheted up when her friend was the target. "That's terrible," Stan said. "If I know Izzy, she held her head high and ignored it." But had she? Izzy didn't tolerate that sort of thing well. And why should she?

"Well, she tried. But it was difficult. Honestly, I've never seen a temper on that girl, but I saw one after that happened," Abby said. "And it wasn't pretty."

Chapter Eighteen

Stan left the general store, her mind racing with uneasy thoughts. Izzy had a negative history with Harold and never mentioned it once last night. Why would she keep that from her? Is that why Jessie wanted to know if Izzy had seen Harold around town since he'd been back? Maybe she thought he'd come to her place to cause more trouble, and Izzy had taken action? And what was up with Abby's vitriol toward Seamus? Head down, thoughts swirling, Stan headed to her car, which she'd parked on the street in front of the store, clutching her container of half-and-half. She didn't see Miss Viv rushing down the sidewalk, arms full of packages, until she bumped right into her. Miss Viv let out a cry of surprise as the packages tumbled to the ground and various items of clothing spilled out.

"I'm so sorry!" Stan exclaimed, reaching down to help her scoop up the bags and boxes.

"Don't worry, dear." Miss Viv knelt also, but she seemed a bit wobbly. Stan reached out to steady her. Miss Viv reached for something small that had rolled away. A cigarette, Stan saw, but on closer look she realized it was an electronic one rather than a real one.

"I'm quitting smoking," Miss Viv said apologetically. "Seamus hates it."

"Well, it's probably a good thing if you do. Let me get this." Stan began gathering up the items.

"Really, you don't—"

"I insist." Stan picked up a dress with rhinestones down the front and brushed it off. "Have you been to my shop yet? Your sister is there with Daisy."

"Oh, goodness, I'm so late." Miss Viv glanced at her watch. "I'll head over there next."

"Good. She's worried. This is so pretty," Stan commented, tucking a purple sweater back in a bag next to a coat. Was that cashmere? It certainly felt like it. She glanced at the names on the bags as she stood and handed them back to Miss Viv. Luna's Boutique. A high-end shop from a neighboring town, one with a much more affluent population than Frog Ledge.

"Thank you." Miss Viv preened a bit, fluffing up her scarf. "I've waited a long time to buy such decadent clothing."

"It's lovely. Is it for a special occasion?"

Miss Viv hesitated. "Sort of." She glanced around to see if anyone was nearby and possibly listening. The few other people scurrying down the sidewalk weren't paying them the slightest bit of attention. "I'm taking a trip."

"You are?" Stan's radar went up. It seemed like odd timing for her to be planning a trip, with Seamus technically still missing. Was she meeting him somewhere? What if she knew where he was right now? "To where?"

"We're going to Turks and Caicos. And we may stay there," she blurted out.

"Turks . . . wait. We? We who?" Stan asked.

Miss Viv frowned. "Me and Seamus, of course."

"But . . . when? I mean, his location is a bit up in the air right now, no?"

"I know, he's not been in touch in a couple of days. But he's coming back. I know he is. And we're leaving right after Christmas. I can't wait. We've been waiting for a chance to be together for so many years, and now we finally have it. There's no way he would let anything ruin that now."

She sounded so hopeful, almost childlike. Stan's heart broke for her. But she was also hearing warning bells dinging loudly in her head. "Miss Viv. You haven't heard from Seamus? You're sure?" Maybe there was something to her gut instinct that he was the key here. Maybe he was trying to disappear. But why?

"Not since he went to Boston, no. Of course, I'm sure." Miss Viv's tone changed to slightly defensive, and Stan smiled to put her at ease.

"That's too bad. I was hoping he'd called you," she said, hoping she sounded properly disappointed. "Your trip sounds so romantic. You two sound like you've had quite the love story. I'd love to hear more about it. Like why you've been waiting so long to be together." It wasn't a total lie. Stan enjoyed a good ill-fated lovers story as much as anyone. She just had an ulterior motive for asking about this one.

Miss Viv sighed, her eyes going dreamy and unfocused. "We've loved each other since fifth grade," she said. "Ever since he beat up that bully Tommy Higgins when he pushed me down and pulled up my skirt at recess, to make everyone laugh."

"Ouch," Stan said sympathetically. "That does sound like the foundation for a long-term love affair."

"He was so mad at Tommy," Miss Viv agreed. "I knew any boy who could be so chivalrous was worth holding on to. But then things . . . went wrong as we got older. We went our separate ways, and Seamus got married. I never stopped loving him." Her eyes got watery, and Stan forgot for a moment that she was looking for information, caught up in the sense of loss Miss Viv must've experienced when she found out that the only boy she'd ever loved belonged to someone else.

"We still kept in touch, though. And after his wife died, we started seeing each other again. It was like we'd never been apart. Then, well, he got in some trouble and moved to Ireland with the boys. He told me I should forget him, that he could never come back here to live full time. But I told him I was sick of his stupidity, that I loved him and I'd do whatever it took. So we've been seeing each other every winter and summer for the past forty-odd years."

"That's quite a commitment," Stan said. "I'm impressed, Miss Viv. Why did he have to go to Ireland?"

Miss Viv's hand fluttered in the breeze, dismissing the question. "Bad business dealings. And he said it was easier to make money there."

"So how come you didn't move there with him?"

"It just didn't make sense for me. And I had other commitments too. Victoria and I were here helping with our parents' farm, and then as our parents got older we had to care for them. It was a lot of work. But now they're gone, and our land had to be sold. All we're left with is that drafty old house, and I tell Victoria all the time we need to get rid of it. And Seamus wants to leave Ireland permanently. It's all falling into place, after so long! And with him coming into some money, it makes it a bit easier."

"Money?" Stan asked casually, her ears perking up. "That sounds exciting."

"It is! He already got some of it. And he's such a love that he gave me some to shop with and buy whatever I wanted. He's so thoughtful like that."

"Was it an inheritance or something?"

Miss Viv chuckled. "Oh no. His family isn't wealthy. No, it's due to his work. He's getting some kind of bonus or promotion. But you mustn't tell anyone, dear. It's still all being worked out."

"Of course not," Stan said. "What kind of work does he do?"

Another frown. "It's a global business," she said finally. "He's very important."

Before Stan could prod her further, a voice behind them made them both turn. "Well, Vivian O'Sullivan. I'm surprised you're out and about. I figured you'd be pining for your love." Abby's sarcasm wasn't lost on either of them.

Miss Viv glared at her. "Abby, you really should learn how to be nicer to people," she said. "Being mean all the time is not very becoming."

"Oh, go cry to your big sister," Abby fired back. "She'll come fight your battles for you. Stop being so pathetic. No wonder Seamus never married you."

Stan's mouth dropped open. "Abby!"

Abby focused on her. "Like I told you earlier, there are certain people within the family you'd do well staying away from."

"Now you wait a second," Miss Viv said indignantly. "My Seamus is a good man. And he's successful now, so you're just jealous he didn't pick you all those years ago!"

"Successful? That's hilarious!" Abby leaned forward, jabbing a finger at Miss Viv. "He won't be successful when we sue the pants off him! He's left us in financial ruin. I've had to raise all my prices in my store just to try to make ends meet. And he shouldn't get away with it!"

The two ladies glared at each other. The standoff would've been amusing if Stan didn't think they were about to start pulling each other's hair.

"Whoa," Stan said, holding up her hands like she was

separating two boxers in a ring. "Miss Viv, let's get going. Abby looks like she has someplace to be." She raised her eyebrows at Abby.

"That's right. I'm on my break." Abby turned in a huff and walked away.

Stan watched her go, then turned back to Miss Viv. "What on earth was that about? Why does she want to sue Seamus? And what do you mean, he didn't pick her? And how did he leave them in financial ruin?" Her head swirled with questions, but at least she had an answer about the half-and-half. Apparently, that was Seamus's fault too.

"We hate each other," Miss Viv said matter-of-factly. "Always have. We both loved Seamus when we were kids. Seamus never liked Abby. She always resented me for getting him." She straightened defiantly, fluffing her scarf again. "And now that he's successful, like I said, she can see what she's missing out on."

"But why does she want to sue him?" Stan pressed.

Miss Viv looked blank. "I have no idea. Did she say that? I must've missed it."

Stan bit back a sigh. Liam and Declan were right about Miss Viv being flighty. "It's okay. Maybe I misheard," she said. "Do you need help getting home with your things?"

"No, dear. I'll be fine. Thank you! It was lovely to see you." She waved gaily, then set off again. Stan watched her until she disappeared around a corner.

Chapter Nineteen

Stan hurried back to the shop with poor Julius's creamer, hoping he hadn't left yet. He hadn't. His dog was still having a grand time playing with friends, and Julius looked like he was enjoying the company of other dog parents. Exactly the outcome Stan had envisioned when she started planning for her patisserie.

She thought about making a beeline for Betty and asking how on earth Seamus had contributed to Abby's money problems, but that would likely just fuel the gossip fires so she kept her mouth shut.

But despite the nonstop stream of customers, Stan couldn't stop thinking about everything that had happened since last night. Her head swirled, trying to fit all the information she'd learned into some kind of answer that made sense. Of course, until they knew how Harold had died, it was pointless. But her conversation with Miss Viv had taken hold of her mind and wouldn't let go.

What kind of money had Uncle Seamus come into recently that would allow him and Miss Viv to take off for an island getaway—and potentially move there? What kind of job was his *global business*? From the way his sons talked, Seamus had never been that successful at any business venture. She'd heard that a failed run at opening a pub up in Boston had prompted his semipermanent move to Ireland. But from what Miss Viv had insinuated, there was more to that story too. She wondered what kind of trouble he'd gotten into that had chased him out of the country. That didn't bode well to his being a savvy businessman who'd figured out how to make a killing.

Of course, it was possible that he'd finally gotten smarter. Or luckier. But the timing bothered her. Had Seamus been up to something not-quite-aboveboard that was netting him some cash? Did this have something to do with his disappearance? She tried to focus on working—it was her first full day of being open and she wanted to enjoy it—but her mind wandered constantly. And she couldn't help but think of Abby's threat. What could she possibly have to sue Seamus over?

When she flipped the sign to closed at four o'clock, her dog-treat case was nearly empty, and she had an order for custom cat treats for two finicky cats. All in all, the day was a success. She did a quick sweep of the floors and tidying up of the kitchen, then left. She planned to head to McSwigg's. Stan wanted a steaming plate of Jake's fries, and a huge hug. Not necessarily in that order.

When she arrived at the pub, the parking lot was mostly empty, but that didn't mean much. Even in the winter here, people walked to McSwigg's. She yanked open the heavy wooden door and slipped inside, her eyes automatically adjusting to the dim light. It wasn't packed. A few late-lunchers and Saturday afternoon beer drinkers were scattered around the bar and some of the tables, but it was otherwise quiet. Although the promise of a loud, happy Saturday night with Irish music, drinks, and friends hung in the air.

Stan loved McSwigg's at this time of day. She loved it anytime Jake was there, sure, but it was special during the off-hours. You could really appreciate the love and care Jake put into creating and maintaining the place—the gleaming mahogany bar, the carefully positioned drop lighting over the stools, the comfortable furniture over by the stage area, the sign over the bar that read YOUR FEET WILL LEAD YOU TO WHERE YOUR HEART IS in Gaelic.

The only thing missing was Jake behind the bar. Instead, Scott dried glasses. When he'd moved in with Brenna upstairs a couple months ago, she'd immediately put him to work in his "free time."

He waved at Stan. "Afternoon. Wow, I can't believe it's afternoon already." He glanced at his watch. "Time flies when you're having fun."

Stan walked up to the bar and dropped her purse. "That it does. How are you, Scott?"

Scott nodded. "Doing fine. Still kind of in shock about what happened last night."

Stan studied him. Scott looked serious today. Then again, he looked serious most days lately. "It's very sad," she agreed, relieved when he didn't mention murder. "Is Jake around?"

Scott jerked a thumb behind him. "Cooking."

Stan thanked him and hurried out back to the kitchen. Jake had French fries going, among other goodies. She could smell them before she even saw them, and the scent made her swoon. Jake made the best French fries. And he put more effort into them because he knew how much she loved them. Duncan sat at attention on the floor near the stove, watching his every move intently.

"Is that my lunch?" she asked innocently, motioning toward the fryer.

He turned around and grinned. "No. I have your salad over there."

"Nice try. You know in stressful times I need French fries." She plucked one off a plate and winced. "Ouch. Hot."

"Yeah, well, I just took them out of the hot fryer."

"Any word on Seamus?" Stan asked.

Jake deftly scooped some recently sliced onions into a sauté pan, then wiped his hands and turned to her. "No. Unfortunately. Have you talked to Char?"

Stan shook her head and popped a fry into her mouth, ignoring how hot it was. "I called her but she was in bed. Can you believe it? My mother brought her cook over to help feed the guests. I have to try her again."

"Bed? She must not be doing well. I feel terrible." He turned back to the stove and stirred. "How was your day? I wanted to get over to your shop this morning, but I got a call from Betty. She wanted me to help with some cleanup from last night. Sounds like you're going to be called into an emergency committee meeting at the beginning of the week. Betty says it's *imperative*"—he used air quotes around the word—"that Christmas gets back on track."

"She told me. Jeez. She puts you to work, but she was the first one at my door this morning, dying to talk about Harold." Jake was the go-to guy around town when people needed help with most things. It didn't hurt that he was strong, agreeable, always around, and just a generally nice guy. So he always said yes. "Anyway, she and Gail showed up. They were full of theories about Harold and were already pointing the finger at poor Lester Crookshank. We don't even know if the guy was murdered, and they've already got him pegged as the number one suspect."

"Lester?" Jake asked. "Why?"

"I don't know. Something about Harold's black eye. And their work history. The whole conversation was making me twitch." Stan took a deep breath. "Hey, Jake? Can I ask you something?"

"Of course you can, sweetheart." He glanced at her. "What's wrong?"

"I bumped into Miss Viv today. Literally." She filled him in on her encounter on the sidewalk with Miss Viv, the fancy clothes, her secret about Seamus's windfall, and their upcoming trip. "The whole thing sounded a little too good to be true," she finished. "Did you know anything about some job that was making him a ton of money?"

Jake shook his head slowly as he spooned his onions onto a dish. "No. But I haven't talked to him much. The last time I saw him was over the summer, and he wasn't here for very long."

"What does he do for a living?" Stan asked.

"He's always been involved in a bunch of things," Jake said. "He finds people to partner on things with. I would say he's a man with many interests."

Which means you have no idea, Stan thought. "So Abby came outside when we were talking and they got into a bit of an altercation. Abby said something about suing Seamus, that he'd left her in financial ruin and that's why she'd had to raise all her prices. Do you know what she's talking about?"

Jake raised an eyebrow and leaned against the counter. "That's the craziest thing I've ever heard," he said. "I think Abby just raised her prices and is trying to find some excuse when people get mad about it. I don't think my uncle and Abby even communicate."

Stan studied him. He wouldn't lie to her—he'd have no reason to—and he genuinely seemed to believe that these crazy stories about his uncle were fictional. But was he simply, as Liam had suggested, too loyal?

"Jake." Stan watched as he turned back to his stove. "Do you think he was involved in something . . . dangerous?"

"Dangerous? No way." Jake dropped his spoon and turned again to face her, shaking his head adamantly.

"Listen, Stan. Miss Viv is sweet, but she's a little flighty. I'm not sure you can take anything she says at face value. You know what I mean?"

Stan wasn't so sure. "But what about the trip?"

Jake shrugged. "Why shouldn't they go on a trip? Seamus has been stringing that poor woman along all these years. He should be taking her on a trip. Heck, he should be marrying her before she dumps him fifty years later. Now come on." He slid his arm around Stan's waist and led her out to the bar. "I'll be right back with your fries. And your salad."

Stan settled onto a stool while he disappeared through the kitchen doors again. She wasn't convinced, but Jake clearly didn't want to hear anything negative about his uncle. Which she understood, but if he and Ray were in trouble and everyone kept their heads in the sand . . .

Jake came back out with a heaping plate of fries and the obligatory salad, which she ignored in favor of the fries. He sent Scott out on a break and took over bar duties, making easy conversation with the customers and cleaning up in between filling orders. Despite the troubles hanging over the town, it was easy to put them out of your mind sitting here. It was just that kind of environment. McSwigg's was Frog Ledge's very own Cheers— where everyone knew everyone.

Well, mostly everyone. Stan had never seen the man who sidled up to the bar wearing a plaid driving cap and a leather jacket. She might not have looked at him twice were it not for his nose. Slightly bulbous to begin with, it looked like it had been broken a few times over the years and finally settled into a position slightly left of where it should've been on his face. He had a pleasant look about him though. When Stan caught his eye, he tipped his hat to her.

"Afternoon, ma'am," he said politely.

"Hello," she said, waving a fry at him.

"I'm lookin' for Jake McGee. You know where I can find him?"

Stan paused, curious now. "He's right there." She pointed with her French fry to where Jake poured a beer from one of his taps.

"Ah, thank you." He winked at her, then moved up to the bar and took a seat. When Jake turned, he raised his cap again. "Afternoon," he said. "I'm a friend of your uncle Seamus. Wondered if I could have a word with you?"

Chapter Twenty

After Jake recovered from the surprise, he called Scott to come back in and cover the bar, then led the man into the kitchen. Stan remained at the bar, dying to hear their conversation. Who was this guy? Did he know where Seamus was? Or was he looking for him too?

Once again, the all-too-familiar refrain of that little voice in her head repeated: *What on earth had Jake's scatterbrained uncle gotten himself into?*

The two of them were out back for nearly forty-five minutes. Stan considered going back to get herself more French fries and eavesdrop on the conversation, but she managed to control herself. When they finally came out, Jake looked grim. His visitor climbed back onto his seat at the bar next to Stan. Jake poured him a bourbon, neat, then turned to Stan. He tilted his head ever so slightly, a gesture that said *Come on*, then disappeared through the door leading to the upstairs apartment.

She waited a few seconds, then slid off the stool and followed. He was sitting on the steps leading upstairs, eyes glued to his phone, scrolling slowly with one finger. Stan sank down on the step below his.

"Who is that man? Does he know where your uncle and Ray are? Are they okay?" She fired the questions at him one after the other. It wasn't until she stopped to take a breath that she noticed how pale Jake was. Her heart hammered in her chest. *Please don't let it be more bad news . . .*

"My God, what's wrong?" She grabbed his hand. "Are you okay? Is your uncle okay? Would you say something? You're scaring me."

Jake glanced at her. His face was even darker than when he'd first emerged from the kitchen. "That guy is apparently my uncle's friend," he said. "Kevin. He says he plays poker with that gang Seamus hooks up with when he comes back to town. He said my uncle never showed up for the game. He came down to see if he'd been home. He's worried about him."

Stan digested that. "That's not good."

"No," Jake agreed. "It's not good at all. But what's even worse is what he heard from another friend."

"What?"

"Someone supposedly saw my uncle at the South Boston harbor last night. Waiting for a cargo ship that was coming in."

"A cargo ship?" Stan repeated, completely baffled. "Why would he be waiting for a cargo ship?"

Jake shook his head slowly. "I have no idea. Kevin was asking me the same question. And then, according to this other person, there was an incident when the freight arrived."

"An incident." Stan knew she sounded like a parrot, but she was having a hard time wrapping her head around this information. "What kind of incident? And who was this other person?"

"I don't know who the other person was. Kevin managed to dodge that question a few times. So I figured I'd check for myself." Jake held up his phone. "According to the Boston news websites, he was apparently telling the truth. The headline news is all about a delivery at Conley Terminal in South Boston. According to the reports, a car that arrived from overseas was hijacked as it was being offloaded. Shots fired, the whole nine yards. The thief got away with the car, but it crashed into a barrier on the highway and burst into flames."

"Oh my God." Stan's hand flew to her mouth. "Was it . . ."

"I don't know," Jake said.

"How many people were in the car?" she asked, although her brain screamed that she didn't want to know.

Jake lifted his hands, palms up, a helpless gesture. "I don't know."

"This is nuts." Stan leaned her head against the wall, trying to process. "You know this sounds like a bad movie, right?"

"For sure. But it's all here." He waved the phone at her. "And if it's true and my uncle was there, it's not clear what role he played. But we need to find out if he was hurt in that car crash. If he was even in the car. And if Ray was with him. But why would my uncle be picking up a car? Unless it was his own? I need to ask Liam if he knows anything about this. And why would anyone want to steal my uncle's car, if that's the case?"

"Do you think he was shipping some of his things here?" She thought about what Miss Viv had said, about Seamus leaving Ireland. "Maybe Miss Viv was right, Jake. Maybe he was planning to move here permanently. Or move somewhere permanently."

"I don't know, Stan. He loves Ireland. I can't imagine him not spending part of his year there."

"Maybe there was something in the car that shouldn't have been." She hesitated. "Something stolen?"

"The story didn't mention anything like that."

"Did the person who crashed the car die?"

"It didn't say."

They were both silent for a minute, then Stan asked hesitantly, "Do you think the car was stolen? I mean before the person at the harbor stole it?"

Jake frowned. "My uncle is a lot of things, but he's not a thief, Stan. I know my cousins can be down on him, but he really is a good guy."

"I'm not disputing that. I know how important he is to you. But even good guys make mistakes. Listen, this all sounds really crazy, especially after what Miss Viv said. Don't you think?"

"I don't know what to think right now," he said. "But I'm definitely not going to assume my uncle's guilty of something. Or assume he was even involved in this. For all I know, this Kevin guy is a complete whack job."

"But the news reports are real," Stan said.

They both fell silent for a moment, pondering the implications of that.

"God. We can't tell Char. She'll freak." She rubbed her temples, feeling her headache returning.

"No, we can't," Jake agreed.

"Should we tell Jessie? Maybe she can make some calls to find out . . ." She trailed off, not wanting to finish the thought. Was Seamus in the hospital? Dead? What about Ray?

"Are you kidding, babe?" he asked incredulously. "If we tell her there was a shoot-out and a car chase and our uncle was spotted in the area, she's just going to say *I told you so*. She's not going to want the Boston police associating her name with that kind of thing. When it comes to Uncle Seamus, she's as unforgiving as my cousins can be."

They trailed off into an uncomfortable silence.

"Should *we* make the calls then?" Stan asked. "I can try the hospitals up there when I get home."

Jake looked relieved. "Yes. We should. I don't know why I didn't think to do that just now."

Stan hugged him. "Because you're stressed. Don't worry. I'll pretend I'm family. Maybe we'll get a hit."

"You *are* family," Jake said, squeezing her fiercely. He held on for a minute, then sighed. "I'd better get back to the bar."

Stan nodded. "Sure. I'll head home so I can get started on those calls. I just have to grab my things."

Stan followed him back out into the pub. Kevin, the dapper, bad-news-bearing Irishman, sat on his stool sipping his drink and nibbling on Stan's French fries. Stan narrowed her eyes at this. A cheeky one, for sure. He obviously didn't know how sacred French fries were around here. He brightened when he saw them.

"Hey, laddie. I heard there might be a place for me to hang my hat for the night? A lovely little inn of some sort?"

Jake and Stan looked at each other. Stan knew they were both thinking the same thing. They couldn't send Kevin over to Char's. He'd blab this story, Char would freak out, and next thing the entire town would be in an uproar even more than it already was.

"The B and B is full," Stan blurted out.

Kevin's face fell a bit. "Ah, shame. I'd heard such lovely things. Well, I guess I have to find another place. It's a long way back to Boston." He started to rise.

"Why don't you stay with us?" Stan said. She had no idea why the words even left her mouth. Jake's gaze bored into the side of her head, a silent *What the heck are you doing?* She ignored him. If Kevin had more information about Seamus and Ray, it might be good to have him close by.

Kevin's face lit up. "You're serious? Well, I accept!" He bounced to his feet and bent to kiss Stan's cheek. "I knew Seamus's family were good people," he declared, throwing his arm around her shoulder. "Shall we go?"

Chapter Twenty-one

"Stan. I just told you I don't know this guy," Jake said. "What were you thinking?" He'd dragged her back into the pub's kitchen, under the guise of needing her to bring something home.

Stan shrugged. "It's your uncle's friend, right? Your uncle's a good guy." She let the silent challenge hang in the air for a minute, daring him to disagree. He didn't. "Besides, that's what friends do," she said. "He made this trip down here because he was worried about Seamus. It's the least we can do."

Jake didn't look convinced. "I appreciate that, but I don't want you taking some guy home that I don't even know. I'm leaving with you." He glanced at his watch. "It's only eight. Maybe I'll come back and help Scott close up if my cousins are sticking around. Does that work?"

"Of course." She leaned in and kissed him. "Maybe we can ply Kevin with alcohol and get to the bottom of this. He could know more than he's telling. Or he could have other insights about your uncle. Other than what he already told you sober."

Jake shook his head, a small smile spreading across his lips. "I should've known you weren't offering out of the pure goodness of your heart."

"Of course I was," she defended herself. "He's a guest in town and Char would want someone to help him if she couldn't. Plus, your uncle will be grateful." *If we ever find him.*

Jake didn't look entirely convinced, but he didn't argue the point. He handed her a bag of potatoes.

She looked at him. "What's this for?"

He shrugged. "I said I had to give you something to bring home."

Stan snorted. "You could've at least turned them into fries. Did you see him eating my fries?"

"Hey, you're inviting him to come stay with us," Jake pointed out. He grabbed his coat and followed her back out to the bar, where she pulled on her own coat and scarf and bundled up against the winter night. "Scott. I have to run out for a bit. I'll be back to help you close up."

Scott flashed him a thumbs-up.

"Now. Do you have a car?" Stan asked Kevin.

He shook his head.

"You don't? How did you get here?"

"Train," he said.

Stan glanced at Jake. "There's no trains that come to town."

"No, but they go nearby and I found a bus. I'm resourceful, you know." He winked at her.

"Okay. Come on, then. Jake, you following us?"

He hesitated.

"It's fine," she said, sensing his worry. "We're just going down the street."

He sighed. "I'll be right behind you." He went out the back door to grab his truck while she and Kevin went out to her car. She beeped it open. Kevin settled into the passenger's seat and closed his eyes.

"Don't get too comfortable." Stan laughed. "We're only going down the street." She pulled out onto Main Street. Out of nowhere, a car came out of a side street somewhere behind her and raced down the road, coming uncomfortably close to her bumper. She kept an eye on it as she accelerated.

Kevin opened one eye and peered at her. "This really is a wee town, isn't it?"

"It sure is," Stan said, glancing in the rearview mirror as she put on her left turn signal. She hated tailgaters.

"So what do you do for fun around here? There can't be much action, right?"

Stan chuckled. "We get plenty of action," she said. "Probably more than we need. Depends on what kind of fun you mean, though. We have McSwigg's, thanks to Jake. That's where people hang out." She cruised past the green, deliberately going slowly. The car, some kind of black sedan, was still behind her, sticking close. She could see Jake's truck a distance behind it. Who was driving so badly in this weather? The roads were slippery most nights, given the cold and the on-and-off snow they'd been getting.

Kevin didn't look all that impressed. "One bar? That's all there is in town?"

"That's all we need. It's a pretty great bar," Stan added. She cleared her throat, not finding another opening to ask the question she really wanted to ask. "Kevin. This . . . incident up in Boston. Did you talk to the police at all? Tell them you think Seamus was there? Since you think he might be in trouble?"

Kevin chuckled. "I don't tend to hang around with the police too much. They never did seem to like me any."

She wasn't sure she wanted to know why. She braked as she came up on her driveway, then swore as the car behind her didn't appear to be braking at all. "What is going on with this guy?"

Kevin turned, craning his neck to see. "That ain't nothin'," he said. "Boston drivers'll push you right outta the way."

Stan pulled into her driveway. The car slowed, and a chill crawled over her skin. Was this person following her? Maybe it was just someone lost, she reasoned with herself. Someone from out of town looking for a street number. It made sense.

Kevin watched her curiously. She shook off her general unease and smiled. "Here we are." And from the looks of it, they had company. Jake's dad's car was in the driveway next to Declan's. Liam's rental was parked at the curb.

"Great. Can't wait to get into a comfortable bed. It's been a long day."

"The couch is the best I can do, but it's pretty comfortable." She waited for Jake to park. "Did you see that car in front of you?"

He nodded. "I thought it was driving pretty erratically. Couldn't see the license plate though."

Kevin followed them to the house. The dogs were all clamoring at the door. Stan could hear them as she inserted her key. They went nuts when they realized she'd brought a visitor home—barking, wooing, whining, tails wagging as they all struggled to be the first in line to meet the new person.

"Easy, guys," she said. "I hope you don't mind dogs. Or cats. We have both."

Kevin grinned, scratching behind Henry's ears. "I'm an animal bloke through and through."

Once they'd gotten past the dogs, they headed into the kitchen. Liam, Declan, and Jake's dad were all in the kitchen. Liam had a beer bottle in front of him. The other two appeared to be drinking tea or coffee. They glanced up, trailing into silence when they saw Stan and Jake had a guest with them.

"Hey there," she said, smiling brightly. "This is Kevin. He's one of Seamus's friends from Boston."

The three exchanged a look. "Kevin," Liam repeated. "My father's friend, you say?" He took a swig of his beer and set the bottle down. "What brings you to Frog Ledge, Kevin? My father isn't here."

Stan could see Jake silently imploring Kevin to keep his mouth shut. Luckily, Paul McGee jumped in. He shot his nephew a warning look, then rose and offered his hand.

"Good to meet you. I'm Seamus's brother Paul. These are his sons, Liam and Declan." He pointed to each. Declan still hadn't said a word. Now he nodded stiffly.

"Good to see you all." Kevin nodded, then took off his hat and ruffled his hair. "Mind if I get a shower, lass?"

"Sure. Kevin is staying here for the night," Stan explained when all eyes turned to her with a question. "The B and B is full and, well, he came all this way, worried about Seamus."

"Worried, eh? So you didn't see my dad this weekend?" Liam asked.

Kevin shook his head. "No. He was supposed to be, ah, at our gathering, but he didn't show. It's not like him, so I thought I'd come down and have a look. See if I could track him down. He's got the lot of us worried, for sure."

Liam frowned. "That's a long way to come look for a missing buddy you only see once a year."

Kevin's smile faded. "He's a good friend. You'd do the same for your friends, yeah?"

"Come on, let me show you the guest bathroom," Stan interrupted, turning Kevin and giving him a gentle shove out of the room. "I can put some tea on if you'd like." What the heck was Liam so angry at this guy about? Did he know him? Or did he just hate all his father's friends on sight?

"No, a shower and a sleep will be just fine. So what's stuck in his arse?" he asked as they walked up the stairs.

Stan shook her head. "You'll have to excuse them. We're all worried about Seamus."

"That didn't sound like worry to me," Kevin said. "*I'm* worried for him. That man has a knack for trouble."

So she kept hearing. "How do you mean?" she asked.

Kevin shrugged. "You know, some people don't have the best decision-making skills, sweetheart. A good heart, but not good common sense. Seamus is one of those." He yawned. "I can barely keep my eyes open."

She wanted to ask him to elaborate, but he was clearly ready for bed. She showed him to the bathroom. "I'll make up the couch downstairs for you. I hope that's okay. We've got a full house this week and I don't have that many bedrooms."

"That's wonderful. You're a gem." He blew her a kiss and disappeared into the bathroom.

Stan grabbed some blankets and a pillow to make up the couch and headed downstairs. Liam met her in the hall and pulled her into the den. "What are you doing with this guy? You don't even know him," he said. "You shouldn't be having people like that just stay at your house, Stan."

"He's your dad's friend, Liam. Why are you so upset about it?"

"Because you don't know my dad's friends." His piercing blue eyes were serious. "My dad has friends in all different places, if you get my drift."

Stan sighed. "He came to see Jake and needed a place to stay. We didn't think it was wise to send him to Char's. And I don't get your drift, actually. No one will tell me anything about him except these vague, general statements about how he makes bad decisions and has sketchy friends. Miss Viv said he had some big successes at work and just came into some money. That they're going on a trip. Did you know anything about that?"

Liam's face said that he didn't. "Came into some money, yeah? She say how?"

"His 'global' job."

"And she didn't say what this job was."

Stan shook her head.

"Because that doesn't sound suspicious," Liam muttered. He turned and paced the room, clearly agitated.

Stan watched him for a minute. "What are you afraid your dad's doing, Liam? If you don't believe he has some sort of good paying job?"

For a second, she thought he might actually tell her. He stopped pacing and looked at her, as if gauging how much he could get away with saying. Then he seemed to change his mind. "I don't know. Believe me, I wish I did." He blew out a breath. "So my cousin agrees with this guy staying here?" He lifted his chin to indicate their guest up in the bathroom. Stan heard the shower stop above them.

"Yeah, he does. It was all me doing the offering, though."

"Jake always was too soft when it came to my dad."

"What do you mean?"

"He's got the favorite uncle thing going on. It's always clouded his judgment."

"What's wrong with your dad being his favorite uncle?"

"Nothing." Liam smiled a little. "My dad just doesn't always deserve it."

Chapter Twenty-two

L iam was clearly done talking. He went back to the kitchen. Stan went to the living room and arranged the blankets and pillow on the couch for Kevin. When she returned to the hall, he was just on his way downstairs, hair still damp.

"Lovely shower," he said when he spotted her.

"I'm glad. Your bed's in here." She showed him to the living room. "I hope it won't be too noisy."

"It's perfect." He winked at her. "Thank you again."

So much for her plan of plying him with alcohol and getting information. She left him and went back to the kitchen. Liam, Declan, and Paul were all sitting in silence. Liam was tightly wound—she could feel his energy crackling through the room. The set of Declan's jaw said he wasn't happy. Paul smiled at Stan, but it seemed to be a strain. Stan felt sorry for the whole family. This couldn't be an easy time for them. Jake had taken the dogs out back. She could see him standing under the floodlights, waiting for them to do their business.

"Can I make you some coffee or anything?" she asked.

Paul shook his head. "I need to get home. Nora will

wonder where I've gotten off to. I'll see you kids tomorrow, most likely. Heard you were getting the Christmas tree and doing some decorating?"

Stan had nearly forgotten about that, with all the excitement. She and Jake were taking Caitlyn, Eva, and Kyle to Lester's tree farm to get their Christmas trees and officially kick off the holiday decorating. The annual house-decorating contest was next weekend, and they needed to get a move on. But she didn't much feel like doing anything holly jolly at the moment.

"Yes, that's the plan," she said, a little unenthusiastically.

Jake came back in. "What's the plan?"

"Christmas tree decorating."

Paul squeezed her arm. "You'll feel better if you do it," he said. "My nephews would do well to join in on the fun." He sent both of them a look. They both looked away.

Paul left, and Jake went back to the pub after making sure Liam and Declan were sticking around for the night. Stan itched to head upstairs and make the calls to the Boston hospitals. She spooned the cats' and dogs' dinners into their bowls and took a bottle of water out of the fridge. "I'm going to head upstairs. I'm beat."

"Night," Liam said. "We'll stay up and keep an eye on things until Jake gets back."

"Thanks," she said. She had to admit it made her feel better, having them there to keep an eye on things. Stan fished in her purse for her phone and headed upstairs, all four dogs on her heels. They all went into her bedroom. She shut the door, leaning against it with her eyes closed for a minute. Then she flopped onto the bed and picked up her phone.

Half an hour and four hospitals later, she tossed the phone onto the far end of the bed out of frustration. None of the hospitals had any record of a Seamus McGee in their patient listings. No one would give out any information relating to the prior evening's "events." And the only John Doe patient one of the hospitals would admit to was a "known homeless person." On the one hand, it was good news. Maybe Seamus hadn't been involved in the cargo ship debacle. On the other hand, it still didn't tell them where he and Ray were.

"It shouldn't be this hard to find someone. It's not *that* big of a city," she said to Scruffy, who was sprawled on the bed watching the whole ordeal. Scruffy didn't even raise her head. Stan decided to go downstairs and get more water and maybe sneak a snack. She wanted to wait for Jake to get home from the pub before she went to bed anyway.

When she opened the door to her room, she jumped a foot to find Kevin standing outside it. He looked almost as startled as she was. The dogs were startled too, and all howled.

"I'm sorry, lass. Just needed the bathroom again. Too much whiskey earlier." He winked at her.

She took a deep breath and tried to calm her nerves. Liam and Declan must be in the kitchen still and didn't hear him. So much for their guard dog skills. "It's fine. There's a bathroom downstairs, though. I should've shown you."

"Ah, it's fine. I'll find it next time." He slipped into the other bathroom and shut the door.

Liam appeared at the stairs. "Everything okay?"

She nodded. "Fine." Stan stood there for a moment after he went back to what he was doing, wondering if Kevin had really needed the bathroom or if he'd been listening at the door to her conversations. Jake and Liam were right, after all. If they didn't know the guy, they couldn't vouch for his character. Or maybe he'd heard her asking about Seamus on his way by and wanted to hear if there was any news on his friend. Or maybe he hadn't been listening at all, and she'd simply opened the door as he'd been on his way past.

She made her way downstairs and ate some cashew-milk ice cream out of the carton until Jake came in. "Hey, babe. Any luck?"

Stan shook her head, swallowing the rest of her food. "No Seamus McGees and no John Does. Other than a homeless guy."

"Well, that's good," Jake said. "Don't you think?"

He looked so hopeful. "Of course, it's good," she said. "Not finding someone in a hospital is always a good thing." She paused as she heard the creak of the stairs. Kevin on his way back down from the bathroom.

Jake heard it too. "Our guest?"

Stan nodded.

"Everything okay?"

"I think so," she said, linking arms with him. "Let's go to bed. I have a feeling tomorrow is going to be busy."

Chapter Twenty-three

Stan set her alarm for the crack of dawn Sunday morning. She wanted to be at the café early enough to bake a fresh assortment of treats. Early services at the churches around the green—a range of Baptist, Catholic, and Unitarian—let out around eight thirty. Plenty of time for them to go home, get their dogs, and head out for their morning coffee and pupcakes by nine thirty or so. Which meant she needed to be in the kitchen by eight. Plus, tonight was Christmas-tree night, so she had to be back early. And she wanted to stop by Char's to see if her friend needed anything.

Plus, she needed to figure out what her new houseguest was up to. She wondered if he'd left, or if he was still sacked out on her couch.

She couldn't imagine what Char was feeling right now. If Jake had been missing for nearly two days with no contact, she would've gone crazy by now. And they hadn't even been together that long. With as many years as Ray and Char had in the same house, his absence must be like a sinkhole in the middle of the living room floor.

She was on her way down the stairs to make coffee when the front door burst open and Liam raced in.

"Oh. Sorry," he said, halting abruptly when he saw her.

"Hi," Stan said. "You're up early. Everything okay?"

"Fine. Great," he said. "I, uh, needed a paper."

Stan noticed his hands were empty. "I get the Sunday *Times* delivered," she said. "Plus the *Frog Ledge Holler*. Well, everyone gets that, whether they like it or not. Did they not come?"

"Oh. I didn't know." He raked his hand through his already messy hair with a sheepish smile.

"So which one did you get?"

"Which what?"

Stan cocked her head at him. "Which paper?" She took a closer look. Liam didn't look great. He had on the same clothes he'd worn last night. His eyes were bloodshot, and he hadn't shaved.

"Ah, none. The general store was closed."

He was right. Abby didn't open until eight on Sundays. But didn't he know that? He came to Frog Ledge every year. "Liam. What's going on? Is everything okay?"

"Fine. Everything's fine, not to worry. Are you heading to the café? Need help with anything?" He fidgeted, shuffling from one foot to the other. His olive-green canvas sneakers were not the best choice for the weather.

"I am going over to the café. I sold most of my treats yesterday, which is awesome. But I need to bake a bunch more to replace them."

"Well," Liam said, "good for you. I'll see you later." He offered a distracted smile, then headed past her up the stairs.

"Hey," Stan said before he could vanish. "Can I ask you something?"

He looked at her warily. "Sure."

"The other night. Of the Christmas celebration. Did

you go over to the museum late that afternoon for something? To the headquarters?"

A range of looks flitted across his face before he settled on puzzled. "Me? I don't believe so. Not on purpose, anyway. I did walk up that way from the house, but that's it." He flashed her that killer smile. "Why d'ya ask?"

Stan couldn't tell if he was lying or not, and it bugged her. "Just wondering," she said. "Trying to figure out who was around that day."

"Ah. Well, like I said, if I was, I was passing through." He turned and hurried the rest of the way up the steps.

Stan watched him go, then detoured from her path to the kitchen and went to the front door instead. She opened it and peered out. Both her papers were sitting on her porch. Liam would've had to step right over them to get back into the house.

Why would he lie about getting a newspaper? Maybe he'd found Abby's closed and came back, too distracted by all the drama to even notice that what he wanted was right in front of him. Or maybe the newspaper was an excuse for going somewhere else.

And worse, was he lying about not being near the museum the other night? Or not being able to recall? His answer had sounded weak. Then again, he could've been walking along, distracted by something, and not really noticed that he was in the general area. Lord knew it had happened to her many times when she had something on her mind. Of course, that was before anyone knew Seamus and Ray were missing, and before Harold died. That wasn't to say he didn't have other things on his mind, but the big things hadn't happened yet.

Still puzzling it over, she scooped up the papers and headed into the kitchen, flipping the *Holler* over first to read the headlines. Of course, Cyril had an update on Harold's death that didn't say anything. And true to his word, he'd also printed the first piece of the essay collection his father had written about the famous Book of Kells.

Reading as she walked, she came around the corner into the kitchen. And nearly jumped a foot. She hadn't expected to see Kevin sitting in her kitchen with coffee brewing. But the smell of a strong, full pot of coffee was heaven.

"Mornin'! Did I startle you? I hope it's okay I made coffee." He jumped up and pulled out a chair for her. "Here you go. Let me pour you a cup. How do you take it?"

"Yes, you startled me. I wasn't expecting you. But the coffee smells so good." She smiled, disarmed in the face of her favorite weakness. "Black is fine." She accepted the mug gratefully. "This is wonderful. And saves me time, so thank you."

"Thank *you* for letting me stay here," Kevin said. "The couch was comfy, the blankets were warm, and I am forever in your debt."

"Are you kidding? Anyone who makes me coffee this good is welcome here anytime." She sipped and smiled, feeling the caffeine hit her system. "Much better. Where is everyone?"

"I don't know," Kevin said. "Haven't seen anyone but you and the cats."

Stan looked around. "Where are the cats?"

"They weren't very interested in me once I told them I didn't know where their snacks were."

"Sounds like them. So what are your plans for the day? Are you heading back to Boston?"

Kevin shrugged and stretched. "I'm going to scope out the town. I'd love to meet Seamus's lady friend. Veronica, is it?"

"Vivian. Miss Viv," Stan said. She hoped Jake talked about her enough to his friends that they knew her name when they met her.

"Ah yes. My mistake." He smiled and held up the mug. "Looks like I need a bit more of the elixir."

Jake poked his head into the room, nodded at Kevin, then looked at Stan. "What are you up to, babe?"

"I'm going to see if Char needs any help before I go over to the bakery," she said. "She was in bad shape yesterday morning. Want to come?"

"Sure. That's a good idea. Did they find anyone to take care of the alpacas?" Jake asked.

Stan shook her head. "Not sure."

"I wonder if we can get someone over to help her? Maybe Ted?"

"That's a great idea. I can stop by the Hoffmans' later and ask." Stan glanced at the clock, then drained her cup. "I'm going to get ready. I have a lot of baking to do today."

"Bakery, eh?" Kevin had been listening intently to the exchange. "I do love a good bakery."

"Well, this one is for dogs and cats," Stan said with a smile.

He gave her a funny look. "Dogs and cats?"

"Yes. That's my business. I bake for dogs and cats."

His face remained blank. She sighed. "But there's a café in town. Izzy Sweet's Sweets. She has some of the best pastries you'll ever eat, and she opens early on Sundays."

"Well now. That sounds like a plan to me." Kevin stood. "Just down the street?"

Stan gave him directions and offered to drop him off, but he said he'd rather walk. When he left, Jake looked at Stan. "Did he say when he's heading out of town?"

Stan shook her head. "No. He said he wants to go see Miss Viv. He'll probably leave tonight, though. Not much for anyone to do down here, right? Especially someone who's used to the Boston scene." She smiled. "I'd guess there aren't very many illegal poker games here in Frog Ledge."

Chapter Twenty-four

Stan and Jake both skipped showers in case they needed to do alpaca duty. It was barely eight when they pulled into the B and B driveway. Stan gave a quick knock on the front door, then stepped inside. She could feel how somber the mood was before she even got all the way inside.

Char's kitchen, dining room, and living room were all basically one large room on the first floor. They'd remodeled years ago to get that open floor-plan feel, and it was perfect. That way, she could cook and still be interacting with her guests at all times, and it made the B and B seem much larger.

Jake's aunt Margaret was at the stove. Char's stove. Char never let *anyone* near her stove, yet Patricia had made breakfast yesterday and Margaret appeared to be making breakfast today. Stan wondered if her friend was in bed again.

"Hey, Auntie." Jake went over and kissed her. "Char around?"

"Hello, my gorgeous nephew. She's outside," Margaret said, hugging Jake and turning to smile at Stan. "Showing my husband how to feed the alpacas."

Jake laughed. "Uncle Frank is feeding the alpacas?"

Margaret shrugged. "We want to help out. Poor woman seems so sad. And I'm mortified that my brother may have caused this." She wrinkled her nose. "Some days I want to shake that man so hard his brain resettles in a better position." She nodded to the dining room table full of other guests, a mix of Jake's family and some other visitors to town. "Anyway, we wanted to help out any way we could. So we're cooking our own meals today."

"You guys are the best. We're going to try to find someone to help her out, but in the meantime, thank you," Jake said. "We'll go talk to her."

Stan and Jake headed to the back door and out onto the patio, scanning the grounds for Char. Stan spotted her friend shepherding Jake's uncle Frank, who hauled a bucket of something through the snow. She wore a shiny purple parka. Her orangey-red hair was held back by a headband that made it stand almost straight out from her head.

"Oh boy." She sighed. "This can't be good. Char is not the best at these outdoor chores."

"We need to get Ted. I'll pay him if I have to," Jake said grimly. "What in God's name is she wearing for shoes?"

Stan squinted. She could just barely make out Char's boots in the distance, but they looked to be some kind of platform heel. "She's going to kill herself. Hey, Char!" She waved, picking her way over the mounds of snow to the fence.

Char turned, wiping her eyes, and waved unenthusiastically. "Hi, honey. And Jake. You're both such darlings to come. Jake, your lovely uncle is such a godsend."

Frank waved at them. "Morning!"

"Oh, Char." Stan rushed over. "Are you crying?"

Char snorted. "Of course I'm crying. Wouldn't you?"

If Jake vanished, she'd be devastated. "God. Of course I would cry. What a silly question. Look, don't you have anyone else who does this? I thought you guys had hired some people."

Char looked at the alpacas strolling around their fenced-in area. "We did, but they're college kids and they're home on break. I don't even know what I'm doing. I just want to make sure my babies don't s-starve." She sniffled, wiping her face with her fuzzy mitten. "I'm showing Frank how to put out food and water."

"I'll help him," Jake said. "Why don't you two go inside."

Stan put her arm around Char and led her away. "I'm going to talk to Emmalee and Ted to see if they can help out with the farm for now. While we figure this out," she added as Char began to protest. "You can't handle the B and B and the animals."

The situation was pretty dire, because Char gave in immediately. "I guess that's probably the smartest thing. You and Jake are such darlings. And his family too. Oh, Stan, I just don't know what to do," she said, letting her face drop into her hands and beginning to cry again.

Stan clasped her friend's hand. "I know," she said. "But you have to hang in there, Char. Trust me."

"But, Stan? I don't know if I can forgive myself. I feel like this is all my fault."

"What on earth do you mean?" Stan asked.

Char opened her mouth, but she was interrupted by a shout, followed by barking. Savannah, their farm dog, announcing the arrival of more guests. Stan turned and her jaw dropped, forgetting all about what Char was going to say.

Her mother and Tony Falco were walking down to the farm. Which in and of itself was a bit shocking, since the most contact her mother had ever had with a farm was driving past the ones in Frog Ledge. The farthest outside she'd ever gone when visiting Char's had been the patio. So to see her making her way down through the muck and snow was . . . interesting.

But even more shocking? Her mother wore jeans. And some kind of outdoorsy boot. Which brand Stan couldn't identify at the moment, but she'd wager the profits from her new business they were some kind of designer brand she'd bought specifically for this moment. Whatever this moment was.

Stan and Char looked at each other, speechless.

"Um," Stan said, "what are they doing here?"

"Well, I have no idea," Char said. A ghost of a smile touched her lips. "But do you think they took a wrong turn?"

Tony waved when he noticed they were watching. His other hand held on to Patricia as she stepped gingerly through the field, a grimace she no doubt imagined appeared as a smile on her face.

"Good morning," Tony called. "Char, sweetie, your guests need you inside. Patricia and I are going to take care of the alpacas."

Stan barely covered her giggle with a cough. Helping with breakfast was one thing, but helping on the farm? She slapped her mittened hand to her mouth and forced out a few violent coughs for effect.

"Kristan, you're not feeling well?" Tony asked, concerned. "You've been out in the cold too much. Come on, you both should go inside. We've got this covered." He beamed, looking quite proud of himself. He looked a bit more dressed for the part than her mother, with boots that actually appeared to have been worn outside before. And Stan knew that despite his many years in politics and suits, he'd worked on farms here in Connecticut as a kid. So he likely did know what he was doing.

"Oh no," Char protested. "I can't let y'all do this. Especially not Patricia," she said, looking at Stan's mother warily.

A glimmer of relief crossed Patricia's face, but Tony waved Char's comment off. "Nonsense, Char. That's what friends and neighbors do. Patricia has been waiting all morning to help out, haven't you, darling?"

"Well, y'all are loves," Char declared, sparing Patricia the pain of answering through gritted teeth. "But Jake and his uncle are already taking care of it. Tony, why don't you go help him and we ladies will go inside and get some grub ready. What do you say?"

"I think that's a grand idea," Patricia said, linking her arm through Char's. "And you need moral support anyway, don't you, Char?"

"Sure do. Come on in for breakfast soon, okay?" Char asked Tony, then fell into step with Patricia back to the house. Stan followed, wishing she could get Char alone again for a few minutes so she could hear whatever she'd been about to tell her when her mother showed up. She had to assume she'd been talking about Ray's disappearance. Why would she think this was her fault?

They stepped inside through the patio door, Savannah circling around Stan, always looking for a snack. The chatter from the kitchen area had elevated a notch or two, and they made their way into the fray, curious.

Margaret and the rest of the guests huddled around the food—which didn't smell nearly as good as Char's, in Stan's opinion—but no one ate. Instead, they all talked over each other, voices rising higher in competition.

Char frowned. "Well, it's lively in here," she said, her booming voice halting the conversation. "What on earth has everyone all in a tizzy?"

A short, plump woman—not a McGee—wearing a velour running suit turned around, eyes glinting with the promise of gossip. "My word, if I'd known this little town was so action packed I would've visited years ago!

We just had the most *exciting* visit from the lady who runs that lovely little general store down the street."

Abby. Stan grimaced, already dreading what news she'd brought along.

"She was looking for you," Velour Suit's friend said, pointing at Char. "But she told us anyway, because she knew we were all at the tree lighting. She said that makes us practically part of the town!"

"Get to the point," Stan muttered.

Char elbowed her. "What is it, honey? Spill it," she said. "We're all dying here."

"Well." The two women exchanged a look that Stan figured was supposed to be somber but held an inkling of excitement. "Funny you should mention dying. Well, not funny of course. Oh heck. She told us that she heard—officially, mind you—that poor man was *murdered*!"

Patricia gasped. Stan's heart sank. Had Jessie put out official word? Or was this just another cog in the rumor wheel at work?

Char wasn't taking the news well. Her face had gone white, and she fanned herself with her mitten. "Come again?" she asked, her voice doing a strange wobbly thing.

"Someone killed him," Velour Suit offered helpfully. "Poison. And she said the culprit probably thought he was the other man—the one who was supposed to be Santa— and that's why they did it!" The little crowd tittered. "Who was the other man? Why would someone want to kill him?" she asked eagerly.

Char looked at Stan. "I feel faint," she whispered.

Stan and Patricia each grabbed an arm and helped her to the couch in the adjacent living room. Char sank down, still fanning herself. The little crowd of guests watched with concern.

"Is she okay?" Velour Suit asked no one in particular.

"Of course she's not okay! Lord's sake." Patricia turned to Stan. "Can we kick these nattering women out?"

"Would you all mind giving us a few minutes?" Stan asked. "That'd be great." She waited until the guests reluctantly filed out of the room and headed upstairs. She figured at least one of them would find a way to linger in the hallway and listen in.

Margaret helped usher everyone out. Once everyone else was relatively out of earshot, Stan leaned over Char. "Water?"

Char nodded. Stan grabbed a bottle out of the fridge. "Listen. You know Abby. She'll say anything to get attention."

"But what if it's true?" Char whispered. "What if someone thought it was Seamus? What if they realized their mistake and then . . ." She trailed off, choking back a sob. "What does that mean for my Raymond?"

Chapter Twenty-five

What if someone had killed Harold thinking it was Seamus? It was the question Stan had been asking herself since Friday night. Amara had asked it too. And now the word seemed to be out on the street—again, likely in rumor format, but still. She needed to talk to Jessie. First to find out if she'd confirmed this had in fact been murder, and secondly to ask her if she'd given any additional thought to who the real target had been.

Char wasn't in any shape for serious conversation after the bombshell. Stan and her mother hovered over her, trying to get her to drink some tea and eat something, but she couldn't be consoled. Finally, they moved into the kitchen area, leaving Char on the couch.

"I'll stay with her and make sure she's okay," Patricia said to Stan. "I'm sure you need to get to the store, right?"

Stan glanced at her phone. "I do. Shoot." And she needed to shower, and eat something, and figure out who was blabbing this all over town. And if it was true. So much for getting to her baking early. "I can't believe this."

"Tony told me that was the rumor," Patricia said in a

low voice, yanking open the fridge and perusing the offerings. "But do you think they have proof?"

"I have no idea. I mean, it's barely eight on a Sunday morning. I highly doubt Abby is on the call list for the tox reports." Stan sighed. "I have to go talk to Jessie."

Patricia found a quiche and popped it into the oven. "This is going to go down as the craziest Christmas season I've ever had, for sure."

"I think that's true for most of us." Stan pulled out a chair. "That darn Abby. Actually, that reminds me." She went over to where Char lay with a pillow over her face. "Hey, Char. Question."

Char moved the pillow slightly and peered at Stan with one eye. "What?"

"Why does Abby hate Seamus so much? Is it because he wouldn't date her?"

Char tossed the pillow aside and sat up. "Date her? Lord, that woman is insufferable."

"That's what Miss Viv said. About when they were kids. Abby got really nasty with her out on the street the other day about Seamus. But she made a comment to me too about him. Something about how he deserved this more than Harold. Do you know why she would say that?"

Char thought about that. "You know, I remember Raymond telling me back over the summer that Abby's husband, Bill, had started working with Seamus on something. Some new business venture. Maybe it went wrong? I really haven't heard, though." She shook her head. "And I highly doubt she's holding on to that much of a grudge from when they were kids. Although with Abby, one never knows."

Stan's antennae rose. "Do you know what kind of business venture?" Maybe Miss Viv did know what she was talking about. And maybe the family had been kept out of the loop for a reason.

"I don't. I think the only thing I said to Ray about it

when he told me was *don't go getting any ideas.* Seamus is fine to have as a friend. But my goodness, working with him could land someone in the looney bin." She glanced around, realizing too late that the house was full of McGees. "Oops."

"I think most of them might agree with you," Stan muttered. She grabbed her phone and texted Jake.

Rumors are kicking up about this being a murder. I need to go find your sister. Are you ready to go?

Be right there, he replied.

"I've gotta go," she told her mother and Char. "Will you be okay?"

Char flopped back down. "Miserable, but okay."

Patricia waved her away. "Go bake."

Stan pocketed her phone and slipped out the front door, her mind on Harold. Jake met her by the car.

"Want me to drop you at home? I'm going to skip the shower for now. Too much to do," she said. "One of the guests heard this was an official murder. Not sure if your sister put anything out publicly yet, but Char's freaking out."

"Oh boy. Yeah, drop me at home. Are you going to see Jessie? Maybe you should give her some time."

"I just want to stop by really quickly," Stan said. "I have to get to the shop anyway."

She dropped Jake at their driveway and drove off. The street was quiet. She drove around the green, heading for Jessie's house on the east side of town. On the way, she passed Lester Crookshank's tree farm, where they'd be going later tonight. And swerved into the parking area when she saw a police car parked out front. She pulled up behind it.

As she'd suspected, Jessie and Trooper Lou were inside. Stan rapped on the window.

Jessie, in the driver's seat, turned. And glared before buzzing her window down. "I know you're eager to win the decorating contest, but you'll have to come back later for your tree."

Lou grinned. "Morning, Stan."

Stan ignored Jessie's comment. "I saw your car. I need to talk to you. I was just at Char's. Abby stopped by the B and B, dying to spread the news that this is an official murder investigation. Is that true? Do you have evidence? Did you put something out to the public?"

"We really should hire her," Lou said to Jessie. "She has a knack for getting information almost before we do. Actually, sometimes you do get it before we do." He turned to Stan. "You want a second career?"

"Shush," Jessie snapped at him. "Don't encourage her. Stan, do you really think I'm going to discuss the details of this case with you?"

"But you admit it's a case," Stan said triumphantly. "Otherwise you wouldn't be here. You're questioning Lester."

"I'm the one who needs a new job," Jessie said with a long-suffering sigh. "Since it will be all over town—no, scratch that, you just said it's *already* all over town—I'll confirm publicly that this is an official murder investigation. Harold was poisoned. No further comment. Now, can you please leave so I can do my job?"

"Not so fast," a voice behind Stan piped up. "I need a statement from you on that."

She spun around to find Cyril behind her, his pencil poised over his notebook. "Man, I have the best timing. I needed some background from Lester on my Christmas tree story and figured I'd get it out of the way before he got busy later. Lucky that I happened on the powwow. So when did you get results? Was there an autopsy already done, or are you basing this off toxicology reports? This is pretty quick for results—how did you get it expedited? What was the method? Do you have any suspects?"

Jessie held up a hand. "Stop. This is not a press conference. If you want to talk, come by my office later this morning. I have work to do."

"What are you doing here?" Cyril asked. "Is Lester a suspect? Are you arresting him?"

Jessie folded her arms and glared.

Cyril smiled, not to be deterred. "Fine. I'll be at your office in an hour. That will give me time to go back to the paper and get the news up online. You sure you don't want to give me a statement to go along with it? And I assume I won't be able to talk to Lester now?"

"We're doing everything in our power to find out who killed Harold Dewey," Jessie said through clenched teeth. "And no. I'm first in line to talk to Lester."

"And get Christmas back on track?" Cyril prompted. "I think we should definitely mention Christmas."

"Christmas is coming on December twenty-fifth, like it does every year," Jessie said, her finger on the window button. "What we do here in town doesn't stop time. Bye, Cyril."

He turned, still scribbling furiously in his pad as he made his way back to his car. Jessie turned to Stan. "You too. Out."

"Wait," she said urgently. "Before you drag this poor man through the mud. There's a serious possibility that your uncle was the target here, not Harold. Have you considered that? Even the people at the general store heard that. I'm not sure from where."

"Oh, for the love of God," Jessie said. "Gossip does not equal facts. How many times do I have to tell you people this?"

"It doesn't matter. The question is out there. Heck, I had the question before anyone said anything. Is that how you're working the case?"

"She's got a point," Lou said to Jessie. "We need to consider that angle."

Jessie rounded on him with a fury that surprised even Stan. "Do you work for her, or me?"

Lou held up a hand. "Relax, boss. I'm just saying—"

"*I'm* just saying." Jessie turned back to Stan. "Obviously I'm not discussing how I'm working the case with anyone except my boss and our team. But since Harold Dewey is my dead guy, I'm looking into who would want to kill him. Now, don't you have a business to run?"

"I do," Stan said. "But one more quick thing—"

Jessie buzzed the window up.

Stan wasn't getting anything else out of her right now. With a sigh, she headed back to her car.

Chapter Twenty-six

Stan didn't know what else to do, so she headed to her shop. First, she stopped at Izzy's for coffee. It felt like she'd been up for days already. The café buzzed with activity. Izzy was behind the counter. Stan was shocked at how tired she looked. The bags under her eyes suggested a long trip. She moved like a zombie from the coffee machine to the pastry case to the cash register. Luckily, Jana, also working, moved a bit faster and deftly worked around her boss. Either she was used to seeing her this way lately, or she was just that good.

"Hey," Stan said when she made it up to the counter. "How're you doing?"

Izzy lifted a shoulder in a shrug. "Surviving."

"Do you have a minute to talk?" Stan asked after she ordered her coffee.

Izzy surveyed the line. Jana gave her a little shove. "I've got this. Go."

Izzy made Stan's drink, then followed her to a table. "What's going on?"

Stan leaned close to her friend so she didn't have to

speak loudly. "Jessie's officially calling this a murder. She's out at Lester's farm now, questioning him."

Izzy's eyes widened. "My God. Did she say how?"

Stan shook her head. "Not officially, but it was obviously some kind of poison. And she's mad at me because I suggested her uncle might have been the target instead of Harold. For some reason, nobody wants to hear that version of events. At least in the family. But for different reasons. Jake is a huge fan of his uncle's. Jessie isn't."

"So what does that have to do with anything?" Izzy asked.

Stan studied her, puzzled as to why she wasn't putting this together. "Because they're looking at people who they think might've wanted to kill Harold. But if they look at people who might've wanted to kill Seamus because they didn't know he wasn't Santa, that's a whole other chain of suspects. Right?"

"Right." Izzy nodded as it clicked into place. "Sorry. I need more coffee."

"And that chain may even include Seamus's own son," Stan said. She leaned forward and spoke softly. "Liam? The older son? He was seen out by the museum earlier in the afternoon Friday."

A horrified look passed over Izzy's face. "That's not— that can't be true."

"Who knows? Neither of Seamus's kids sound like they adore him." She looked more closely at Izzy. "You look like you need more sleep. Are you okay?"

"I'm fine. So, are they focusing on Lester?"

"I guess he's at the top of their list. It's a shame. Sounds like he's spent years helping Harold out, and this is what he gets for it." Stan shook her head. "I don't know. My gut is telling me Seamus is the way to go here."

Izzy said nothing.

"Iz?" Stan leaned forward. "What's wrong? Is Junior okay?"

Izzy opened her mouth, but at the last minute she stopped. "Nothing. Junior's a little better. Look, Stan, I have to get back. I need to finish up here and get over to the bookstore this afternoon. We'll talk later, okay?"

Stan watched her get up and hurry back to the counter. Everyone was acting so darn weird around here. It was starting to freak her out.

She rose to leave and paused when she saw Trooper Garrett Colby walk in. He was in uniform, which wasn't surprising. Colby worked a few days a week in Frog Ledge with Rosie, his K-9 partner. He was probably starting his shift and needed his morning caffeine. But instead of joining the line, he went around the counter and motioned to Izzy.

Stan frowned and started walking toward them, but Colby and Izzy were already heading down the hall to the door leading up to Izzy's apartment. She hurried to the counter and grabbed Jana. "What was that about?"

Jana shook her head and turned her back to the line so none of the customers would hear her. "He wanted to talk to her in private. That's all I heard."

Stan left Izzy's and called Jake as she headed to her shop. "Your sister is out of control. She's at Lester's questioning him, and she has Colby at Izzy's."

He was silent for a moment. "She's just doing her job, Stan. She'll get on the right path."

"Jake. Neither of you are listening to me, but I'm telling you. Harold is not your answer here. My gut is telling me—"

"Stan. I'm accepting a delivery at the pub. I'll call you in a while, okay?"

Stung, she didn't respond for a few seconds.

"Stan?"

"Yeah. Fine. Call me in a while." She disconnected and shoved her phone in her pocket. Muttering to herself, she stalked inside and found Brenna already at work.

"Thank God." She sighed, dropping her purse on the counter.

Brenna turned and eyed her. "What's going on?"

"Nothing. Everything. I'm so frustrated right now." She pulled off her coat and tossed it over a chair, then began gathering ingredients. "And so behind."

"You're not, really," Brenna said. "I've got a bunch of stuff in the oven. What's my sister doing?"

Stan laughed. "You're so smart."

"Nah, I just know what to expect when she does something that riles everyone up."

"She claims to have gotten the official word that Harold was murdered. And she's got Lester and Izzy being questioned."

"No!" Brenna put down her mixing spoon and stared at her. "For real?"

Stan nodded. "I wish I was kidding, believe me."

"But that's crazy. All of it. I mean . . ." Brenna trailed off and turned back to her mixing bowl. "Jeez."

"Yeah."

The oven timer dinged. Brenna opened the door and pulled out three cookie sheets, one by one, and set them down to cool.

"Those look gorgeous," Stan said, coming over to admire them.

"Thanks. These are the tuna treats for the cats." She pointed to a tray full of smaller treats. "I hope they're a hit."

"I'm sure they will be. Hey, Bren? Do you know what your uncle does for a living?"

"Seamus?" Brenna chuckled. "He loves get-rich-quick

schemes. I would say he has a master's degree in finding the worst ones."

"Seriously?"

Brenna nodded. "He's never been one to love hard work. He'd much prefer to have things be fast and easy. Of course, when they don't turn out that way, it's even worse than just doing work in the first place, but he doesn't seem to get that. I mean, I don't think he would do anything that would harm anyone. I just think he doesn't always make the best decisions about making a living. And . . ." She hesitated. "I've heard a few times over that he loves to gamble."

"That makes sense, if he's involved in these poker games," Stan said. "Has he gotten into trouble over it?"

"I have no idea," Brenna said. "It's more like I hear my dad saying something to my mum, but they stop talking around us, you know?"

"So if someone told you he was coming into some money because of a business decision he'd made . . ."

"I'd ask them what the heck they'd been smoking."

Brenna went out front to open the door and work the counter. When Stan had filled the oven again, she took a quick break to call Izzy. No answer on her cell, but she answered on the café phone.

"What happened?" Stan asked. "Are you okay?"

"You mean with Colby?" Izzy snorted. "What a bunch of crap. I mean, he's nice and all, but was there to do Jessie's bidding. He wanted an official statement about Friday. Said they might have more questions for me." She tried to laugh it off, but Stan could tell she was bothered. "If that doesn't sound menacing, I don't know what does."

Chapter Twenty-seven

"It feels kind of wrong to be picking out a Christmas tree when there are so many crazy things going on," Stan said. They were in Jake's truck, driving to Lester Crookshank's tree farm. Caitlyn, Kyle, and Eva were behind them in Caitlyn's car. They hadn't spoken all day after Stan had raised the question about Seamus with him earlier this morning. And when they'd met at home this evening, Jake had avoided the subject entirely. Stan just hoped the tree farm was open—that Jessie hadn't done anything foolish, like arrest Lester.

"You'll be glad we got a tree once it's up," Jake said, pulling into the parking lot. "Plus, you know we have to compete in the house-decorating contest. Especially if your sister is. We need to win."

Stan looked at him. "I didn't know you were competitive."

He laughed. "Babe, everyone in this town is competitive when it comes to things like this. Haven't you learned that yet?"

"Looks like I still have a lot to learn about Frog Ledge." She looked out the window, relieved to see the tree farm open and cars jammed into the lot. The activity level was high at the farm tonight. "I hope this doesn't have a negative effect on Lester's business," she said, half to herself.

"Lester will be okay. Jessie's just covering her bases, given his relationship with Harold," Jake said. "Don't worry about it, Stan. You don't need to be involved in this. Jessie will figure out who really did it. Hey, by the way. I called Ted Brahm and he's going to help Char at the farm until Ray's back."

He sounded like he thought Ray was away on vacation somewhere. Stan shook her head, but forced herself not to say anything. "That's great. Thanks for doing that."

"It's for Char. We'd both do anything for Char, right?"

"Absolutely. I wish we could solve this whole thing for her. Jake, seriously. Who do you think it could've been? Who would've wanted to kill Harold?" Stan pressed. "If it really was directed at him. I mean, you knew him pretty well, right?"

"I did, but only as well as you know someone who comes to town every few months and does some work for you."

"Seems like most people felt sorry for him," Stan said. "I mean, I'm sure he could try people's patience, but sounds like people understood his limitations and tried to keep them in mind."

"Most people did." Jake parked the truck and turned off the engine. "Really, Stan. I think you should put it out of your head and enjoy the evening. Okay?" He reached over and squeezed her hand.

"I guess." She didn't feel very festive, though. She shoved open the door and got out of the truck.

Kyle parked next to them and hoisted Eva out of the back seat, taking her hand once he'd deposited her on the ground. "Ready?" he asked, slinging his other arm around Caitlyn's shoulders.

Caitlyn slipped her arm around his waist. "Ready," she announced.

"We're gonna get the biggest tree, Auntie Krissie," Eva told Stan.

"Oh yeah? What if I want the biggest one?"

Eva looked horrified. "You can't have it."

"Good evening, folks," Lester Crookshank said, coming out of the little shed he used for his office. "Welcome to the Christmas tree farm." Lester embodied everything Stan had always thought a New England farmer would be. Tall, rugged, a head of thick silvery-gray hair. He had to be in his late fifties, maybe even older, but she could still see how solid he was from years of hard outdoor work. His face had permanent lines around his eyes and mouth, and his complexion was that of a man who'd spent too much time in the sun over the years. Still, he had kind eyes. Tonight, they looked sad despite the festive atmosphere he'd tried to cultivate around him.

"Hi, Lester," Stan said. "This is my sister, Caitlyn, and her fiancé, Kyle, and my niece, Eva."

"Good to meetcha," Lester said. "What kind of tree are you looking for?"

"A big one," Eva piped up.

Lester grinned. "You've come to the right place. We have a lot of different kinds of trees. Balsam fir, blue spruce, Douglas fir, white pine . . ." He led them away, still listing trees.

"Guess we're on our own," Jake said, taking Stan's hand. "Let's go see what strikes our fancy."

They wandered around the rows of trees, enjoying the smell of the firs and the Christmassy atmosphere. Stan felt herself relax for the first time since Friday. This was how she wanted to spend the Christmas season—with Jake, doing festive, homey things, holding hands and being happy. Not arguing about potential murderers and crazy family members. The place was packed, with families and couples all traipsing through the snow to find their prized tree, while Lester's workers helped drag trees over to the netting machine to wrap them for the ride home. That made Stan think of Harold, which brought all the drama of the past two days rushing back to her head.

"You're thinking again," Jake said, squeezing her hand.

She sighed. "I am. Thinking about Harold."

"I thought we agreed you weren't going to think. About that, anyway."

"I'd love to shut it off, believe me." She pointed. "How about that tree?"

Jake assessed the tree she'd indicated, walking around it, looking at it from all angles. "I think it's perfect," he finally pronounced. "I'll get cutting."

"Okay. I'll go find someone to grab it and net it for us." She headed back toward the pay area. Lester was sitting at a small table when she arrived, counting out some cash.

He glanced up when she came in. "Hi, Stan."

"Hey. We found our tree." She smiled. "You have a great farm here, Lester."

"Thank you." He rose slowly, as if his body hurt, still arranging cash in a pile. "I'll send one of the boys over."

"Thanks." Stan hesitated. "How are you doing?"

His hands stilled, then he shoved the rest of the cash back in the box and locked it. "I'm fine."

He so wasn't. And she didn't blame him. "Look, Lester. I know Jessie talked to you today. I also know she's feeling some pressure about this case. She knows you wouldn't—"

"She doesn't know anything of the sort," he interrupted. "That's why she was here asking me. In full view of the whole town. I'm surprised people are here tonight." He smiled a bit sadly. "Although I think some are here to be nosy."

"Lester." Stan grabbed his arm and pulled him into the corner, where people coming in to pay for their trees couldn't hear the conversation. "Did you give Harold that black eye?"

Lester pressed his lips together. "I don't know how that's any of your business. I talked to the police. I don't need to say anything else."

"It's not my business. But if you didn't, that takes a lot of the suspicion off you."

"You don't think I know that?" He folded his arms across his chest and glared at her. "Listen. Harold could be one of the biggest thorns in my side on any given day. He was also a good worker when he had his act together. Did we have our problems? Sure. I also felt sorry for him. And I did a lot for him."

"What were you fighting about?" Stan asked.

"Who said we were fighting?"

"You're avoiding my answer about the black eye. That says to me that maybe you two were fighting."

"You didn't even know him, did you?" Lester asked.

Stan shook her head.

"Then why are you so worried about it?"

Stan looked around the small room, wondering how much to say. "Because I don't believe you or Izzy would do such a thing, and you guys are at the top of the list," she said finally. "Because I don't think anyone knew that he was the one in the Santa suit." She looked at Lester. "Did you?"

Lester shook his head slowly. "I knew he blew me off for work that night, which made me mad because that's a big night for us. But I didn't know why. Look, Stan. I appreciate you worrying for me. I didn't kill anyone. I can't believe anyone would think I could. That's what makes me the most sad."

"Dad?"

They both turned to see a young man, almost as tall as

Lester, with the same build. He wore a cap pulled low over his forehead.

"What, Edward?"

"We're almost out of net. Where'd you put the new order?"

Lester looked at Stan. "I have to go."

"Can I pay for my tree?" She pulled some cash out of her pocket.

Lester waved her off. "It's on the house this year." He walked out, putting his arm around his son on the way. The boy turned back to look at Stan as they walked out.

"Thank you," she called. He didn't answer. Stan watched them go. She still believed Lester would never harm anyone, but something about their conversation bugged her. Just a feeling, really, but she got the sneaking suspicion he wasn't telling her the whole truth. On her way out, she slipped a twenty under the register.

Chapter Twenty-eight

When they got back with the tree, the house was full. Stan could hear the voices, rising and falling in tone, all the way from the front hall. From the sounds of it, the topic was—no surprise—Seamus. Jake looked at Stan. "So much for a quiet night of decorating."

When they reached the kitchen, they found Liam, Declan, and Jake's parents crowded around the kitchen table, eating Chinese takeout. Kevin wasn't there. The four dogs were sitting at attention around the table, watching them all intently. Or rather, watching the food intently. Nora McGee was making a point to Liam, pointing a chopstick at him as she did so, as her husband watched with amusement.

They all turned when Jake and Stan walked in. The dogs hadn't even noticed, they were so focused on the food potential.

"Hello you two," Nora said, getting up to give them each a hug.

"We hope you don't mind us invading your space," Paul said once his wife had released them. "We did save you some food. Although Henry tried to convince us you weren't hungry."

"Of course not. We're happy you're here," Stan said, and realized she meant it. She liked Jake's parents, though she'd been cautious about getting too close to them too quickly. At first she'd been worried they wouldn't approve of her. She wasn't a small-town girl, after all, and Jake's heart had been broken in the past by someone who didn't want to settle for small-town living. She'd anticipated they would try to talk him out of being with her, citing the argument that she'd eventually want to go back to her corporate public relations life—the travel, the expense account, and all the rest that went along with it.

But they'd accepted her without question from the beginning. And she'd realized recently she had been the one keeping them at arm's length, not the other way around. Now she was making a concerted effort to change all that. They were both lovely people. And Nora was so different from her own mother. Not bad, she thought now, a bit surprised at her change of heart about Patricia. But different, all the same. Nora was warm and loving and didn't hide her emotions. What you saw was what you got. And Paul, well, he reminded her a lot of her own dad, gone more than ten years now. Solid, levelheaded, always willing to lend an ear or give advice.

"Help yourself," Declan said, motioning to the food. Paul got up and grabbed some extra plates. "We didn't feel like cooking. Or eating anything healthy."

Jake nodded. "Dad, want to give me a hand bringing the tree in?"

"You bet." Paul grabbed his jacket off the back of his chair. "Be right back."

"Sit," Declan said to Stan, pulling out a chair for her. He looked exhausted. His hair, cut short compared to his brother's, stood up in tufts—he'd been running his hands through it when Stan walked in. His eyes were bloodshot.

Liam hadn't said a word yet. He was picking at some rice on his plate, just moving it around, really. For two guys so angry at their father, they appeared to be losing a lot of sleep over the situation. She knew all too well how it was to love someone but not like them. And to lose sleep over them.

"Any news on Seamus or Ray?" Stan asked lamely into the silence.

"Nothing," Nora said with a sigh. "Margaret and Frankie are going to stop by. Hope that's okay. The rest of the clan has taken over Jake's pub for the night. They want to spend some time with Brenna."

"I can't believe she's working there tonight." Stan shook her head. "She's been putting in more hours than me, trying to get the shop open and running smoothly. I have no idea what I'd do without her."

"She loves working with you," Nora said. "I'm glad of it. She struggled with what she wanted to do. I don't think she wanted to be away from home, but wasn't finding a lot of opportunities to do something she cared about. You came along at exactly the right time." She winked at Stan.

"Oh. Wow. Thank you," Stan said, not sure what to say to that. "I love having her. She's great at what she does."

The front door banged open as Jake and Paul maneuvered the tree inside. "Hey, Stan," Jake called. "Where are we putting this again?"

She hurried out to the hall and surveyed the tree, which looked a lot larger in here than it had on the farm. "I think probably the living room," she decided. "Let me grab the stand."

She hurried to the basement to grab it. When she returned and set it down, Nora joined her to watch the proceedings. "Are we having a decorating party?" she asked gleefully, rubbing her hands together. "I love decorating trees. If I could have one in every room, I would. But my husband can be a party pooper on that front."

Paul shot her a look through the branches as he and Jake wrestled the tree into place. "One is more than enough," he said. "Especially when you get to just watch this part and do the fun stuff, like hang things on it."

"Where are the ornaments?" Nora asked, ignoring him.

"Mom. We have to let it set for a bit." Jake laughed. "Go finish your dinner. Maybe we let it settle tonight and do the ornaments tomorrow. What do you think of that?"

Nora pouted a little. "I guess. As long as you don't do it without me. This is a big year for you, Jake. I want to see you decorate your first tree in your new home."

Jake cringed. "I'm not in fifth grade, starting a new school, for crying out loud."

Stan hid a smile. They were so different from her own family. And she was smitten.

They all trooped back to the kitchen to pick up where they'd left off with their food. Liam had given up on the rice. Instead, he fidgeted in his seat, looking like he was about to jump out of his skin. He kept checking his watch, like he was expecting someone. Declan was reading the paper. He kept cracking his knuckles, a sound that threatened to drive Stan out of her skin.

She tried to ignore it and filled her plate with some rice and broccoli.

"So," Paul said, "we've decided to keep our McGee party on schedule for Wednesday night."

Liam looked at him, surprised. "Yeah?"

Paul nodded. "We have all our relatives here. I think it makes sense. Do you boys feel differently?"

Liam shook his head. "No. Just surprised."

"Declan?"

Declan looked up, clearly not paying attention. "Yeah?"

"The party," Paul repeated. "Are you okay if we go forward with it?"

"Why wouldn't I be?" Declan asked.

"Well, I know it's hard, not knowing. About your dad."

Declan snorted. "Oh, you know, Uncle Paul. You're just too nice to admit it."

Stan wondered what the heck that meant.

"Declan." Paul sighed. "No one knows anything yet. We shouldn't pass judgment on your dad when we have no information at all to go on."

"It's the same story and you know it," Declan said flatly. "My dad is the least dependable person on the planet. He's proven it time and again." He jerked his shoulder in a shrug, his foot tapping a staccato beat on the floor. "Something—or someone—obviously came up and he had a better opportunity than hanging around here for the weekend. And since he's thoughtless, he wouldn't think to tell anyone before he took off. I'm just sorry he took the other bloke along for whatever ride he's on. You know, I may skip the party this year. I should get home to my family."

Before Paul could formulate a politically correct answer to that, the front door banged open. All of them jumped. Jake was out of his chair and in the hall before Stan could even move. But it was only Jessie, who'd taken full advantage of the unlocked door to make a dramatic entrance. She stormed past Jake and into the kitchen, pointing a finger at Stan.

"What do you think you're doing?" she demanded.

Stan glanced down at her plate. "Eating dinner?"

"You know what I mean. Why were you poking your nose into my business with Lester Crookshank?"

"Jessica," Nora commanded. "What's wrong with you? You don't come into your brother's house and—"

"Not now, Mom," Jessie said, holding a hand up, still glaring at Stan. "I'm serious, Stan. You need to mind your own business on this one."

Stan stood so they were on an even par. "I'm not sure what you're so upset about. I had a conversation with Lester when we were there buying our Christmas tree. I didn't realize that was against the law."

"Talking about an ongoing investigation—*my* investigation—is against the law!"

"Jessie." Jake stepped in front of his sister. "Can you relax?"

"I won't relax. I'm trying to work on a murder case and your girlfriend has some crazy notion that she knows better than me what's going on." Jessie peered around Jake to focus on Stan again. "I'm telling you. Forget my uncle. Stay away from Lester Crookshank. And any of my suspects. Are we understood?"

Stan felt a flare of anger at this unreasonable demonstration of control, but she didn't want to add fuel to the fire by arguing with her in front of her entire family. "Fine," she said coolly.

"Great." Jessie turned and flounced out of the kitchen, almost slamming into her aunt Margaret and uncle Frank, who'd walked in during her meltdown.

On second thought, Stan didn't want to give her the last word. She started out of the kitchen after Jessie, just in time to hear her say, "Who are *you*?"

Rounding the corner into the hallway, she saw Jessie face-to-face with Kevin, who'd also just walked in. Stan had almost forgotten all about him.

"Kevin," he said, taking off his cap and offering his hand. "And you are?"

"The police," Jessie said. "Are you one of my uncle's crazy friends?"

"Jess. Please," Stan said. "What is going on with you?"

Jessie ignored her and jabbed a finger into Kevin's chest. "If you've come here to cause trouble, or drum up sympathy for my uncle, you can just leave now," she said. "We're all on to him. He's off doing something insane. And probably illegal. But he's still managed to convince some people that he's a poor, innocent victim. Well, if you see him, tell him it's not going to fly this time. Got it?" And she shoved past him and out the door, slamming it behind her.

Kevin watched her go with wide eyes, then turned to Stan. "Well then. Fiery one, she is. And she's got the hair for it." There was a touch of admiration in his voice.

"Yeah," Stan muttered. "Fiery, all right."

"I hope you don't mind I'm back. I spent the day walking around, visiting with people, and decided I didn't want to go back right away. If you'll have me for a bit longer, that is?" He smiled winningly at her.

"Sure," Stan said, suddenly too tired to care. "The couch is yours. Enjoy."

She turned to go back to the kitchen when her cell rang in her pocket. It was Betty.

"Can you be at the town hall meeting room first thing in the morning?" she asked. "We have to have an emergency Christmas committee meeting."

Chapter Twenty-nine

"Honestly. The tree is lit. All is well in the Christmas realm. Why are we even here?" Izzy muttered in Stan's ear, handing her a coffee. "There's a murdered man and two missing men, and we're still talking about the Christmas celebration. It's one of those things I'll never get about places like this. People sure do get depressed about their traditions getting messed with."

Stan accepted the coffee gratefully and sank into one of the folding chairs that had been set up in the town hall meeting room to accommodate this emergency meeting. She glanced around to see who was in attendance. After Jessie's outburst last night, she felt like she might get hauled off to jail just for sitting next to Izzy, who remained with Lester at the top of the suspect list in Harold's death. She'd called Char this morning, and her friend was out of bed, but listless and distracted. Stan had no idea how to help her. Kevin, Seamus's mysterious friend, had been asleep on her couch. So basically, all was weird in the world.

"I don't know," she said. "I got the same call as you." She'd been relieved that her duties on this committee were coming to an end. Now it appeared they'd been extended. To say the Christmas holiday was important in Frog Ledge was a gross understatement.

Izzy swept her braids up into a ponytail. She literally looked like she'd rolled out of bed and come straight here. She wore leggings and a flannel shirt, and despite the cold weather, she had no socks on with her sneakers. Her scarf didn't match her coat, either, which was so not Izzy. It was probably just the stress of this murder. It was getting to everyone.

"I remember the first year I was in town, the city council voted against Christmas lights, to save money, and there was a huge uproar. You'd have thought they voted to cancel Christmas altogether," Izzy went on.

"Voted against Christmas lights? Who *does* that?" Stan shook her head.

The door blew open and Kyle appeared, carrying a tray of cookies. Izzy's eyes narrowed. "What does he think he's doing?"

Kyle saw Stan and made a beeline for her, oblivious to Izzy's death stare. "Hey," he said, sliding into an empty chair next to Stan. "Where should I put the cookies?"

Stan's gaze dropped to the tray overflowing with cheerful, yummy-looking Christmas cookies—wreaths, presents with bows, Christmas trees with frosting lights, reindeers and candy canes and snowmen. The only thing missing was . . . Santa.

"I left it out on purpose," Kyle said, reading her mind when she lifted her gaze to his. "I figured people may not want a reminder."

"Did someone ask you to bring cookies? Because that's my job," Izzy said.

Kyle looked instantly contrite. "I'm so sorry. I didn't mean to intrude. I just thought people might need something this morning, and I know it was a last-minute meeting."

"Are you even on this committee?" Izzy asked.

"Izzy. Jeez. Relax," Stan said. "Did you bring anything?"

"No," Izzy said. "I had no time. And I don't do things last minute on people's whims anymore."

"Okay then. Why do you care?" She couldn't help it—she was losing patience with everyone. And with Izzy so distant and . . . secretive lately, she felt no remorse about it.

"Good morning, everyone!" Betty Meany had arrived and was holding court at the front of the room, saving the moment from deteriorating even further. Kyle slipped away to put the tray of cookies on a table to the side of the room. "I'm sure you're wondering why I've brought us all together, since technically our celebration is over."

A murmur of agreement rippled through most of the committee members. Only Curtis Wallace, Stan's least favorite councilman, looked smug. Like he'd had something to do with this. The door opened again and Tony Falco came in. He nodded briefly at the group, then took a seat next to Stan and Izzy.

"Morning," he murmured. "What's going on?"

Stan shrugged. "We're about to find out."

Betty waited until everyone had settled down before speaking again. "I gathered everyone because I wanted to talk about doing a second holiday stroll. Since the last one was a bit . . . disrupted. And I know one of our merchants"—here she found Stan and beamed at her—"is working on new dates for her official grand opening. Curtis and I have discussed this and we think it's a viable solution. It would also bring added revenue to the town. So what does everyone think?"

"And it's more work for everyone," Mona Galveston chimed in. "During a very busy time of year. That should be taken into account."

"Agree," Emmalee Hoffman said. "Plus it feels a bit

disrespectful. Given . . . everything going on. Do we really need to do another event?"

"We have a very good reputation in the area for having one of the best Christmas celebrations, despite our size," Curtis Wallace said in that pinched, nasally voice that reminded Stan of nails grating on a chalkboard. "Our celebration this year was lacking, to say the least. We have a chance to repair the situation."

Cyril Pierce slipped in just in time to catch that quote. He made a beeline for Stan also. "What'd I miss?" he whispered loudly, pulling out his notebook.

Stan was busy texting Brenna that she'd be late to the store and didn't answer.

"They want to have another holiday stroll," Izzy muttered. "Because they're crazy."

"We had a man killed, for goodness' sakes," Neil, the guy who ran the laundromat near Izzy's, pointed out. "I think maybe people will forgive us for the celebration being a bit rushed."

Out of the corner of her eye, Stan could see Cyril furiously scribbling in his steno pad. She could see him pulling at least three stories out of this meeting—one, a report on the town's Christmas celebration and the conflict surrounding it; two, a reason to speculate on the missing men and the toll it was taking on the townspeople; and finally, an update on the murder itself and the reaction to Harold Dewey's death. How Santa dying would affect the town for generations to come.

Good Lord. She was starting to think like Cyril.

"Besides," Mona continued, "if we go through the motions of a stroll again, we'll need a Santa, and we'll need a signature event. Have you given any thought to that? Where will we find another Santa?"

Blank stares all around. "You think Seamus will turn up by then?" Neil asked. "I'm sure he'll do it."

"Yeah, but someone might try to kill him. I mean, isn't

that what they're saying? That Santa got killed because they thought it was him?" Tom, a long-term Christmas committee member and volunteer at the town's historical War House, asked.

Stan rose to her feet, unable to keep her mouth shut any longer. "Hey. You haven't even picked a date for this thing. Maybe do that before you argue about Santa?"

"And that's what we're trying to do," Curtis Wallace said, his tone snotty. He hadn't liked Stan much since she'd questioned him about his relationship to someone who'd ended up dead last summer. "But we need a Santa."

"Well, pick one you know is available," she said, exasperated. "Unfortunately, no one knows where Seamus is."

"When's your grand opening, Stan?" Betty asked.

"Next Saturday," Stan said.

"Great. We'll do the stroll next Saturday, then. What about Paul McGee for Santa?" Betty suggested, turning back to the rest of the committee. "Seamus has always done it, but Paul would be wonderful! He's such a kind man. And he loves children."

The group seemed to agree on that. Satisfied, Betty turned to Stan. "It's settled. Stan, will you do the honors?"

"What honors?" Stan asked.

"Ask him, of course. You're practically related," Betty said with a laugh.

Stan bit back a sigh. She loved Betty, but sometimes she could be too laser-focused on her town duties. "Guys. Come on," she said, trying for a reasonable tone. "The man's brother is missing. The whole family is stressed. You really want me to ask him to play Santa? Can't we think outside the box here?"

Betty's lips pushed together in a pout. "Paul is a wonderful man who's able to put aside his feelings to help people. You know that, Stan. I'm sure he wouldn't take offense at being asked."

"Maybe so, but . . ."

"Excellent. So we have a plan. Is everyone willing to pick up their former responsibilities? Except for those associated with the tree lighting, of course. I have plenty of new jobs for you. See me when we're done and I'll get you assigned. We should do some things differently. Like have carolers going around to all the stores. And maybe a front window competition for the stores. I'll get an entertainment subcommittee going."

Next to Stan, Izzy's phone dinged. She checked it, then stood up and slipped out of the room without a word.

"Stan?" Betty demanded.

"What?"

"Will you help with the entertainment?"

"Betty, I don't know if I can—"

"Great. Thank you. Anything else? No? Well, that was productive. Everyone have a lovely Monday!" With that, she dismissed them.

Stan turned to Tony, who offered a sympathetic smile. "At least you'll have a subcommittee," he said.

"Yeah. Great." She blew out a breath, then looked at Kyle. "Can you work with me on Saturday?"

"Of course. Wouldn't miss it."

That was a relief. "Thank you. Truly."

Neil made his way over to them and sat in the row in front of Stan. "Hey. Meant to ask. No word on ol' Mackey yet?"

Stan shook her head. "Not that I know of."

"You think he's having a midlife crisis?" he asked earnestly. "I mean, these things happen, you know?"

She shook her head vehemently. "No. That's not Ray."

Neil laughed. He reached over and patted Stan's hand as if to reassure her that she knew nothing about the ways of men. Stan felt her free hand instinctively close into a fist.

Kyle saw it and leaned forward too, cutting off any further commentary the guy had. "Hey, man, I'm new to town and all, but maybe those rumors would be more directed at you?"

Neil's smile faded. He frowned, opened his mouth, then closed it again before he whirled around and marched out the door. Kyle winked at Stan. "Much as I'd love to see you lay someone out, it's probably not the time," he said. "We've got to get your grand opening planned and find our friend Ray."

Chapter Thirty

Stan drove straight to the patisserie, her mind spinning with all the new chores this revised holiday stroll would add to her already stretched to-do list. Really, she wanted to shake some sense into Betty, but it would be no use. Once Betty got an idea in her head, she wouldn't let it go. So, she was helping plan another Christmas stroll.

Stan let herself in the back door. The scent of cinnamon and pumpkin hit her full on.

"Morning!" Brenna called. "I started a few batches."

"As usual, thank you." Stan dropped her bag and took off her coat. "Sorry to be late."

"The meeting, I know." Brenna grinned. "What's going on?"

"They want to have another Christmas stroll. Which they're timing around my grand opening next weekend. I mean, we've got one dead guy and two unaccounted-for guys, and this is what they're worried about. So now the committee has more work to do. What's next on the list?"

Brenna handed her the day's recipe list.

"And now I have to ask your dad to be Santa. Because

we still need a Santa." She grimaced. "I would think most people wouldn't want to see Santa at this point."

The bell out front rang, signaling a customer. Stan checked her watch. "Yikes. Almost ten already. I keep losing my mornings." Stan hurried out front to greet whoever had arrived.

Emmalee Hoffman and Ted Brahm were in the entryway. "Hey, guys," Stan said. "How's it going? That was quite the meeting this morning, huh, Emmalee?"

Emmalee shook her head. "I'll tell you. There's no need to make everyone do all this work a second time, but there was no getting around it gracefully. And in case he hasn't told you himself, Tyler is available to help you again. Whether it's with the entertainment you were voluntold for, or your grand opening. I know you need a photographer and a number of other things done."

"That would be wonderful," Stan said. "He's on my list to call, but I just haven't had a chance. Do you know if he can come by this afternoon?"

"I'll text him right now." Emmalee pulled out her phone. "I'll tell him to bring Eddie too."

"Eddie?" Stan asked.

"Eddie Crookshank. Lester's boy? He and Tyler are friends. Tyler's been trying to help him through some tough times lately. It will be good for him to do something constructive. He can help with the manual labor portion."

Tough times. Lester's boy was having problems of some sort. Stan wanted to ask more about it, but didn't know if Emmalee would think her interest was odd. But she wondered if the problems had anything to do with Harold or working on the farm together. She made a mental note to try to find that out. In the meantime, she needed to act like the store proprietor. "Great. Thanks. So what brings you here?" she asked, smiling brightly. "Treats for the cat? Or the farm animals?"

Emmalee smiled. "Neither. Well, of course we can get treats for the cat. But . . ." She looked up at Ted, beaming. "We're adopting a dog."

"You are! That's wonderful. What kind? From where?"

"He's a golden retriever. Only a year old. From a golden rescue, way down the other part of the state," Emmalee said. "We're very excited. His name is Ollie."

"Congratulations. When is he coming home?"

"Today," Emmalee admitted. "And we realized we have no idea what to do for food. Of course, Tyler reminded me about your meal plan for dogs. I'm not sure how I'd forgotten about that, but that's what happens when you get old like me." She smiled. "Anyway. Can you recommend some meals for him? We'd love to sign up for the monthly plan. We know how important good food is to these babies."

"Of course. We can get you going on that. Why don't you sit and I'll bring over the menus?" Stan pointed toward a table on the human side of the café. "I'll be right back."

She slipped out back to get the booklet Brenna—thank God—had gotten made for her, which outlined the meal choices and delivery plans she offered. "Guess what!" she said in a stage whisper to Brenna. "The Hoffmans want a meal plan! They're adopting a dog. This is the first real meal plan customer I've had! Besides Char, who I always thought was buying them just to be sweet."

Brenna dropped her mixing spoon and clapped. "That's amazing! And Char buys them because she knows it's the best food for her dog, silly. Here's your book." She winked. "Aren't you glad I had you put it together?"

"Totally. Thank you so much. I'd be lost without you." She hurried back out to her guests. "I wish I had some coffee to offer you," she said, sliding into a chair. "But I didn't order any from Izzy today."

Ted winced a little at that. Stan covered her mouth. "I'm sorry. Are you doing okay, Ted?"

Emmalee rubbed his arm. "He's so upset. Aren't you, dear."

"It's just very sad," Ted said. "I can't believe it. Harold wasn't a bad man. I mean, I'd only come to know him last season after I moved to town, but he was always very helpful. He spent some time on the farm with us."

Stan remembered what Tyler had told her, about Emmalee giving Harold a break while his father had less patience for him. Ted apparently had the same good heart as his wife.

"He got a bad rap around town," Emmalee confided to Stan. "Especially thanks to those cousins of his."

"Cousins?" Stan hadn't heard anything about Harold having relatives around Frog Ledge.

"The O'Sullivan sisters. Vivian and Victoria." She shook her head. "They treated him so poorly. I mean, it wasn't his fault that their mother left him a portion of the property the sisters felt they had a claim to."

"Wait." Stan held up a hand. "Harold was related to Miss Viv? Seamus's Miss Viv?"

Emmalee nodded, pursing her lips. "Yes."

She sat back, her head spinning. Why on earth had no one mentioned this? Like Jake? "Do a lot of people know?"

"I'm not sure they do," Emmalee said. "It's not like the ladies ever wanted to acknowledge him, especially given his challenges. But their mother always felt sorry for him. He was her sister's son, you see, and her sister had her own problems. So Viv and Victoria's mother, Louisa, basically raised him and always felt responsible. My mother was close to her. She died about a year ago, and her will really sent everything into an uproar. Once Harold found out he was an heir, he requested the money for his portion of the property." Emmalee shifted in her chair, leaning forward as she got to the juicy part. "The ladies wanted to buy him out, but they couldn't afford it. So they were forced to sell most of the land. They made some money, but had to sink it into house repairs. So out of their parents' formerly immense acreage and share of the town, they're basically left with that drafty old house. A developer bought the rest. I think they're putting up condos or something. The work started in the fall. I'm sure it's eating away at them, watching that construction day after day."

"The land that Kyle wants to build his restaurant on," she said, half to herself. "It's zoned commercially because Harold made them sell it? Wow. So they had a good reason to hate him."

Emmalee shrugged. "You could say that. If money is a good reason to hate someone. Although I guess on their part it was more the nostalgia factor. They wanted to keep the land in their family. And losing it to someone they consider a worthless drunk has stuck in their craw, for sure." Her phone dinged. She glanced down at it and smiled. "Tyler and Eddie will be here for you at four. Does that work?"

"Perfect," Stan said. "Hopefully this will be the last time we have to plan this grand opening."

Chapter Thirty-one

After Emmalee and Ted placed their order and left to pick up their new family member, Stan went back to filling her pastry cases. But despite her vows to forget about this whole Seamus/Harold mess, her mind was on the information she'd just learned. Harold and Seamus had a history, sure. She'd already known that. But what she hadn't realized was they had this other connection point—Miss Viv.

If Miss Viv and her sister had a beef with Harold, and Seamus knew about it, he could've done something to retaliate. The McGees were loyal—that much Stan knew. Had Miss Viv put him up to it?

And would that revenge consist of setting Harold up to be killed?

What if she *had* been wrong about Seamus—what if he hadn't been the target, but the orchestrator? Could Jake's favorite uncle really be that cold-blooded? She didn't want to think so, but who knew. After hearing some of the stories about Seamus, she had to assume he had a whole other life that probably most of his family members knew nothing about. If the whole freight-yard story was true, for one, it certainly seemed like he could run with a rough crowd. And men who ran with rough crowds had to know how to take care of themselves—and their loved ones—to survive. So if Seamus thought Harold had hurt Miss Viv, maybe he'd feel like he had to do something about it in her honor, like he had all those years ago in grade school.

Brenna came out with another tray of cookies. "Here's the last batch. I think we've got enough for today, don't we?" She surveyed the case, hands on hips. "Looking good."

"It sure is," Stan said. "Hey. Were you planning on being here for the day?"

"Of course." Brenna grinned. "Where else would I be?"

"Great. Can you cover the counter for a bit? I need to run a quick errand."

"Of course. Take your time."

Stan headed down the street to the pub, hoping Jake was there already. He was. She caught him on a trash run to the dumpster outside.

"Hey," he said. "What are you doing here? I thought you were at the store all day."

"I am. But I need to talk to you."

He tossed the trash into the dumpster and wiped his hands on his jeans. "What's wrong? Are you okay?"

"Yeah. No. I don't know. Can we go sit for a few minutes?"

"Come on." He slipped an arm around her shoulders and led her inside, calling to Scott that they were going upstairs for a few minutes. Scott waved his agreement.

"Does he think it's weird that we just use their apartment whenever we feel like it?" Stan asked as they climbed the stairs. "I probably would."

"Nah. Brenna doesn't care. I don't think Scott cares. I think he's worried I'll throw him out if he doesn't agree." Jake grinned. His overprotection toward his little sister kept Scott on his toes. He unlocked the door and pulled out a chair for Stan at the little kitchen table. "Now what's going on?"

Stan took a deep breath, saying a silent prayer that she hadn't made a bad decision to raise this with him. "I just had a conversation with Emmalee Hoffman. Unsolicited. She mentioned it to me, but I feel like it's another piece of the puzzle. And I know Jessie is mad at me and thinks I'm poking my nose where it doesn't belong, but I'm not. I just want to make sure everyone's thinking through this the right way."

She saw his whole body go still. "Thinking through what? What do you mean? Stan, you're not still worrying about Harold, are you? You need to leave that to Jessie. You heard her loud and clear last night."

"Emmalee just told me that Harold and Miss Viv are related."

"Cousins," Jake said. "So?"

"You knew that? And never thought to mention it?"

Jake shrugged. "I didn't know it was a big deal."

"It sounds like Miss Viv and her sister lost out when some property they felt should've been theirs partly went to Harold, and he made them sell it."

"It was a bunch of farmland," Jake said. "They actually profited from the sale. Otherwise they were just going to let it sit there. I don't see the connection, Stan."

She caught the slightest hint of defensiveness in his tone and tried to figure out how to approach this differently. She didn't want to upset him, but at the same time, she felt like everyone was sticking their heads in the sand over Seamus for varying reasons.

"Look. I'm just saying. If Harold really was the target, like Jessie insists, was this why? Because, Jake, it's either that or Seamus was the target here. Izzy didn't kill anyone. I'd stake my life on it. And Lester Crookshank may have had his problems with Harold, but at the heart of it he's a good man. I know he is. And those are the two people the investigation is focused on right now. If not them, it begs the question, is everyone looking in the right place? And if Seamus's girlfriend felt wronged by Harold, would Seamus have come to her defense? And maybe made a bad decision on how to do that?"

She held her breath. Jake didn't say anything for a long moment. She could see the clock on the microwave behind him flash to 12:01, then 12:02. Finally he spoke.

"I'm not really sure why you think my uncle is such a bad person, Stan, but I assure you he's not. He certainly didn't set Harold Dewey up to be killed, not even out of love for his girlfriend. And as for your other theory, that someone was trying to kill him—I won't even pretend to understand where that came from."

"Jake," Stan said, incredulous. "You heard the story with your own ears about the cargo ship. That had to raise a red flag. I'm not saying he's a bad person. I'm just saying, maybe he made some bad decisions."

"If you're saying my uncle set somebody up to be killed, that sounds to me like something a bad person would do. And if you think he did something worthy of being killed for, that's not much better. So I guess I don't understand how you *can't* think that. Listen, I really have to get back to work."

"Wait. Please." She rose, reaching out for his hand, but he stepped away from her touch. Hurt, she yanked her hand back. "I wanted to talk this through with you because I thought we could put our heads together and figure something out," she said desperately. "I know how much he means to you and I want to help you find him. And I know how much Ray means to Char and I want to help her find him. If we keep ignoring the idea that this has anything to do with Seamus, we're never going to get there. And two innocent people are getting their names dragged through the mud. The whole thing is a mess."

"Billing my uncle as a criminal isn't going to help find them either," Jake said. "And it's certainly not going to make him want to come back. You know, Stan, just because your family isn't super loyal to each other doesn't mean that's the right way to be. And it's definitely not the way everyone's family is." He turned and walked out the door, back down the steps into the pub.

Stan watched him go, tears pricking at the backs of her eyelids. He'd never walked away from her like that before. And the family comparison was kind of a low blow. She felt terrible about hurting his feelings enough that he'd felt the need to lash out, but she also felt a twinge of anger that he was so willing to brush off her concerns. Her gut continued the drumbeat that something was off with Uncle Seamus. Her gut was hardly ever wrong. In fact, the times when she'd gotten in the most trouble had been when she'd ignored her gut completely.

Whether Jake or anyone in his family wanted to believe it or not, Uncle Seamus had more to do with this than anyone realized. But no one seemed invested in figuring out how.

Chapter Thirty-two

Stan left the pub through the back door. By the time she'd walked back to the patisserie, she was more angry than upset. It wasn't like her whole life hadn't been disrupted here too. From the extra committee time she'd be serving to get the holidays back on track, to having to reschedule her grand opening and double her expenses by buying everything again, to having not only Jake's cousins living at her house but now Seamus's friend Kevin, who'd obviously decided he liked Frog Ledge so much he was never going to leave. She'd heard him snoring on her living room sofa again this morning.

Of course, that was her own fault. She laughed a bit ruefully. It had only been two nights that he'd been there, and she'd done the inviting. She was letting everything get to her.

But add to that a friend under suspicion for murder and another friend paralyzed by the temporary loss of her husband, and the whole holiday season was simply not turning out the way she'd envisioned. And she hadn't even added poor Harold to that list of bad turns.

She shoved open the front door, certain steam was

now coming out of her ears. Brenna noticed right away that something was up.

"Uh-oh," she said. "What's happened?"

"Nothing," Stan said.

Brenna shot her a skeptical look. "Right. Last time you looked like that, your mother was trying to tell you how to design this place and you were ready to gag her and stuff her in a closet."

Despite herself, Stan had to laugh. This was much more serious, but she remembered that day well. "Yeah, well, my mother and I have had a few of those days. Honest, Bren, it's nothing. Don't worry about it." The last thing she wanted was to alienate another McGee.

Brenna looked around. There were two customers in the patisserie—a young couple with their two dogs. They were snuggling together on a bench in the dog area while the dogs, two Labs, contentedly munched on treats on the floor next to them. "Let's go out to the kitchen," she said.

Stan reluctantly followed her. "What if someone comes in?"

"We'll hear the bell. Now what's up? Does this have to do with my brother? 'Cause he called here before you got back."

"He did?"

"Yeah. To see if you'd gotten here yet."

"Great. How nice of him. I'm not calling him back." Stan resisted the urge to cross her arms and pout.

Brenna stifled a smile. "Why are you two arguing? You never argue."

"I can't tell you. You'll be mad at me too." Stan grabbed a bottle of water out of the fridge and leaned against the counter. "We need a table back here in case we want to sit," she grumbled. "Why don't we have a table?"

"It wasn't in your mother's design. Of course you can tell me. I won't be mad, Stan. I promise."

"You don't know that," Stan pointed out. "You have no idea what I'm going to tell you."

"Oh, I think I do," Brenna said.

Stan paused, surprised. "You do?"

Brenna nodded. "It's about my uncle, right?"

"Yeah, actually."

"Let me guess—Jake doesn't want to talk about what's going on with him."

"How'd you know that?"

Brenna rolled her eyes. "Really? It's my family. I know them like the back of my hand. They can all be ridiculous at times. This is one of Jake's times. He thinks Uncle Seamus is out having fun and forgot to come home."

Interested now, Stan took a swig of her water and set it down. "So what do you think's going on?"

"I think my uncle was up to something," Brenna said. "I have no idea what, but the way he was behaving before he left for Boston was totally sketchy."

"Really? How so?"

"He was antsy. Disappearing a lot to make phone calls. I spent that night with him and Miss Viv. The night before he left? He was having massive mood swings. Alternated between super happy to crazy nervous. Whispering a lot to Miss Viv and making her giggle. Victoria was getting so annoyed with them. I thought it was kind of funny at the time, but now I'm guessing something serious was going on."

"Do you have any idea what he was telling Miss Viv?"

Brenna shook her head. "I heard her say she couldn't wait to pack, but I didn't know what she meant and I didn't feel like I should ask. I thought they were just being silly, you know? But then . . ." She hesitated.

"What?" Stan prompted.

"When I was going to the bathroom, I heard him on the phone in one of the bedrooms. I swear he said something like *what do I do if something goes wrong?* I tried to listen, but I think he was walking around and he got too far away."

Stan felt a rush of excitement. Maybe she'd been right after all. "Did you tell anyone?"

Brenna nodded. "My sister."

"What did she say? Did she believe you?"

"I'm sure she believed me. She just doesn't care," Brenna said, her tone more amused than bitter. "She said whatever foolish thing Seamus is involved with is not her problem unless it's illegal and happens in this town. And since he's clearly not in town, she's washed her hands of it. We actually had a fight about it. I was upset at myself for not paying more attention before everything happened."

"Did he mention Ray at all?" Stan asked.

"Not that I heard. So what was your fight with Jake about?"

"I merely raised the question that this Harold thing was tied to Seamus somehow."

Brenna's thought process clearly hadn't gotten that far. She paled. "What do you mean?"

Stan explained her theory about Lester and Izzy being weak suspects in Harold's death. "If you think about it, no one really knew Seamus had passed the Santa hat to Harold, right? So what if he was the target?" She left out the part where she'd wondered if Seamus had orchestrated Harold's death. That might be going too far right now.

"Jeez." Brenna paced the kitchen. "I didn't even think of that. You think whatever he was into was that serious?"

"I have no idea what he was into," Stan said. "But I don't believe they're just up there having fun and avoiding coming home. Ray wouldn't do that to Char, no matter what Seamus wanted."

The bell on the door tinkled. Brenna jumped up. "I'll take care of it. Just breathe." She hurried out front, but was back in less than a minute. "You're going to want to come out here," she said.

Chapter Thirty-three

"Oh God. What now?" Stan groaned.

"No, this is good. Trust me," Brenna said. "Bad timing, but this is really good."

Curious now, Stan followed her out to the store. A woman stood at the pastry cases, admiring them and their contents. She had short, curly blond hair. Her black wool coat and high-heeled boots looked expensive. When she turned to smile at Stan and offer her hand, her grip was firm.

"Stan Connor. It's so great to meet you in person. I'm Megan Flynn from *Foodie* magazine. We spoke over the phone about the feature we ran on you a few months back?"

"Ms. Flynn! Yes, of course," Stan said, wishing she'd dressed a little better this morning. "What brings you here?"

"Please, call me Megan. I've been dying to come and see this place. I heard your grand opening was this weekend and I really wanted to get here then, but I was called away on something else."

That was a blessing in disguise. "Actually, it's been

postponed. I did more of a . . . soft opening this weekend, since I still wanted to stay on track. But my official grand opening will be next Saturday."

"So I didn't miss it! That's wonderful. I'll see if I can make it. Listen, I came down on behalf of our editor. He wanted me to scope out the place for a follow-up, but he also wanted me to gauge your interest in something else. An ongoing feature we're thinking of piloting." She looked around. "Is there somewhere we can talk?"

"Of course." Stan led her to a table on the people side of the shop, her mind racing. An ongoing feature? For *Foodie* magazine? What on earth could they want from her?

Brenna raised her eyebrows from behind the counter. Stan grinned, knowing her assistant would be eavesdropping hard on this conversation.

She sat down across from Megan Flynn. The other woman didn't waste any time jumping in.

"Pet food is serious business these days, as you know," she said. "People are way more interested in it than they've ever been. The article we did on you and Nutty got a ton of attention. Where is that little darling, anyway?" She craned her neck, looking around the store.

"He's at home," Stan said. "With all the dogs that come in, I'm still trying to decide if it's a good idea to have him here."

"Understandable." Megan nodded. "Anyway, we're thinking of running a monthly column on pet food and nutrition. Each column would include a recipe for some yummy treat or meal. And we'd like you to be our contributing editor for that column. What do you think? Of course, it's a paid position."

"Contributing editor?" Stan repeated. "Paid position? Me?"

Megan Flynn laughed. "Yes, you. Why not? Look at what you've done here!" She waved a hand at the shop.

"And we interviewed some of your customers when we did that story. They say you're the real deal. Plus, we don't know of any other people who've taken pet food to this level and been successful. And I should also mention—if this is successful, we're considering a *Foodie* spinoff focused entirely on pets. Very much down the road, of course, but wanted to make sure you knew that as well. So what do you think?"

"Um," Stan said. Megan cocked her head, clearly impressed with Stan's articulate nature. "I mean, I think it sounds really great. What would you want the focus of each column to be?"

Megan beamed. "Our editor, Carol, will discuss all of that with you. She's great. She'll be calling you. I think they're really looking for a variety of insights into why people should put more into feeding their animals than buying some canned food online and tossing it in a bowl. Make sense?"

"Sure, yes," Stan said, already wondering how she was going to fit this into her crazy schedule. "It sounds fabulous. Thank you for thinking of me."

"My goodness, it's a no-brainer." Megan rose and flicked some dog hair off her pristine coat. "Would you be open to me bringing a photographer Saturday?"

"I would love that," Stan said. "Thank you."

"Excellent. It's a date. I'll have Carol call you. Bye now!" And she swept out the door, leaving Stan staring after her.

Brenna rushed over. "I only heard some of that. She was from *Foodie*?"

Stan nodded, still kind of shell-shocked.

"Well?" Brenna demanded. "Aren't you going to tell me what she wanted?"

"She wants to do a follow-up article. So she's coming back Saturday during the grand opening," Stan said.

"That's awesome!"

"It is. And . . . she—well, the editor—wants me to do a monthly column on pet nutrition for the magazine."

"*What!*" Brenna screeched. "That's amazing, Stan!"

"It is pretty cool, isn't it?" Now that it had sunk in a bit, she was smiling. It felt good to be noticed for all the hard work she'd put in over the last year. And it took away, at least a little bit, from the sting of her earlier encounter with Jake.

Chapter Thirty-four

Stan spent the next few hours in a completely different mental space than the one in which she'd spent the last three days. She felt happy. Her shop was doing well. The townspeople loved it. The dogs who'd visited loved it. She'd sold out of most of her treats all weekend long, and she hadn't even had her official grand opening yet. And now? She was going to get more recognition in *Foodie* magazine. And a paying writing gig. Cyril would be proud—she was a journalist, after all.

But after the euphoria lifted a little, she realized she was mentally exhausted. And annoyed.

Annoyed at people getting angry at her when she was just trying to help. Annoyed at people who were pointing fingers at her friends for a serious crime, when they wouldn't listen to any alternate solutions. Annoyed at Jake—yes, even her beloved Jake—for ignoring what seemed so obvious, what was right in front of his face. And for shutting her out and walking away from her. Something they'd promised not to do to each other.

And she was annoyed at herself for worrying about the whole Harold/Seamus/Ray debacle. She had enough going on: a new store, houseguests, a Christmas decorating contest, her mother's wedding, Kyle's restaurant. Yet she continued to focus on things that really had no direct bearing on her life. And that netted her no gratitude for any help she tried to provide.

So maybe she should just forget about it. Be like everyone else and go about her business. Ask Kevin to hit the road, and reclaim her couch. Forget about what anyone else was going through. That made her feel guilty when she thought of Char, but that was a different story. She could still try to help Char without putting herself through the turmoil of trying to talk sense into Jake or Jessie, or worry about finding their Mysterious Vanishing Uncle.

"Yes," she said out loud, startling the guy who'd just walked in with his dog. "That's exactly what I'm going to do." She smiled at him. "Hi. How are you?"

Once she'd served up some pumpkin cream-cheese treats for his dog and the store was empty again, she stuck her head in the kitchen. "I need to run one more quick errand."

Brenna sent her on her way. This time, she hurried to town hall and took the stairs to the second floor. Jessie's office door was open, and she sat behind her desk, head down, intently focused on some papers in front of her. Stan rapped sharply on the door with her knuckles and strode in.

Jessie looked up, startled. Before she could say anything, Stan went straight to her desk, slapped her hands on it and leaned forward.

"Don't ever come into my house and yell at me again. Especially not in front of your family," Stan said. "Just because you don't want to listen to reason and you want to control the story. You're bothering people who didn't do anything wrong, and I don't like it. But you know what? You win. I don't care anymore. Do whatever you want, arrest whoever you want. I have better things to do than waste my time worrying about something that no one wants me to worry about."

She paused and took a breath. Jessie stared at her like she'd never seen her before.

"Stan," she began, but Stan cut her off.

"I'm not done. I have one more thing to say. I know you don't want to hear it, but too bad. I also know your brother won't tell you because God forbid he shares something that makes his precious uncle look bad. The guy you yelled at, also in my house? He came down to tell Jake that your uncle may have been spotted at the South Boston freight yard trying to accept a delivery. A car that got hijacked and crashed into a highway barrier. No one knows if he was in the car or not, but there are no records of him at any of the Boston hospitals. How do we know that? Because I called them all! So when you all try to tell me that I'm crazy for thinking your uncle may have been the target in this catastrophe, let me point out that anyone who can ignore all that is even crazier than I am. Now I'm done."

With that, she spun on her heel and stalked to the door. She'd almost crossed the threshold when Jessie said, "Stan. I know you're right."

Stan stopped, waiting for the punch line. When it didn't come, she turned. "You do?"

Jessie sighed and got up, walking around to the front of her desk. "I admit there must be some element of truth to it," she said. "I don't have blinders on like my brother. I've been in touch with the Boston police. I know what happened the other night. I don't know what it means, but I agree something's not right."

Stan heaved a sigh of relief. "You do? Thank God!"

Jessie held up a hand. "Don't get too excited. That doesn't mean that I'm not pursuing people who had a problem with Harold Dewey. It just means that I understand my uncle may have been involved in something, and I'm going to keep an eye on where the trail leads."

All the relief that had whooshed through Stan left her body. "So you're still looking at Lester and Izzy," she said flatly.

"I have to. I have evidence . . . that I can't discuss with you. But I have enough to talk to them both again."

"Why aren't you looking at people who had a problem with your uncle? Heck, what about Abby? She threatened to sue him. Said he was the cause of her financial troubles, the reason she's jacking up her prices at the store. And she said he deserved to die more than Harold. If that's not an incriminating statement, I have no idea what is!"

Jessie's face didn't change. She had that uncanny ability to keep her cop face in place during all sorts of confrontations. It was part of what made her a pro, Stan figured. But sometimes it was so infuriating she couldn't stand it.

"And," Stan went on—now she was on fire—"Seamus's own girlfriend told me he's coming into some money and they're taking off together! To Turks and Caicos, for goodness' sakes! Viv is out buying fancy dresses. What's that about? You mean to tell me Seamus got some kind of corporate bonus out of nowhere? Come on, Jessie. You're a cop. You have to think that's suspicious."

Jessie set her jaw. "Stan. I'm sorry about last night. I really am. I heard from Lester that you spoke to him and it made me mad. The stress of all this is getting to me. You're right, I shouldn't have come to your house and spoken to you that way. But I have to ask you—please stay out of this. I know what I'm doing. Okay?"

She turned and walked back to her desk without waiting for an answer. Stan left without giving her one. She'd made up her mind anyway. She was staying out of it. Let Jessie figure it out and be the hero. She only hoped that the truly innocent people involved didn't suffer need-lessly. As for Jake, well, he'd have to figure out where he stood too. She couldn't keep trying to talk sense into him. She had to start taking care of herself.

Stan left town hall and headed back to her shop, deter-mined to do as everyone wanted and forget about this whole business. Good thing she had plenty to keep her mind occupied. And she needed to hurry back. Tyler and Eddie were due at the shop. She called over to Izzy's— Izzy wasn't there—and ordered coffee to go and a dozen cupcakes. Then she texted Brenna that she was picking up some goodies and she'd be right over.

When she arrived, Brenna had closed up and was clearing away dirty dishes. Tyler and Eddie were sitting at one of the tables, both texting furiously on their phones. They both brightened at the sight of cupcakes.

"Oh, sweet! Food!" Tyler exclaimed. "I've been at the paper all day and had to skip lunch."

"Some days you just need cupcakes," Stan said, de-positing the goodies in the middle of the table. She smiled at Eddie. "Hi, Eddie. I don't think we've met offi-cially."

"Nicetameetcha," Eddie mumbled, shoving his phone in his pocket.

The boys helped themselves to cupcakes. Brenna even came over and selected one.

"Yum," she said. "So what are we talking about?"

"Grand opening," Stan said. She grabbed a cupcake too. Why not? "You're working that day, right?"

"Wouldn't miss it," Brenna said.

"So we're doing photos again?" Tyler asked.

"I'd like to, yes. I have to line up Santa, but as long as you're able to take pictures."

"Let's offer a free Christmas cookie to every dog and cat who comes in to get their photo taken," Brenna said.

"I love it." Stan made a note. "I was thinking a gingerbread-type cookie this time. We did cranberry-apple candy canes last weekend to go along with the red theme, but let's maybe do stockings or trees this time?"

"I like stockings," Brenna said, making a note on her phone. "Who are we naming the treats after?" Brenna asked. "Or are we using Chuckie's Christmas Cookies and Houdini's Holly Jolly Catnolis?"

"We'll keep the original winners," Stan said. "It's only right. I think I'll get more food from the Italian place. It was amazing. They'll deliver it. Tyler and Eddie, can I enlist you to help with getting the tables back here to set up the food? And maybe pick the food up that morning?"

Eddie nodded. "Where are you getting the tables? My dad has some I can just throw in the truck and bring over."

"I was going to borrow them from town hall, but if you have some, perfect."

"I'll check with my dad, but I'm sure it will be fine." Eddie hesitated. "Hey, I have a suggestion," he said.

Stan looked at him expectantly. "Sure."

"If you don't have any luck with finding a Santa, I think my dad would love to do it. He was pretty bummed that Harold was doing it this year."

Stan frowned. "Bummed?"

"Yeah, when Harold told him, I don't think he could believe it. You know, Harold didn't have a rep for being, well, jolly." Eddie shifted uncomfortably, as if just realizing he was talking about a dead man. "Anyway, wanted to offer him up."

"Thanks," Stan murmured as the boys walked out the front door. She remembered the feeling she'd gotten last night at Lester's. That he'd been lying about something. Well, she'd just learned what he was lying about. He'd known Harold was going to be in the Santa suit taking Seamus's place.

Chapter Thirty-five

After Stan closed up the shop for the day, Brenna headed to the pub to pick up a shift while Stan headed for home. When she got to her driveway, she paused a moment, then continued walking down the street toward Char's. She really wanted to see her and make sure she was as okay as possible.

When she got to the B and B and let herself in the front door, she was surprised to see Char at the stove while four men crowded around the dining room table. They were all in varying stages of conversation. One was a red-head. Another was bald. The third man had thinning blond hair, and the last guy wore a hat that looked a bit like the one Kevin had been wearing. All eyes turned to Stan when she walked in.

"Hello," she said, meeting Char's eyes with a question.

"Stan! Honey, come sit." Char's voice sounded more alive than it had since Friday night, and there was a sparkle in her eyes. "You won't believe who came to visit me. These are Seamus's friends. From the poker game." Stan's eyes traveled back to the table. The men raised their hands to wave to her. "Stan is Seamus's niece, pretty much. As soon as she marries his nephew, anyway."

Stan shot her a bewildered look. Char must be feeling better. Where had that come from?

"How'dya do," the redhead said, his voice thick with Irish.

"They think Seamus and Ray are in some kind of trouble," Char went on, her voice rising in pitch with every word. "Maybe now someone will believe me! I knew my Raymond wouldn't just up and disappear." She jabbed her wooden spoon into whatever was bubbling in her Crock-Pot, like she was trying to spear it.

"Wait, hold up," Stan said, eyeing the four men. "It's three days later and now you're here?"

The men looked at each other—a little nervously, Stan thought.

"We didn't really know what to do," the bald guy said when none of the others spoke up. "See, Seamus kinda left us in the lurch. He was supposed to bring all this cash to our game. Promised us it was the real deal, that we could start inviting the big boys and really up our payouts, right?" The guy with the hat nodded encouragingly, so he went on. "So we found some guys to bring in. First they didn't wanna, you know? Thought we were just jokesters. But they finally agreed to come and put some money in the kitty. Then Seamus doesn't show."

"Really kinda messed us up," the blond guy added. "Our new additions were not real happy with us. So we weren't real happy with him, you know? But then, we started to get worried."

"About Seamus?"

"About all of us," Redhead said. "These guys were mad. And they could . . . do things, ya know? We started getting a little worried for ourselves. And for Seamus. So we thought we'd skip town for a few days. Maybe bump into Seamus down here. 'Course, we'd been hearing about the B and B all these years from Ray and had to come here and meet his lovely wife."

Char blushed.

"So none of you saw Ray or Seamus this weekend?" Stan asked.

"Nope. They never showed up at the game, like we said."

"I knew it. I knew they were in trouble," Char said triumphantly. "Do you think these goons caught up with them? Have them kidnapped somewhere?"

Redhead frowned. He seemed to be the spokesman. "Nah. These guys are too classy for that. But maybe they had people . . ." He trailed off when he saw the look on Char's face.

And Stan had been worried about Kevin coming here and freaking Char out. Now there were four of them.

Kevin.

"Hey," she said. "Why did your other friend come without you then? Was he more worried?"

Blank looks all around. "What other friend?" the guy with the hat asked.

"Kevin." She realized she didn't even know the guy's last name. And she'd been letting him stay in her house. Maybe Jake was right and she was crazy.

More blank looks, then Bald Guy brightened. "McCready? He's here? Get outta town."

"I don't know his last name. He showed up at the pub the other night."

"Gotta be him. I didn't know he was even coming to the game this weekend. He hasn't been round lately. But see? Still loyal to his old pal," Bald Guy said. "He staying here too?"

"He's staying at my house," Stan said, avoiding Char's gaze. She could feel her friend's eyes boring into her head wondering why she hadn't told her. She decided against mentioning the whole freight delivery and car chase incident in front of Char.

"We'll have to go say hello," Redhead declared. "Meantime, where can we get a drink around here?"

Chapter Thirty-six

Stan went home thinking of Lester. Her first instinct, of course, was to talk to Jake about it. But she didn't think she could. He was still upset, and she wasn't supposed to be involved. It might just make things worse if she brought it up, even if they agreed to disagree.

When she got there, Declan was hauling a suitcase to his car. "Are you leaving?" Stan asked, surprised.

He nodded. "I have to get home. I'm really not in the mood to do a family Christmas party, with all this stuff going on with my dad."

"You don't want to wait to . . . find out what's going on?"

Declan shrugged. "I'm not that far away. My brother will call me." He hugged Stan awkwardly. "Thanks for everything. Really. I'll stop by the pub and let Jake know."

Stan watched him drive away, thinking about how sad it was when families made such a mess of things with each other. Hers included. She went inside and peeked into the living room. Kevin's bag was in there, but there was no sign of him. Liam, as usual, wasn't around.

She let the dogs outside and fed all the animals dinner—a special salmon and spinach dish she wanted to test for her meal delivery menu. They all approved, so she added it to her schedule. Then she made herself a salad and sat in her kitchen, enjoying the peace and quiet for a few minutes. When she finished eating, she picked up the phone and called Char, relieved when her friend answered. She'd worried about leaving her there with those men.

"How are you?" Stan asked.

"I'm still here," Char answered. "I guess that's all any of us can hope for."

"Did those four have anything useful to tell you after I left?"

"No." Char was silent. "The more time that goes by, the more hopeless it seems, doesn't it?"

"It's not hopeless, Char. Don't say that." But she didn't have a good reason to offer her about why she shouldn't feel hopeless, so the words sounded lame even to her own ears.

"That other friend of Seamus's came around here today," Char said, changing the subject slightly. "The one who's staying with you?"

"Kevin?" Stan said, surprised. "He did? Did he see his friends?"

"No, they were out. He said he wanted to meet me. Said not to worry. That Seamus has a lot of friends and everyone's looking for him. Charming fellow. I gave him some gumbo."

"Did he say where they were looking? Or what he thinks happened?"

"No. Just that Seamus is very resourceful."

At least he didn't mention the freight yard incident. "I'm sure he's right," Stan said. "Sounds like Seamus's friends know him best of all."

She ended the call and nearly jumped a foot when she

realized Kevin stood in the kitchen doorway, a small smile playing across his lips. "You're right about that, lassie," he said. "We do know our friend Seamus well. I'm sorry to eavesdrop," he added. "The door was open. I imagine you were speaking to the lovely Southern lady?"

"Yeah," Stan said, trying to slow her pounding heart. "Do you always sneak up on people like that? And if you all know Seamus so well, why don't you know where he is?"

Kevin moved into the kitchen. He reached into a cabinet for a mug like he'd been living there forever. He chose a tea bag and turned the hot water on, then turned back to Stan. "It's just a matter of time before he turns up," he said. "Trust me on that."

Stan tried to go to sleep early. Mostly because she didn't want to get into some sort of discussion—or argument—with Jake. He came in, climbed in bed next to her and gave her a kiss on the forehead, then fell asleep. She spent the rest of the night tossing and turning. When she finally did sleep, she had dreams about Harold and Seamus hiding on the tree farm, and Lester was angry at both of them and trying to find them. She woke up feeling unsettled, but a shower helped.

When she went downstairs, she could once again smell the fresh coffee. But the room was empty. She poured herself a cup and let Scruffy and Duncan, who'd followed her downstairs, out into the backyard and watched them from the window while she mentally planned her day. Treats, meal planning, grand opening chores. She wanted to try a new recipe she'd been playing around with. And she needed to update her website with the new grand opening details.

But that annoying piece of her brain kept drifting back to the larger matter at hand. She wanted to know why

Lester had lied about not knowing Harold was Santa. And what it meant. She thought about what Eddie had said as she let the dogs back inside. Lester was upset that Harold was Santa. She had to imagine, based on everything else she'd heard, that the Santa slight was just a piece of it, the icing on a cake full of frustration and animosity.

No one would get that angry over not being asked to wear a Santa costume, would they? And especially since the choice hadn't been officially sanctioned by the town or anyone close to the planning committee. It had just been Seamus, looking to get out of his duties for whatever reason. Maybe Lester didn't know that, but still.

She let out a cry of frustration, startling Scruffy, who sat at her feet waiting to see what the plan for the day was. "I'm not supposed to be worrying about this anymore," she told the dog.

Scruffy lay down and hid her face between her paws. Her dog knew her well.

She wasn't kidding anyone but herself. She couldn't let this go. The only way she was going to get on with her life was to figure out who killed Harold and why, and where Seamus and Ray were. Especially where Seamus and Ray were, because until Ray was home, Frog Ledge—and Char—would never get back to normal.

She heard the front door thunk shut and poked her head into the hall to see who it was. Kevin leaned against the wall, completely engrossed in the newspaper in his hand.

"Morning," she said.

He glanced up and in the second before what she'd come to recognize as his normal, charming smile crossed his face, something else was there. Concern? Anger? She couldn't tell.

"Morning, lass. I see you found your coffee."

"I did. Thank you."

"It's the least I can do. I hope you don't feel I'm overstaying my welcome," he said, scuffing his toe against the floor apologetically. "I'm enjoyin' your wee town, and I'm also not ready to leave until Seamus turns up. I hope that doesn't sound silly. And I'm happy to find lodging somewhere else if you please."

"That's not necessary," she said. "So you haven't told me what you've been doing around here. Aside from visiting Char and Miss Viv. There can't be that much that interests a big-city guy like you." She was curious. He never mentioned where he went during the day. She made a mental note to ask Miss Viv if they'd had dinner.

"Ah, you know. Wandering. Visiting all your historic sites. It's all fascinating."

That didn't really answer her question, but she didn't push. Instead, Stan nodded at the paper. "What are you reading?"

"A fascinating piece about the Book of Kells. Seems one of your locals did a lot of writing about it?" He waved the *Holler* at her. "And there's going to be a talk at the library tonight."

"A talk?" Stan took the paper and glanced at it. It was true. Cyril and his father were going to be at the Frog Ledge Library doing a joint conversation on the Book and all Arthur's research. "That's very cool. Are you going to stick around for it?"

Kevin nodded. "Wouldn't miss it for the world. I'm one of those Irish who likes our history. Shall I save you a seat?"

"You know what?" Stan said. "Yes. Please do."

She was in a much better mood when she and Scruffy got to the patisserie. Henry had chosen to stay in bed today. She even beat Brenna there today, and enjoyed having some time to herself in her new kitchen. Scruffy was getting into the routine now too. First she went out front and sniffed around to see what dogs had been visiting recently that she may not have known about. Then she poked around to see if there were any abandoned treats, or at the very least, crumbs, on the floor. Finally she went out back and settled on the special bed Stan had gotten for her.

While Scruffy did her thing, Stan jotted down a list of ingredients she needed to order and inventoried her cases. After making her list of what she wanted to bake for the day, she got her first batch of treats going. This way when Brenna arrived she'd know exactly what she needed to do.

Her hands were fully immersed in her batter, kneading away, when her cell rang on the counter. She glanced at it, half expecting to see Jake's or the pub's number come up, and didn't plan on answering. But instead, it was Izzy's number. She hurriedly wiped off one of her hands and pressed the button to answer.

"Stan?" Her friend was almost whispering. Stan's stomach flipped.

"Izzy? What's wrong?"

"I need help. Jessie wants to bring me in to the barracks to talk about the other night. I . . . I think she's going to arrest me."

"Arrest you?" Stan repeated.

"I think so," Izzy said. "Otherwise, why would she want me to go there?"

She was right. As the resident state trooper, Jessie's office was in the town hall, and she used that for common inquiries or casual conversations. Bringing someone to the official state police barracks twenty minutes outside of town was serious business.

"Can you help me? Does your mother know a good lawyer or something?" Izzy asked desperately.

"Of course I'll help you. If that's what's even happening, Izzy. You know Jessie. This could just be her way of shaking things up. Making the real criminal think he or she is okay so they'll get complacent. You know?" She was reaching here, but she needed to make her friend feel better. "When is she asking you to come in?"

"Later today. I stalled her as long as I could, said I was needed here at the café. So what should I do?"

"I don't think you have any choice but to go," Stan said grimly. "I'll call my mother. See if she can get someone to meet you there. What time are you going in?"

"Three." Izzy sounded on the verge of tears. That never happened. She was the most cool, calm, and collected person Stan had ever met.

Stan closed her eyes, seeing her blissful state of noninvolvement in this murder rapidly fading away. "Listen, Izzy. I think whatever happened the other night, it had to do with Seamus and not Harold. Something was going on with him. He was coming into some money, I heard—and from what I know about him, he was not a savvy businessman of any sort. Nobody wants to listen to that theory, but I can't help but feel like that's where the story is. It'll all shake out. Just hang tight and answer her questions. You don't have anything to hide."

"Right," Izzy said, but her voice sounded funny. "Nothing at all." She disconnected.

Stan swallowed back the panic rising in her chest. Jessie couldn't believe Izzy had anything to do with this. It was nuts. But Izzy was right—she needed a lawyer.

Which meant Stan had to talk to her mother.

Chapter Thirty-seven

Once Brenna arrived and took over the baking, Stan put Scruffy's leash on and they hurried out to her car. She'd decided to go to Patricia and Tony's house rather than calling. She had to make it quick so she could get back and man the counter, but this conversation would best be had in person.

It still felt weird to have her mother within a five-minute drive, she reflected as she put the car in gear. When she pulled up in front of Tony's semi-mansion a few minutes later, she had to swallow back the memories of the engagement party. Every time she came here she was reminded of the events of that night, when one of her former coworkers had been killed. She hoped over time the memories would fade a bit. Or maybe Tony and her mother would move.

She rang the bell. Patricia answered immediately.

"Kristan. This is a surprise." Patricia leaned forward to kiss her cheek, surprising Stan with the affection. "Hello, Scruffy." She bent and patted the dog's head. Scruffy wagged her stubby tail.

"Hi, Mom. Is this an okay time?"

"Of course. Come on in. We'll have tea." Patricia motioned her in and started toward the living room. "Is everything alright?"

"Not really. Izzy might need a lawyer."

Patricia stopped in her tracks and turned back to Stan. "For what?"

"Jessie's questioning her about Harold's death. She wants to bring her in today."

"She's what? That's nonsense! Why on earth would Jessie do something like that? I've a mind to call her myself and tell her what I think of her investigating skills."

"Wow, Mom. I didn't think you felt that strongly about Izzy."

"I like Izzy. She makes delicious pastries. And I think it's wrong when police officers abuse their power. Look what happened when that other . . . unfortunate situation occurred."

When Stan's former coworker had been found murdered in Tony's upstairs bathroom during the engagement party, a lot of finger-pointing had gone on, not to mention the mistaken arrest of Stan's ex-boyfriend.

"I don't think Jessie's abusing her power. But I do think she's got it all wrong." She sighed. "And I promised myself just yesterday I was staying out of this. I'm in a fight with Jake, Jessie and I had a brawl about it, and most of the McGees are sniping at each other or just generally cranky. I don't want to be involved anymore. But if Izzy is in trouble, I need someone to listen to me. I really think they're looking in all the wrong places."

"Come into the kitchen while I heat the water," Patricia said. "I want to hear what you're thinking. Would Scruffy like anything? Water?"

"You do?" Stan followed her. "And sure, she can have some water."

"Of course I do. You're smart, Kristan. And Lord knows you've had experience in this area lately. Which is a whole other problem, but we don't need to discuss that today." She turned the kettle on and put tea bags—Queen Anne breakfast tea—in two mugs, then filled a china bowl with water and set it on the floor. "Go ahead."

Stan held back a smile at her mother's choice of water bowls. She confided her fears about Seamus and his potential involvement, while part of her wondered when hell had frozen over. If someone had told her a year ago that she'd be sitting in her mother's kitchen in Frog Ledge, telling her secrets, she'd have personally driven them to a hospital for psychiatric counseling.

Patricia listened attentively. "So you think someone was trying to kill Seamus? And Jake doesn't believe that?" She pursed her painted lips and thought about that. "He has to have a good reason, Kristan." Patricia adored Jake.

"He does. Seamus is his favorite uncle. Brenna told me. I guess it makes him blind to some of the things he does. Liam made a comment about that too. Has Tony mentioned any of this to you? He was asking me a lot of questions about Seamus the other day."

"Not really. I mean, he's worried about Ray, of course. But nothing that stands out. I don't think he knew Seamus well." The kettle whistled and Patricia turned to the stove.

Stan still thought there was more to Tony's interest. She'd have to ask him herself when she saw him next.

"Jessie doesn't believe it either?" her mother asked, pouring the tea.

"She does. She's more than willing to believe Seamus is doing something wrong, but she's still wary about saying that's why there was a murder. Clearly she's still investigating down the Harold track. But I went to her office yesterday and told her everything. Miss Viv's story, Kevin's story, how Abby said it was too bad Seamus wasn't the one who died—all of it. She said I was right, but she had to keep investigating the evidence. Whatever that means."

"Let's focus on the immediate problem—Izzy. We'll go sit." Patricia led Stan into the living room. Stan settled on the sofa. Patricia sat in the chair across from her and tapped her manicured nails against the coffee table. "I'll make a call. When does she need this lawyer?"

"Three o'clock today. Mom, I don't think she has a ton of money to spend on this either," Stan said.

"Don't worry. He's a family friend," Patricia said.

Stan raised an eyebrow. "So he doesn't charge you?"

"If he needs payment I'll handle it, Kristan. Tell me why Jessie suspects her."

"Because she was in charge of the refreshments, she had access to the room where Santa was going to hang out, and it turns out she has a bit of a history with Harold. I heard about this secondhand, mind you, so I have no idea if it's true." She filled her mother in on what Abby had told her about Harold and Izzy's alleged altercation last year. "I have no idea about anything else. I don't know what kind of poison it was, and if that's making Jessie lean a certain way." She hesitated. "Truthfully, Izzy's been acting strange lately too. She was supposed to be around all night the night of the tree lighting, but she sent someone over with her stuff and had them just drop it off. Which meant the room got left open, which clearly caused all sorts of problems. She's not been herself lately."

Patricia thought about this. "Maybe she's simply busy. Isn't she trying to open her bookstore also?"

"That's what I thought too. I don't know. I guess this whole thing is making me crazy. Of course I don't think she hurt anyone, but I feel like there's more to it than just being busy."

"Well, let's see what happens with the lawyer. Now.

There's something else that's been occurring," Patricia said.

"Something else?" Stan repeated with a sinking feeling. "Something bad?"

"Something troubling. Char's B and B is getting some odd calls. Hang ups. It happened a couple of times while I was there and answered the phone for her when she didn't want to. I asked her if it had happened at other times, and she said maybe a couple." Patricia shook her head. "I don't think she's paying much attention to things."

"Do you think it's Ray?" Stan asked. "Maybe he's trying to call her but he can't talk! We should get the line traced." She jumped up, ready to go do . . . something, when Patricia held up her hand.

"I don't know, Kristan. I guess it could be, but I didn't like . . . what would you say? The vibe. Yes, that must be it. I didn't like the vibe I got when I answered. I told Char that if it continues to happen she must call the police."

"So do you think it's connected to Ray and Seamus somehow?" Stan asked.

"Well, I've no idea," Patricia said. "But it does seem awfully coincidental that all these things are happening while those two are missing in action."

Chapter Thirty-eight

Stan left her mother's and called the shop. Brenna answered.

"Hey. You busy yet?" Stan asked.

"Not too. I've got a bunch of things in the oven and I'm out front for a while now."

"Okay. I have to make one more stop, if you don't mind."

"Not at all."

"Thanks, Brenna. I'm sorry our first week is so insane."

"Stan. I'm loving being here. Truly."

Stan hung up, thinking about how lucky she was to have Brenna. It might be time to make her more than a staff member, she thought. She'd actually been thinking a lot about that lately. Brenna had been with her from day one, when she'd started baking a few batches of treats and selling them at the farmers' market at Jake's urging. She was still with her today, and she devoted just as much time as Stan, if not more, to the business. Making her a partner would mean Bren wouldn't have to supplement her income at the bar, unless she chose to.

She turned to Scruffy. "We'll deal with that later. We're going to see Izzy," she announced. Scruffy sat at attention in the back seat of the car. "I'd say it's about time we figured out what the heck is going on with that girl." She could use the excuse that she had to prep her for the lawyer, and then poke and prod until she unearthed something that would explain Izzy's odd behavior of late. Although she hoped she didn't hate whatever she unearthed.

She started at the café, but Izzy wasn't behind the counter. Jana said she wasn't out back either.

"Haven't seen her yet today," she said. "Maybe upstairs?"

Stan hoped it was just nerves about the meeting today that was keeping her friend hiding in her apartment. What if she was sick or something and that was the reason she was acting so oddly? She and Scruffy went up to Izzy's apartment and rang the bell. The dogs barked inside, but everything else was quiet. Just when she figured Izzy wasn't home, her friend yanked the door open. She looked flustered.

"Hey. What's up?" she asked, pulling the door a bit wider. The dogs clamored around Stan for kisses and probably treats. Even Junior, poor old guy. Scruffy jumped into the mix, excited to see her friends. Stan crouched down and gave them each something from the stash she kept in her purse, slipping Junior an extra. He wagged his tail appreciatively before lumbering back to his bed.

She stood up and faced her friend. "Can we talk? I just left my mother's."

"Sure." Izzy glanced over her shoulder, then motioned Stan inside.

"What are you looking for?" Stan asked, following her in and closing the door behind her.

"What do you mean?" Izzy asked, sounding distracted.

"Is someone here?"

"No! Why?"

"Because you're looking around like you expect to see someone walk in." Stan glanced around. She hadn't been up here in ages. Izzy was barely ever up here. They'd had more conversations sitting at a café table downstairs than Stan imagined she'd ever had up here in her actual apartment.

She'd painted, though. The walls in the kitchen were a light shade of yellow. It looked like a recent project too, as her pictures were still on the floor waiting to be re-hung. There were fresh flowers too, a bouquet of white roses and another vase full of brightly colored blooms. Stan could smell fresh coffee and her mouth watered for it.

Izzy recognized the look. Without asking, she reached into the cabinet for a mug and filled it. "Here."

Stan accepted it and sat at the table without waiting for an invitation. Izzy hesitated a moment, then joined her.

"My mother has someone meeting you at the police barracks today," Stan said. "An attorney. Apparently he's a family friend."

Izzy winced. "Which means I'll need to re-mortgage one of the buildings, right? Don't get me wrong," she added hastily. "I'm grateful. I'm just . . . strapped at the moment. The bookstore is costing me more than I planned."

"Don't worry. My mother's taking care of it," Stan said.

Izzy frowned. "Why?"

Stan shrugged. "Because she knows the whole thing is bogus."

"Glad someone does," Izzy muttered.

"Why didn't you tell me about the episode with Harold?" Stan asked. "Where he stole from you and then badmouthed you all over town?"

"Oh jeez. How did you—"

"Doesn't matter. I wish you would've told me."

"It was stupid. And it was a long time ago. If people

think I killed the guy over that, then they have no idea of the crap I've put up with over the years." Izzy barked out a laugh. "That was mild. It was a drunk guy having a temper tantrum."

"I'm sure it seemed personal, though. It would've to me."

Izzy shrugged. "Just because some people still, in this day and age, have a problem with other people's skin color, it's not my problem. I say they're the ones who have to deal with the fallout of being bigots. Doesn't affect me any."

Stan was silent for a few minutes, sipping her coffee. "Izzy. What's going on with you lately?" she finally asked. "And don't give me some story about how busy you are. I get that. But it's not like you to not be around the night of the tree lighting, especially when you had a part to play. And I know how much you love Christmas. That's got people talking. Right or wrong, it's all about perception. But you know that." She leaned forward and grabbed Izzy's hand. "You are one of my very best friends. Talk to me."

Izzy didn't speak for long enough that Stan feared she was angry. But then she sighed and stood up. Without a word, she walked down the little hall leading to her bedroom.

Well then. Not sure what her exit actually meant, Stan stayed where she was and finished her coffee. Had Izzy dismissed her? Should she go after her and try again? Or just leave and wait for her to calm down?

She was saved having to further analyze her friend's odd behavior. Izzy reappeared a minute later, tugging someone down the hall behind her. Stan's mouth dropped.

"*Liam?*"

If he'd worn a hat, Stan felt certain he would've tipped it at her. Jake's cousin smiled, a bit sheepishly. "Mornin', Stan."

Stan looked from him to Izzy and back again. "Are you guys . . ."

"Seeing each other?" Izzy nodded. "Yeah. There you go. Secret revealed."

"But why is it a secret?" Stan asked. "I mean, wow, I'm totally surprised, but I think it's great."

They looked at each other. "You do?"

"Why wouldn't I?" Stan asked. "Would you two sit down and explain? I feel like I'm missing something here."

Liam pulled out a chair and sat. Izzy poured another round of coffee for all of them. "Should I make more?" she asked, waving the empty pot.

"Depends on how long this story is," Stan muttered.

Izzy grinned, the first real smile Stan had seen on her friend in at least two weeks, and got another pot ready to go. When the beans were grinding, she joined them at the table. "We've kinda been seeing each other on and off the last year."

"The last *year*? Wow, I can be obtuse sometimes." In the year and a half Stan had known Izzy, she hadn't had any idea her friend was dating someone. The closest Izzy came was insisting that she'd snag Johnny Depp someday. True, Stan had never asked, but she didn't think it was any of her business. If and when Izzy wanted to tell her anything, she would. But right now she reminded Stan of a lovesick teenager, the way she was smiling and blushing, stealing looks at Liam.

"I guess we were good at hiding it, right, babe?" Izzy winked at him. "You should tell her how it started."

Liam actually looked embarrassed. "Really?"

"Come on. I love a good romance," Stan said.

Liam drank some coffee. Stalling.

"He's shy," Stan said to Izzy. "That's adorable."

Liam shot her a look, but he was grinning. "When I came to town for our Christmas gathering last year, I knew I had to get up the nerve to talk to her. I mean *really* talk to her. I'd seen her the other times I'd been here and thought she was amazing, but last year I got up enough courage to start hanging around her café." He glanced at Izzy, adoration written all over his face.

Izzy reached over and linked fingers with him on the table. "He was still kind of seeing someone in New York," she explained to Stan. "So it already had its complications. But we totally hit it off. I mean, neither of us had ever felt so connected to another person." She looked to him as if for validation. He was already nodding in agreement. "We spent a lot of time together while he was in town, and it just made us realize—this was it. For both of us."

"But my dad caught on," Liam said, his eyes darkening. "He had a few choice things to say about it."

"Seamus?" This surprised Stan. Even though she didn't know him well, she had him pegged as someone easygoing and nonjudgmental. "Why would he care?"

"Because he's a racist too," Izzy said. This time, she didn't sound bitter. She sounded sad. "He and Harold actually had a lot in common. He didn't think his Irish son should be dating a girl with my kind of genes. Or my color skin."

"You're kidding."

Liam shook his head slowly. "I wish I was. Far be it from me to care what my dad says—I think you've gathered that, Stan—but I didn't want trouble for Izzy. Especially in town here. So of course we kept seeing each other, but we kept it on the down-low. My dad . . ." He shook his head. "He can be nasty. That's what Jake doesn't see. He only sees the fun Seamus. The *aww, shucks* guy who screws up constantly but is always so sorry about it that everyone forgives him, just like that." He snapped his fingers. "But there's another side to him."

"I have to say, you two hid this well," Stan said.

"We had to. We were still trying to figure everything out," Izzy said. "But we love each other." She said it so matter-of-factly that Stan felt her throat choke up with tears. Partly because it was lovely to hear her friend happy, and partly because she was sad about Jake right now.

"As soon as he came back to town, we decided we were going to be together. No matter what. We're just trying to figure out what that means. And I didn't want it all over town while we did."

"And then all this nonsense with my father occurred," Liam said. "And we just thought it best to see how things played out. Although it's been getting harder to sneak around out here. I even ran into you a few times when I was trying to be stealthy. People are really interested in what everyone else is doing in this place, yeah?"

"You don't know the half. And that story about the newspapers was a little weak," Stan said. "Especially since there were two of them on my porch."

Liam grinned. "I'm sorry, Stan. I didn't want to lie to you. But we were just . . . being careful."

"You don't have to apologize to me," Stan said. "I'm glad there's a good reason you two were acting so strangely." She hesitated. "Is that why you were at the museum the other night, Liam?"

He nodded. "Izzy and I got our wires crossed. I thought I was meeting her there, but she'd sent Jana to take care of the delivery." He cocked his head at her. "You were thinking I'd tried to off my own dad, then?"

Stan felt her face heat up. "I didn't know what to think. Someone saw you there and said . . . it didn't look like you wanted to be seen."

"Well, I didn't," he said with a laugh. "But not for that reason."

"You do know you have to tell Jessie, right?" Stan

said. "This will eliminate a lot of suspicion. And maybe get her moving in the right direction faster."

Izzy looked horrified. "We're not ready for that."

"Izzy, she's dragging you down to the police station, for God's sakes. I would think that's reason enough to go public, no?" She looked at Liam, hoping for an advocate. "Liam. Tell her."

"I agree with you, Stan," he said. "But I have to respect what Izzy wants." He squeezed her hand. "Even though I want, more than anything, to tell everyone. And especially to tell my cousin to stop with the nonsense. Anyone who thinks Izzy would hurt anyone or anything doesn't know her at all."

At least they were all in complete agreement about that.

Chapter Thirty-nine

Liam left a few minutes later, promising to be back when Izzy got back from her meeting with Jessie. Stan and Izzy sat in silence for a few minutes.

"Why did you think you couldn't tell me?" Stan finally asked.

Izzy dropped her face into her hands. "I'm sorry, Stan. A lot of reasons, like Liam said. But I think—I didn't want to jinx it."

"Jinx it?" Stan repeated.

Izzy nodded. "I've had crap luck with men for so long, I'd given up on ever finding anyone. And then I do, and it's unexpected and crazy and wild and totally right, but it's a McGee, for God's sakes. How do I reconcile *that*?"

Stan smiled despite herself. Izzy and Jake had gotten off on the wrong foot a long time ago, and there were days when they still fought like cats and dogs. "What's so bad about the McGees, again?" Other than Jake freezing her out for the past two days.

Izzy snorted out a laugh. "You tell me. You've been involved with one, after all. Living with one, even."

"Yeah." Stan sighed. "Two days ago I would've said it's pretty great."

"Uh-oh. I don't like the sounds of that." Izzy propped her elbows on the table and put her chin in her palms. "What's up?"

"This whole thing with Seamus." Stan waved her hand dismissively. "Jake doesn't want to hear a negative thing about his uncle."

"Ah. Well, this story'll go over well then, won't it?"

"You're not kidding. But in fairness, I stuck my nose in probably where it didn't belong. I told him I thought everyone had their heads in the sand about Seamus. I think he may have been the reason Harold died. We had a huge fight about it and we're really not talking much."

"You said something about that on the phone. About Seamus being the target, not Harold. Why do you think that?"

"A few reasons." She gave Izzy the same replay she'd given her mother earlier. "And what Liam said a few minutes ago makes me even more sure of it. Then again, I found out Lester lied about not knowing Harold was playing Santa. His son told me. So I don't know. The whole thing is just so convoluted. Every time I think something makes sense, something else happens to send me down another crazy path."

Izzy got up and paced the room. "Even if she focuses on Seamus, she'll still have a reason to look at me. Given all this."

Stan shook her head. "I don't understand. Is there more to the story? Because I didn't get that from what you just told me."

Izzy went to her kitchen window and looked outside. Without turning around, she said, "He was really nasty, Stan. He came into the café one day last year and said some terrible things to one of his friends about me, making sure I could hear. I cried for days. I think Liam did want to kill him." She turned. "It was way worse than anything Harold Dewey said about me, for sure. And I know people think he's this lovable goofball, but he's got a dark side for sure."

"Does anyone else know about that?" Stan asked.

"I'm sure everyone in the café that day heard him," Izzy said. "He wasn't being shy about it."

The more Stan heard, the worse she felt. For all of them. Jake, because his beloved uncle didn't deserve his unwavering dedication. For Izzy, for being the target of bigotry in this day and age. And for Liam and the difficult position he was in. "So what were you and Liam going to do? If this whole disaster hadn't happened?"

Izzy shrugged. "Liam was going to confront him. Tell him once and for all that we were together and if he continued to disrespect me, he'd see to it Seamus never came back here."

"Whoa. How was he going to manage that?" Stan asked carefully.

"I don't know," Izzy admitted. "He told me to let him handle it. I suspect he was going to tell Jake's dad. Paul's a good guy, right? He wouldn't allow his brother to be doing that kind of thing if he knew about it."

"Absolutely not. I think he'd be mortified. Wow, Izzy. I'm sorry you had to go through all this."

"Hey. You know what? He's worth it." That goofy grin reappeared on her face as she toyed with her braids. She poured more coffee and came back to sit down. "But now I'm worried. I mean, you and Jake seem disgustingly happy most of the time. But there's gotta be something that's bad. Is there something? Come on, girl." She leaned forward, encouraging. "He leaves the toilet seat up? Plays bad music too loud? Scrapes the bottom of the soup bowl with his spoon for so long that you want to beat him senseless with it?"

Stan stared at her, then burst out laughing. "Now I need to know who made you so angry about a soup spoon. No, Jake doesn't do anything like that. I know this is going to sound stupid and totally honeymoon stage, but he's really perfect. For me, anyway. Which is why stupid arguments are so hard. I don't want anything to ruin it. And I know it's silly. I mean, we live together now. We're bound to argue at some point, right?"

Izzy squeezed her hand. "Listen. I know any argument stinks. He'll come to his senses. And I bet he'll be really sorry when he finds out some of this stuff about his uncle. Now. If Jake's that perfect, his cousin must've gotten the crap genes. I'm sure there's tons of things wrong with him. Dammit, I knew it!" She threw her hands up. "I finally find someone I can stand to be around for more than an hour, and he's got everything stacked against him. Maybe he's a closet drunk. Or a really bad singer. Do you know?"

"Izzy. Stop freaking out. Why are you trying to talk yourself out of this?" She paused. "You must really love him."

"God, I do," Izzy admitted. "I can't think of anything else but him—when I go to bed, when I wake up, while I'm making lattes. It's been like this since that day we really started talking. I have no idea why, except that he's perfect and dreamy and likes *everything* I like—even old Howard Jones songs—and we can finish each other's sentences. But . . . the other problem is, he doesn't live here. And I don't think he'd want to. And I own two businesses here! Why do these things always happen?"

"Have you talked about this?" Stan asked.

Izzy shrugged. "We've kind of had other things to worry about. But a little bit, yeah. He always talks about how much he loves New York."

"But from the sounds of it, he loves you more," Stan said. "Listen. Don't worry so much about the outcome. If you guys are a good match, why not see where it goes? Stranger things than relocation have happened to two people in love."

"He thinks the town's too small and that nothing happens here."

"Jeez. Even after all this?" Stan shook her head. "He must not have been reading the papers for the past year and a half. Listen, my sister thought the same thing. Then she spent some time here, and look what happened." Stan rolled her eyes. "Now she's got more friends than I do. *And* a husband-to-be who said he'd never leave Florida." She spread her hands wide. "Love does strange things to people. Now"—she pointed to the clock on the microwave—"you better get ready to go. I'm standing by my recommendation that you tell Jessie about Liam, that you guys were together the night of the tree lighting and that's why you were MIA."

"I'll think about it," Izzy muttered.

"Good." Stan rose and went over to give her friend a hug. "I'm happy for you. I want you to be happy," she said. "You deserve it."

Izzy hugged her back. "Thanks. And I'm sorry I didn't tell you."

"You don't owe me an apology. It was your story to tell when you were ready. Call me later."

She slipped down the stairs and decided to leave by the back entrance. She didn't feel like going through a café full of people today. The topics of conversation would surely be Harold, Seamus, and Ray, and she just couldn't handle it.

As she rounded the dumpster she almost bumped into Kevin, who stood on the sidewalk. He appeared to be looking up at Izzy's place, but it was hard to tell with his sunglasses on. He looked as surprised to see her as she was to see him.

He recovered quickly, though. "Hi, lassie. Fancy meeting you here."

"Yeah. The entrance is out front," Stan said, pointing around the building.

Kevin laughed. "I know, m'dear. Trying to decide if I need more coffee or if I'm about to get an ulcer, that's all."

"Oh. Well, the dumpster's not going to help you figure that out, is it?"

"I suppose not." He walked with her toward the front of the building.

"Heading anywhere in particular?" Stan asked casually.

He shook his head. "No. Just killin' some time until I pick up the lovely Miss Vivian for a late lunch. I enjoy her company. I'm hoping Seamus'll show up and try to punch me in the face for stealing his girl while he's away," he said with a wink.

"Have you seen your friends yet?" Stan asked.

He stilled. "What friends?"

"The rest of the poker group. They're staying at Char's. I guess they got to town yesterday. One of them has red hair." She stopped, acutely aware and embarrassed that she hadn't bothered to ask any of their names.

"Ah, no. I haven't yet. I'll have to take a jaunt over and visit them." The easy smile was back on his face. He tipped his cap at Stan. "See you at the library later. I'll have your seat waiting." And he walked away, whistling.

Chapter Forty

Kevin had joined the crowded cast of characters in Stan's mind now, and moved into a lead role. What was his deal? Things had been so crazy in general that she had to admit, she probably hadn't given enough thought to the crazy story this guy had shown up with out of the blue. She knew Jake wasn't thrilled about Kevin staying with them. In any other situation, she'd have been more cautious, but since he was a friend of Seamus's and it felt like, in some way, that meant he was part of Jake's extended family, she'd been a bit more lackadaisical in her assessment.

She wondered what he was really doing with his days. Frog Ledge history, while mildly interesting, wouldn't be enough to keep someone like Kevin so enthralled that he'd choose to stay indefinitely. Also, there wasn't that much history to read. A few hours and you'd be done. Add in a trip to the museum and the War House, and maybe you could stretch it to a full day of learning.

No, she couldn't help thinking he was up to something else. Conducting his own investigation into Seamus's whereabouts, most likely. But the fact that he wouldn't discuss it told her there was more to the story. She decided to let him stay on her couch for the time being, but maybe tonight she could find a way to press him on the real story after Cyril's talk at the library.

Decision made, she hurried back to the shop, surprised—and happy—to find Jake waiting at one of the tables. "What are you doing here?" she asked, giving him a kiss.

He rose and wrapped her in a hug. "I missed you. Took a break. Where've you been?"

"I had to go see Izzy. She's got a meeting with Jessie this afternoon. My mother's getting her a lawyer." Stan went behind the counter and began tidying up.

"A lawyer, huh? That serious?" That troubled Jake; she could tell.

Stan nodded. "Hey, are you going to be at the pub all night?"

"Probably. Scott's off tonight and I didn't get anyone else to cover. Why, what's up?"

"I'm going to go to Cyril's talk at the library tonight. On the Book of Kells. His dad is speaking too, so it should be interesting. But I'm going to stop by Miss Viv's first. I want to get her thoughts on Kevin. I think they've been spending time together and I'm wondering if he knows more than he's saying."

She held her breath, waiting for his reaction. He didn't say anything for a long moment, then he nodded. "I think that's a smart idea," he said. "If I can get away, I'll join you at the library."

He gave her a kiss, then left. She stood behind the counter smiling. Maybe they'd actually turned a corner.

She used her GPS to get to Miss Viv's and Victoria's house, out on the east side of town. She'd never been out to their neighborhood before. When she turned onto their street, the first thing she noticed was all the construction. The condos Emmalee had mentioned were in various stages of being built. Some open space still surrounded them, and Stan imagined that was where Kyle envisioned his restaurant. It was a good location for it, and she imagined other merchants would follow suit.

Which wouldn't please the sisters, from the sounds of it.

Their house stuck out like a sore thumb at the end of the block, and looked to be in dire need of repairs. She parked out front and went to the door. Miss Viv opened it before she rang the bell.

"Stan! Hello. What a lovely surprise. Daisy, no," she said, scooping up the little dog as it ran toward Stan's ankles, barking and growling. "Please, come in."

"Thanks." Stan stepped inside. "I hope this isn't a bad time."

"Not at all. Victoria and I were just about to have some tea. Would you like some?"

"Sure." Stan followed her into the kitchen. Victoria turned from the kettle. "How lovely. We never get much company anymore. Is chamomile satisfactory?"

"It sounds perfect," Stan said.

Once they had their mugs of tea, she turned to Miss Viv. "I hope you don't mind my asking, but I'm curious about Seamus's friend Kevin. The man who's staying with me. I know you've spent some time with him."

Miss Viv beamed. Her long hair was braided today, and she wore what Stan had come to recognize as her signature makeup. Her dress suggested she was ready to leave for a nice evening out—or a trip—at a moment's notice.

"He's so nice," she confided. "I was so pleased to finally meet a friend of Seamus's. I've only met one or two over the years, you know."

"There's probably a reason for that," Victoria pointed out.

Miss Viv ignored her. Stan guessed they had this routine down to a tee after a lifetime of living it. "He took me for a lovely dinner the other night, and we met up for lunch today. He says he's staying in town until Seamus shows up, safe and sound. It makes me feel much better."

"Does he have any thoughts on where he is?" Stan asked. "Is there a reason why he's here, when Seamus was up in Boston?"

Miss Viv looked blank. "Why, I don't know. He didn't say that. I guess he figures this is the first place he'll turn up, because of me." She smiled, the cloud clearing. "Yes, that must be it, don't you think so?"

"I'm sure it is," Stan said. Victoria shook her head in resignation and drank her tea.

Daisy barked from Miss Viv's lap. "I think she needs to go outside. Excuse me one moment." She slipped a rhinestone-studded leash on the dog and led her to the front door.

Stan looked at Victoria. "Have you met Kevin?"

Victoria nodded. "He came here to pick her up. I don't trust him."

"You don't? Why?"

Victoria thought about her answer before she spoke. "I suppose part of it is that I don't completely trust Seamus," she admitted. "So I struggle with trusting his friends. My sister is so . . . naïve sometimes. But more than that, it's just a feeling. I can't completely explain it. But I do believe he knows more than he's telling."

Chapter Forty-one

Stan called her mother once she got back to the shop. Since she'd already gone down the road earlier today of doing something she never thought she'd do—confiding in her mother—she figured it wouldn't hurt to ask her to spend the evening with her.

"Do you want to go to the library tonight? Cyril and his dad are doing a presentation on the Book of Kells. Not sure if you heard that it was stolen recently. Remember Dad took us to see it?"

"I do remember," Patricia said. "That would be lovely, Kristan. Shall I meet you there?"

"You're sure?" Stan asked, surprised. "I mean, if you have wedding stuff, I understand."

"Kristan. Do you want me to go or not?" Her mother sounded amused.

"Of course I do. That's why I asked."

"Then I'll see you at the library. What time?"

"Seven." She paused. "Maybe you can get Char to come?"

"That's a wonderful idea. I'll make sure she does."

"And if you want to come over to the house after, maybe we can . . . have coffee or something."

"That sounds lovely. I think Tony might be interested also. Will Jake be there?"

"He was going to try to get away for the talk, but probably has to go back to the pub after."

"Good. So things are better?" Patricia asked.

"They're getting there," Stan said. "I hope."

"And have you heard from Izzy since her meeting?"

"No. Which worries me. I just wish this whole thing was over. I'll see you later, Mom. Thanks."

When Stan arrived at the library a few minutes before seven, her mother and Tony were already there. Stan was relieved to see that Char was with them. Kevin was there also. A few other Frog Ledge residents were also in attendance, as were three other men Stan didn't recognize. They sat together in the back row. They all looked very serious.

Kevin saw her and waved, pointing to the chair next to him. She veered over. "Hey. Thanks for saving me a seat. I have to go say hello to my mother."

"Of course! Bring her back here to sit with us. If she's as lovely as you, I'm delighted to meet her."

Stan blushed a little and went over to Patricia and Char. Patricia air-kissed her cheek. Char hugged her.

"So good to see you out," Stan said to her friend. "Want to come sit over there with me and my houseguest?" She pointed to the seats.

Tony turned. "Houseguest?"

"One of Seamus's friends. He showed up at the pub the other night and wanted to stay in town. We offered him the couch."

"That was generous of you," Tony said. "Especially

since you don't know the man. Sure, let's go." He got up and headed for Kevin.

Stan looked at her mother. "Did you get a chance to ask him about what we talked about?"

Patricia nodded. "He said he didn't know anything more than any of us. We better change our seats now then, before it starts."

"Where are Seamus's four friends?" Stan asked Char.

"They went out for a drink. That's all they seem to do."

Stan smiled. "They are Irish, after all. Which I can say because I'm Irish."

Tony had already introduced himself to Kevin and they were talking quietly. Before she could butt in and see what they were talking about, Jake's parents came in and took seats right in front of them. Nora turned and blew Stan a kiss. Paul reached over and squeezed her hand.

"How are you doing?" he asked.

"I'm okay," Stan said. "I'm glad you're here." She'd just remembered she needed to ask him about playing Santa at the new holiday stroll, and Betty would surely ask for a status update tonight. "Can we catch up after this?"

"Of course."

The room was filling up fast. This was a hotter topic than Stan had apparently realized. Even Miss Viv and Victoria were here. They took seats off to the side. Miss Viv saw Stan and Kevin and waved happily.

Stan faced the front of the room as Betty came out to introduce Cyril and Arthur, who waited off to the side. Stan was sad to see Arthur was in a wheelchair. His health must be worsening.

"Good evening!" She beamed at the crowd. "Thank you all for coming out tonight. We've got a treat in store for you. As most of you know, the *Frog Ledge Holler*, our local newspaper, has been owned and operated by the

Pierce family since, well, forever! And while they've kept their focus strongly on our very own little community, there are certain subjects for which they'll go outside our town boundaries. One of those topics that's near and dear to their hearts is the crown jewel of their Irish heritage— the famous Book of Kells, which has been in the headlines lately. I won't spoil it for our speakers, so with that, I'll turn it over to Cyril and Arthur."

Betty led the room in a round of applause, then took a seat in the front row just as Jake slipped into the room. Patricia pushed Tony over a seat so Jake could slide in next to Stan. He wrapped an arm around her shoulders and she snuggled into him, feeling better for the first time in days. She vowed not to let all this external drama come between them again.

Cyril pushed his dad over to the front of the room, then surveyed the crowd. He had his serious face on. And why wouldn't he? It was a serious topic.

"Anyone of Irish descent has likely been following the tragic story of the recent theft of the Book of Kells from the Trinity College Library in Dublin," he began. "About two weeks ago, maybe a bit less, one of the greatest robberies in our history occurred. The two books on display were stolen without a trace. The last time a theft of these national treasures was even attempted was back in the late sixties, and it was unsuccessful." He paused for dramatic effect. "My father, Arthur Pierce, was a scholar of the Book of Kells, as you've seen from the pieces we've run in the paper this past week."

Cyril went on to give his dad a long-winded introduction about his studies on Irish artifacts, his research on the Book of Kells, and his various expeditions to see and study the book. "But I think what you most want to hear about is the last time a theft was attempted," he finished. "And then we can talk about why this time it may have been successful."

He turned the floor over to his dad. Kevin leaned forward, intent on whatever Arthur was going to say. It took Arthur a bit to get warmed up—illness and isolation had taken their toll. But within a few minutes, he was talking animatedly about his interview with the last known thief who'd tried to steal the book—a "maverick" member of the Irish Republican Army who had found support, interestingly enough, from some Boston members.

"The whole thing ended up being anticlimactic," he said. "When he realized he couldn't get to the book, he turned his attention to a different artifact, the Brian Boru Harp, which he did steal and held for ransom."

"He just gave up that easily?" Kevin called out. "Not a lot of imagination, yeah?"

A ripple of laughter went through the crowd.

One of the serious men Stan didn't recognize from the back row stood. "So what's different today? How'd this supposed mastermind pull it off? And do you think they'll ever find it?"

Arthur nodded confidently. "A lot's different today. We're fifty years smarter, better technology, better surveillance, better ways of getting intel, if you're smart enough. Problem with this other guy—and don't tell him I said so—is he wasn't smart enough. As for finding it, well, I don't see how it wouldn't turn up. You try to sell it, everyone will be all over that. So I'm not sure what's to gain from stealing it, other than you might go down in history as one of the greatest thieves of all time. But you'd better have a good hiding place for it. These things aren't pocket-sized." He rolled his wheelchair forward to make his next point. "The bottom line is, you get away with stealing these things, you better be ready for a life on the run."

Stan froze in her seat, feeling her heart start to pound. She glanced at Jake to see if he'd had the same thought as her, but he appeared to simply be listening to the conversation. No one else looked like they'd had an epiphany. But for some reason, her gut was screaming at her.

Was it possible Seamus had been involved in this heist?

Chapter Forty-two

"**Y**ou coming?"

Stan realized Jake had stood to go and was waiting for her to get up. "Yeah. Sorry. Are you going back to the pub?"

"I am." He looked more closely at her. "What's wrong?"

"Nothing. I just . . . nothing. I have to talk to your dad for a minute. About the stroll this weekend. I'll see you at home later?" She squeezed his hand and smiled to reassure him. But her mind raced with the possibilities. She needed to talk to Cyril.

Jake didn't look like he believed her, but he nodded. "Okay." He kissed her and walked out.

Stan turned to where Paul waited. "Good talk, eh?" he said. "That Arthur always was such an interesting guy. What a career he had. People think you work on a tiny newspaper and you don't get to do anything exciting. Boy, are they wrong. So what did you want to talk about?"

Stan focused on the task at hand. "The stroll we're doing this weekend. Can you be Santa? Which would also mean being Santa at my shop for pet photos?"

Paul's eyebrows arched in surprise. "Santa? Me? I'm flattered."

"So you'll do it?" Stan itched to get to Cyril, who was talking to Kevin off to the side of the room.

"Of course. I'd be honored."

"You're wonderful." Stan kissed his cheek. "I'll be in touch with the details."

She made a beeline for Cyril, who was still speaking with Kevin. "Sorry to interrupt. But actually, I want both of you."

Kevin beamed. "Well, that's the best news I've heard all week."

"Will this take long? I have to bring my dad back to his place." He adjusted his glasses and took a closer look at Stan. "What's up?"

"I need to talk to you. Can you come by my place on your way back?"

"You have a story for me?"

"Maybe," she said impatiently. "Just come over. Kevin, will you be there too?"

"Wouldn't miss it. I'll head back there right now."

"Great." And if Tony and her mother were going to be at the house also, it was her chance to get Tony's reaction on all this too. Hiding it from her wasn't helping anyone.

Now she just had to get them all talking. Honestly.

Cyril must've been more eager than he'd let on. He was at Stan's door within an hour.

"I enjoyed your talk tonight. Your father is certainly passionate on the subject," she said as she led him into the kitchen.

"I'm glad. Yes, he is. It was good for him to get back into the news world, even if it's just for a night." He glanced down at the dogs surrounding him and awkwardly patted each of them. Cyril wasn't a huge dog person. "So what've you got for me?" He paused when he saw Patricia and Tony sitting at the table with Kevin. They'd dropped Char off at the B and B at Stan's request. "Hello."

"Cyril. Excellent talk tonight," Tony said. "We need more events like that."

"I agree," Cyril said. "I was pleasantly surprised by the turnout."

"It was very impressive," Patricia agreed.

Small talk exhausted, all heads turned to Stan. She'd only mentioned that she'd asked Cyril to come by to talk about something to do with Seamus, but hadn't said what. She figured they'd all think she was crazy, but what the heck.

"Thanks for coming over," she said. "Cyril's talk got me thinking and I wanted to see what you all thought. I know this is going to sound insane, but bear with me." She took a deep breath. "Did anyone else think perhaps Seamus was involved in the Book of Kells theft?"

The room went completely silent. Even the dogs seemed to be holding their breath, waiting for a reaction.

Patricia finally spoke. "Kristan. I'm worried about you. Have you been getting enough sleep?"

Kevin sat back, arms crossed, an amused smile on his face.

"Why is that so far-fetched?" Stan demanded. "Think about it. He disappears and you"—she turned to Kevin—"come here with this crazy story about a cargo ship from Ireland and a carjacking that happened the same night. He promised his friends some high stakes poker money, according to his pals. He told his girlfriend he was coming into some money and they were going to disappear to Turks and Caicos. He had to know he wouldn't be back, because he got a replacement Santa. So why couldn't he be part of it?"

Patricia frowned. "Cargo? Carjacking? Whatever are you talking about?"

"I wondered if anyone would put two and two together," Cyril said.

All heads swiveled in his direction.

"What?" he said.

"You thought the same thing?" Stan asked.

"Once I started having some of the same conversations you mentioned, absolutely. It makes perfect sense," Cyril said. "It's going to be the story of the year. And it originated here in Frog Ledge." He rubbed his hands together gleefully. "See, Stan, I told you you're cut out to be a journalist. I'm impressed."

"We need to think through the repercussions of this," Tony said. "And we need to make sure we're safe. Because if Seamus tries to come back here with the goods, there could be trouble."

Patricia's jaw nearly hit the table. "You think this is true?"

"I've been doing some research on Seamus," Tony said. "Purely from the perspective that this is my town and I want to know what's going on here. After learning about some of his . . . acquaintances, I don't think it's as far-fetched as it sounds."

Stan sat back, not sure what to say. She'd put the idea forward but hadn't been sure anyone would buy into it— or whether or not it had any merit. But if Tony was taking it seriously, that was something. "What about you?" she asked, turning to Kevin. "Do you think he could've been involved?"

Kevin's amused smile stretched even wider. "Never underestimate the power of a man who loves money."

Which was as good as a *heck yes*, in Stan's mind.

"Are you writing about this?" Tony asked, turning to Cyril.

He shook his head. "Not until I have some facts confirmed. But when I do . . . hoo boy, will I write about it."

"Do you have evidence?" Stan asked, surprised.

Cyril shook his head. "I don't know anything more than what we've speculated on." But he looked like the cat that had swallowed the canary. He would be terrible at poker.

"So you think someone killed Harold—thinking he was Seamus—because they think he stole the book?" Patricia asked. "Jessie really should know about this, then. Given that she's bothering Izzy and that other poor man."

"Well," Cyril cautioned, "it's possible there are still two lines of inquiry here. Lester Crookshank is a valid suspect in Harold's murder. So, I'm afraid, is Izzy Sweet." He cast a sidelong look at Stan. "Although you don't agree."

Tony held up a finger. "Let's get one thing clear about Lester. He may have known that Harold was going to be in the Santa suit, but he didn't kill him."

Stan gaped at him. "You knew he lied about that?" She'd completely underestimated Tony. He was way more engaged in the goings-on around here than even she was.

Tony nodded. "He had a good reason. He was protecting his son."

"Eddie? What happened to Eddie?" Stan asked.

"Harold caught him . . . selling an illegal substance on the farm. He tried to hold it over Lester's head. It didn't end well. The boy gave Harold the black eye. Lester panicked and tried to protect him. No one else knows this, but he actually took Eddie to see a counselor Friday, late afternoon. He wasn't even in town when this would've happened. He's reluctant to tell anyone—especially Jessie—because of the potential ramifications to Eddie."

Stan felt like doing a fist pump, since the Izzy theory was wrong too. Although the more the two of them tried to hide their real alibis to protect themselves or others, the more damage it was doing. "So I've been right all along. This is related to Seamus." She could barely contain her excitement. "We should be able to get some real traction on this now, no?"

"I'd be very careful about how you go about looking into this," Kevin chimed in, more serious than Stan had ever seen him. "If our friend has gotten himself involved in this caper, chances are good there are some bad people looking for him. If they haven't already found him. I wouldn't recommend discussing it outside of this room."

Chapter Forty-three

When they arrived at Jake's parents', it was a full house. All the McGee relatives who'd come to town for a party were getting their party. Except for Declan, who'd gone home to his wife and kids. Stan couldn't help but wonder, after the conversation with Izzy and Liam, if Seamus had been equally horrible to Declan's wife for some reason and that was why she didn't interact with the family.

It was too bad, she thought. She'd wanted to like Uncle Seamus. Especially since Jake adored him. But someone who'd treated Izzy that way would have a long way to go to come back into favor. If he'd survived his latest expedition to come back at all.

The gang of four staying at Char's B and B were also in attendance, which Stan thought was hilarious. Kevin was not, even though they'd extended the invitation. Or maybe he'd arrive later. Who knew—he seemed to be having a grand old time in town doing his own thing. Miss Viv and Victoria were there too. Miss Viv stood in the middle of Seamus's friends, clearly enjoying the attention, while her sister sat alone on the couch. Stan felt sorry for her and made a mental note to go sit with her once she'd greeted Jake's parents.

"I'll go put our coats in my parents' room," Jake said, helping Stan off with hers. "Be right back." He gave her a quick kiss and headed upstairs.

"Thanks for coming, honey." Nora McGee swept over and gave Stan a welcoming hug. "I know there's a lot going on for you right now." She stood back, holding on to Stan's arms, appraising her with knowing eyes. "How are you doing?"

"I'm okay," Stan said. "It's been a long week for everyone, right?"

Nora chuckled. "That's an understatement. Come, let's get you a drink." She led Stan into the kitchen, where they'd set up a makeshift bar on the kitchen counter. Stan had to smile. If her mother was in charge of this party, there'd be a "real" bar with a bartender on staff. She much preferred Jake's family's way of doing things.

"What'll you have?" Nora surveyed the offerings. "I make a nice gin and tonic. Or I do have wine."

"I'll take the gin and tonic," Stan decided. As she waited for Nora to mix the drink, she leaned against the counter. "How are you and Paul doing? With . . . Seamus and everything?"

Nora sighed. "That man has been a thorn in my side for years," she admitted.

Stan's eyes widened. "He has?"

"Sure. He's the classic younger son. Can't get his act together, expects everyone to bail him out constantly, always in some kind of trouble. Not big trouble, but enough trouble. And a womanizer. Good Lord, such a womanizer." She shook her head, then dropped her voice, shooting a guilty look over her shoulder. "I shouldn't say that with Miss Viv in the next room. I'm starting to sound like her sister. Victoria has never liked Seamus. Thinks he's always treated Viv poorly. I can't say I disagree with her."

"Wow," Stan said. "I had no idea. I mean, I thought—"

"Don't get me wrong, he's family," Nora said. "And we are loyal to family. Paul loves his brother, so of course I love him too. And my son has always adored him. But sometimes I want to wring his darn neck. This is one of those times. To leave all of us hanging, and that poor woman . . ." She trailed off and shook her head. "I just wonder what foolishness he's gotten himself involved in this time. And to drag Ray Mackey into it is so wrong." Nora stirred the drink and handed it to Stan. "But listen. I know my son can be as pigheaded as my husband sometimes. Don't let him get away with it, okay?" She winked. "He's got himself a good match in you. You keep him on his toes."

Stan didn't quite know what to say to that. She'd wondered what Jake's parents really thought of her. This had to be a good sign. She sipped her drink. It was perfect. "I think we've both found a good match in each other," she said.

Jake popped his head into the kitchen. "I always worry when I see you conspiring with people, Ma," he said. "Especially my girlfriend."

"Well, you should worry," Nora retorted. "Now come make sure your girlfriend is having a good time." She linked arms with Stan and pulled her back into the dining room, where people clustered in small groups, laughing and talking. "I'll see you in a bit," she said, giving Stan a kiss on the cheek, then went to mingle with her guests.

Jake slipped his hand into Stan's. "Why do I get the feeling I was the topic of that conversation?"

"Oh, get over yourself." Stan poked him. "We are perfectly capable of having a conversation that doesn't revolve around you. Now, is it weird that everyone is having such a good time, with everything still so . . . up in the air?"

"Not in this family," Jake said. He nodded toward the

corner of the room. "Although there's one person not having the best time."

Stan followed his gaze. Liam leaned against a wall by himself, a beer in his hand and a miserable look on his face. Clearly he hadn't told anyone about Izzy yet, because she wasn't here. She felt sorry for them. It wasn't a fun way to have a relationship. "Let's go talk to him," she said, tugging Jake over.

"Hey," she said, giving Liam a hug. "We weren't sure you were coming, since you weren't at the house when we left."

Liam shrugged. "I was at Izzy's. She's working. I wanted to spend some time with her."

Stan nodded. "I figured. She never called me. What happened at the barracks?"

"They pulled her into a room and asked her a bunch of questions about her run-in with Harold. The lawyer advised her not to say anything, so she didn't. It was pretty anticlimactic, from the sound of it."

"That's good news, right?" Stan asked.

"I guess if you call being brought to the police station and questioned about a murder, sure, it's good news," Liam said with a humorless laugh. "Makes me want to throttle my cousin, for sure."

Jake sighed. "I know she's tough. But she'll figure it out, Liam. Trust me. Stan'll tell you. She's been on the receiving end of this before."

Liam looked at Stan, new respect in his eyes. "You have?"

Stan nodded. "When I first came to town. Jessie was sure I killed the town vet. Took me a while to convince her otherwise."

"Wow." Liam thought about that. "I don't doubt she'll figure it out," he said finally. "But she's dragging Izzy's reputation through the mud along the way."

"Well, an easy way to stop it would be to tell her Izzy's

alibi," Stan said reasonably. "And while you're at it, get the rest of the family on board with your relationship. Seamus won't stand a chance when he gets back, if he's still trying to fight it."

"Jakie!"

The three of them turned, Jake cringing slightly at the use of the nickname, to find Miss Viv wobbling toward them on heels that seemed way too high for her. "Hi, Miss Viv," he said, giving her a kiss on both cheeks. "Careful," he added, when her ankle turned beneath her.

"I told her not to wear those silly things," Victoria said, joining them and handing her sister a glass.

"They're not silly!" Miss Viv said indignantly.

"When you fall and break your neck they'll seem really silly," her sister said.

Liam slipped away into the kitchen before he could be pulled into this conversation.

"Why don't we go sit." Stan interrupted the sisterly bickering by taking Miss Viv's arm and leading her to the couch.

"I had to wear my nice shoes tonight. Seamus's friends were going to be here," Miss Viv explained, leaning on Stan. She looked behind her to see if her sister was listening. Victoria was talking to Jake. Miss Viv whispered to Stan, "And I hope tonight will be the night Seamus comes to get me."

"To get you?" Stan repeated.

"Why, yes, dear. For our trip that I told you about." Miss Viv stared at her somewhat reproachfully. "You were listening, weren't you?"

Before Stan could reply, they were both startled at the sound of shouting from somewhere behind them. Stan whirled just in time to see Liam deliver a perfect right hook to Redhead's face, sending the other man down to the floor in a listless heap. Someone screamed. Within seconds Jessie was there, grabbing Liam, who looked like he was literally about to kick the other man while he was down.

"Stop," she commanded.

Liam wrenched his arm away. "Don't talk to me."

Redhead's friends crowded around in shock. "You can't do that, man," said Bald Guy.

"Just did," Liam said. "You want to be next?"

"Liam. For God's sakes. Let's go." Jessie clamped her hand on his arm and began to pull him away.

"What, are you going to arrest me too? Go ahead," he said defiantly. "At least you'll have a reason to. Unlike Izzy, who was with me the whole afternoon and night that Harold was killed. So why don't you let her off the hook!"

Stunned silence settled over the room. Stan hid a smile. That was one way to make an announcement.

"You should arrest him," Redhead slurred from the floor, gingerly feeling his jaw. "I think he broke my face."

A crowd had gathered. Nora went to reach for her nephew, but Jessie sent her mother a look. "Are you asking me to press charges?" Jessie asked Redhead.

"Jessica," her mother murmured.

"Hell yes," Redhead said. "He just punched me out for no reason!"

"No reason?" Liam's voice rose. "You don't call making a racist comment about someone *no reason*?" He looked like he was about to go after him again. Jessie planted herself in front of him and gave him a shove in the other direction.

"Are you telling me you're seeing Izzy?"

Liam nodded.

"And you're her alibi for Friday?"

"Yes, alright? My father and his friends"—here he glared at Redhead on the floor—"had opinions about it. So we were keeping it to ourselves. But since you're crazy and you're trying to pin a murder on her, I'm telling you!"

"Are you still going to arrest him?" Redhead demanded.

Liam raised his foot as if he was going to step right on the guy's face. Stan silently cheered him on.

Jessie grabbed him, pulling him off balance. "Let's go," she said. "We're going to the barracks. You need to cool off."

Chapter Forty-four

The entire room watched as Jessie led her cousin out of the house. Nora looked like she was about to go after the two of them, but Paul restrained her. "Let it be," he said quietly. "She'll do the right thing."

Miss Viv turned back to the room full of people. "Well!" she said brightly. "Who wants a drink?"

As people started to chatter amongst themselves again, Stan was distracted by her ringing cell phone. She pulled it out of her pocket and glanced at the caller ID. A local number, but no name attached. She answered.

"Hello, this is Alarm Central. We're getting an alarm report from 140 Revolutionary Road?"

Her shop. Stan felt her heart sink. "I'm not there right now. Can you send someone?"

"Yes, ma'am. The police have been dispatched."

Stan thanked her and hung up, turning to Jake. "The alarm's going off at my shop."

"I'll get our coats." He took the stairs two at a time while Stan fidgeted impatiently. When he returned, he veered off and said something to his mother, then helped Stan with her coat and ushered her out the door.

"Why would the alarm be going off?" she asked, buckling her seat belt.

"Probably a glitch in the system. Don't worry." He pulled out of the driveway and drove the two miles to her shop. When they got there, a state police car was parked out front, lights flashing. The alarm had been silenced, but as they hurried up to the front door Stan felt her heart stop. There was a gaping hole in her front window.

"Oh my God," she breathed, grabbing Jake's arm.

Lou met them outside.

"What happened?" Jake asked.

Lou shook his head. "Someone broke in. Looks like they smashed the window with some kind of pipe and started to trash the place."

Stan shoved past him and yanked the front door open. She stepped inside, her boots crunching on a pile of broken glass. Whoever had broken in must've been startled by the alarm—thank goodness her mother had insisted on it, even though Jake hadn't thought it was necessary—but still tried to inflict the most damage they could in a short amount of time.

Her café tables were overturned. Chairs and stools were strewn around the room, and one of the stools had been smashed, a leg lying forlornly in the middle of the floor. All the vases she'd lovingly picked out for each table were broken. The Christmas tree had been toppled, leaving broken ornaments and a puddle of water. The rest of the Christmas decorations had been torn down, some of them left broken on the floor. She did notice with some relief that they hadn't made it to the pastry cases. If those had been ruined, she would've been closed indefinitely.

They'd wreaked as much havoc as possible in a short amount of time.

Her throat tightened, a sure sign that tears were about to follow. She'd worked so hard. She was so proud of her shop. Who would want to wreck it? Even as she asked herself the question, she knew. This had to do with whatever was going on around here. All of it—Seamus's disappearance, Harold's death, Ray's no contact, whatever had gone on up in Boston. She'd been right all along, and someone was afraid of her being right. Someone didn't want Seamus to be the focal point. That was the only explanation.

A chill raced up her spine as she thought of the dogs and cats. What if her house was next? Would someone hurt her babies? She thought of Kevin, the houseguest that everyone had warned her against. And Seamus's other "friends" who'd come to town. And the three men who'd been at the library tonight that she'd never seen before. Who were all these people? Had one of them done this? Did it have something to do with the Book of Kells, as she'd suspected?

She felt Jake come up behind her and slide an arm around her shoulders as he surveyed the damage. "Who would do something like this?" he said, almost to himself. "Lou. Was this kids? I can't imagine any of our locals doing this, though. Some college kids out on a prank?"

Lou's face said he didn't think so, but he shrugged. "I can't say for sure, Jake. It looks a little too . . . calculated to me to be kids screwing around on a dare or some kind of fraternity initiation. Besides, why would they come all the way out here and pick Stan's store? And it doesn't seem like a robbery. There's still money in the cash register. I don't know." He looked at Stan. "Anyone you've had problems with lately?"

"No. But I think this has something to do with Seamus," Stan said grimly.

"How so?" Lou asked.

Stan looked at Jake. She hadn't filled him in on the Book of Kells conversation from the other night. No time like the present. She spilled the highlights of the conversation. Jake looked like his eyes were about to pop out of his head. Lou just listened until she was done.

"What about this guy who's been staying with you?" he asked. "You think he's on the up-and-up?"

Stan shrugged and looked at Jake.

"We took him at face value that he was Seamus's friend," Jake said. "But do I know that for a fact? Nope. We were way too trusting."

"I don't know," Stan said. "I don't get a bad vibe from him. But I do think he knows more than he's saying. What about those four that are staying at Char's?"

Lou grinned. "I heard your cousin decked one of them," he said to Jake. "It's why Jessie couldn't answer this call."

"I know even less about them," Jake said. "But now I'm worried for Char. Heck, I'm worried for all of us."

Jake called Scott to bring a piece of plywood from the pub. Stan waited in the car while they boarded up her window. Lou had taken the report and left, promising to do his best to figure out who'd done this. He also promised to have extra patrols going by the pub, Stan's shop, and Izzy's place until they'd figured this mess out.

When they finally got home, Stan wanted to crawl into bed. But first, she needed to make sure everything was okay. The house was empty save for the animals. She'd never been so happy to see her furry friends. The dogs clamored around her, barking and demanding hugs and pets. Nutty sat in the front window watching them with disdain, and she saw Benny peeking around the corner from the den. Everyone was accounted for, and no one was acting strangely. That made her feel better. Still, she made Jake check the entire house—all the windows, the back door, the gate outside, under the beds—before she allowed herself to completely relax.

She wondered where Kevin was. His bag was still in the living room, but his absence stood out for her. He hadn't been at the party, either. And it was near midnight. He didn't usually come back so late, since he didn't have a key—at least Stan hadn't been *that* trusting.

And Liam. Would he be back, or had Jessie arrested him? Or maybe she'd just made him stay overnight and cool off. "Would she do that?" Stan asked Jake. "Make Liam sleep in a cell?"

Jake shook his head. "He probably went to Izzy's."

Her cell rang. She recognized the number. Cyril was on the job.

"Hello."

"Stan. I heard what happened at your shop. Can you comment?"

"I don't really know what to say, except how devastated I am that someone would do this," she said.

"Was anything taken?"

"No. Just destroyed."

"Is this going to halt plans for Saturday's celebration? Boy, someone wants our Christmas spirit wrecked this year, eh?"

Saturday. The grand opening, take two. She'd nearly forgotten about it. She closed her eyes, suddenly weary. "I honestly don't know, Cyril. I have to see when I can get someone in to fix it. And I have to replace some furniture. So probably, yeah. Because even if I can get it fixed, I don't think I'll be in the mood to have a party."

She could hear him tapping on keys on his end of the phone, taking down her comments. When he stopped typing and spoke again, he'd shifted from reporter mode.

"Hey. Off the record. Can we talk tomorrow?" he asked. "About that . . . matter we discussed the other night. I have some things I want to run by you. I'll call you. Oh, and there's a meeting about your sister's boyfriend's restaurant. The sisters are planning to publicly oppose it, I heard."

"You're not serious."

"I am."

"Well, that's just what we need. And how are they finding time to do that, anyway?" She shook her head in disgust. "Thanks for the heads-up, Cyril. I'll talk to you later."

Chapter Forty-five

After yet another mostly sleepless night, Stan finally got out of bed at five and went into the shower. She stood under the hot spray for a long time, trying to find a way to feel better about everything. Of course, there wasn't much to feel better about. Last week her biggest problem had been being too busy to Christmas shop yet. Now she wished she could rewind. Or fast forward to when everything got resolved, even though that seemed like an unattainable goal at this point.

With a sigh, she shut the water off and stepped out of the shower, dressing hurriedly in an old pair of jeans and a sweatshirt. Since most of her day was going to be spent cleaning up the shop, she didn't worry about how she looked. She ran some styling product through her hair and let it air dry while she went down to make coffee. The cats were waiting, so she heated up some of their food and let them eat before the dogs got up and tried to steal it. She gave them extra treats and tried to reassure herself that they'd be okay in the house alone today, that no one was going to break in and hurt them.

She wished she believed it.

But there was nothing she could do about it, unless she asked Jake to stay here all day. And since he ran a business too, she felt bad asking him to do that. She'd just have to trust that they'd be okay.

After making a piece of toast with cashew butter and drinking more coffee than any human should consume in an hour, she grabbed her coat and snuck out before Scruffy—or Jake—realized she was leaving. She didn't want her little dog running through the broken glass over at the shop. And she wanted to let Jake sleep. He'd been up as much as she had lately.

Stan drove as slowly as possible up the street. She dreaded today's chore, dreaded pulling up to her beautiful little shop and seeing it in such a state. She felt a tad guilty for feeling so upset about it, when other people were facing worse challenges. Like their husbands missing for nearly a week, or being suspected of murder.

So when she pulled into the front parking lot, her mouth dropped open. It was barely seven, but the lot was jammed full of cars. And a van she recognized as belonging to Frank Pappas, the contractor who'd worked on Jake and Izzy's building and who'd installed the new kitchen here at her shop. She saw Frank himself standing near the front door, smoking and overseeing a crew of his workers who were installing a new window.

She parked and hurried over to them. "Frank? What are you . . . how did you—"

He glanced at her and held up a finger, then focused on his crew. "It's not straight!" he hollered. "To the left!" Shaking his head, he tossed his cigarette butt to the ground. "Gotta watch every move they make, I swear to God. Yeah. Stan. Jake called me last night. Said there was an emergency. What the hell happened?"

"Someone broke in," Stan said. "Not sure who or why. But thank you, Frank. I appreciate you coming so quickly."

He waved her off, obviously uncomfortable with the praise. "It's a job." He jerked his thumb toward the building. "You got some people inside."

"Yeah. Thanks." She hurried in and stopped in her tracks. The place had already been mostly cleaned up, but that wasn't the most surprising part. Char herself was overseeing the operations in here, much like Frank outside. She held a broom in one hand, and with the other directed Betty and Brenna on how to rearrange the undamaged tables and chairs. Her mother stood behind the counter, surveying the room, looking for anything else out of place.

"You guys? Mom? What on earth are you doing here? Char, my God. This is the last thing you need to worry about." She went over and hugged her friend.

"Sweetie. Don't be silly. I heard you had some problems, and I knew I needed to pull myself together and get over here to help you. Lord knows you've been trying to help me all week, and what a thankless job that's been for you." She gave Stan a squeeze, then stepped back. "Now. Once we get this place cleaned up, I'm taking you to my friend's place down the road a ways. She sells lovely furniture, and we'll get you some things to tide you over until you can replace these pieces. You can be chic and mismatched for a while, but you'll be up and running. What do you say?" She beamed at Stan.

Stan assessed her friend. Char had lost some weight, and she wore about half her usual makeup. Her lively orange hair wasn't quite as vivacious as usual, and instead of one of her brightly colored outfits she wore a pair of black pants and an oversized red sweatshirt. But being back in the mix of the living was clearly helping. Some color had returned to her cheeks, and her eyes were the brightest Stan had seen them since Friday, when everything happened. It made her feel a bit better. "So Jake did all this?" she asked. "He got all of you?"

Her mother nodded. "He called me last night. I was going to call you, but he said to give you some time. He organized us to come in and help this morning."

How sweet. She thought she might cry, but managed to hold it in.

"I can't believe this happened, Stan." Brenna looked distraught. "I mean, when Jake told me . . ." She shook her head. "Who would want to do this?"

"Some degenerate kid, that's who," Betty declared, dumping a pile of glass into the trash can. "I swear, parents don't control their children nowadays, and look what happens. Innocent people just trying to make a living are the ones who suffer."

"Betty, I'm not sure this was a kid," Stan said. "Lou didn't think so either."

Betty scoffed. "Then who was it? Someone who wants Christmas canceled? Hmmm. Maybe you're right," she said, tapping a finger against her chin. "I've a mind to call that cranky goat farmer down the way. He's been badmouthing our Christmas celebrations for the last ten years. I bet you he paid someone off to do this."

"Why would a goat farmer want to destroy my shop?" Stan asked, exasperated. "That's not going to get Christmas canceled!"

A rap at the front door pulled them all away from the conversation. Lester Crookshank poked his head in. "Delivery," he called. "Can I come in?"

"Of course!" Stan hurried over to hold the door for him, watching in amazement as he brought in a brand-new Christmas tree. She felt the tears well up again. After her last encounter with Lester, he had every right to be sour with her. Instead he was bringing her a Christmas tree from his farm to replace the one that had been ruined. In that moment, she loved this little town more than she had ever loved a place before in her life. Including her favorite beach.

"Lester," she murmured, "you didn't have to—"

"I'll get this all set up for you," he interrupted her. "Not to worry. You finish what you were doing."

"What a dear," Char said. "Thank you, Lester."

Lester shrugged, turning red. "It ain't nothing."

"It's absolutely something," Stan said. "Thank you."

"Now," Patricia said briskly, "I called your sister, Kristan. You know how obsessed she is with Christmas decorations this year. She's going to come down later, with Eva, and put some new things up for you. You'll be just like new by the end of the day, as long as we find the right furniture."

A cell phone rang in someone's purse. Each of them felt around to see if it was theirs.

Char looked surprised to see it was hers. "Who's calling me at this hour?" she wondered aloud. "Hello?" Then her eyes widened, and her face went deadly white. Stan rushed to her side.

"Char! What's wrong? Who is it?"

"Raymond?" Char asked, her voice shaking like a leaf.

Stan gasped, tugging on her arm as Patricia, Betty, and Brenna crowded around too. "Where is he? Are they okay? Is he with Seamus?"

"Tell me that again? I can't hear you. Raymond?" Char pulled her arm free and moved around the room. "Darn signal! Raymond? Who is Kelly? You tell me right now what is going on!"

They all held their breath, waiting to see what would happen next. Char held the phone away from her ear and looked at it. They all heard the familiar beeping that signaled *call failed.*

Chapter Forty-six

Char looked like she was about to cry. She hit redial, but the call wouldn't connect. Covering her mouth with her hand, she fled into the kitchen.

They all looked at each other.

"At least he called," Brenna offered, always the optimist. "So we know they're okay. Or at least, we know he's okay." She looked unhappy at the thought of her uncle not being okay.

"Let me go talk to her." Stan hurried back into the kitchen. Char leaned against the counter, weeping. Stan went to her and hugged her.

"Char. Talk to me. What did he say? Is he okay?"

"I couldn't tell what he was saying," Char whispered. "I could barely hear him. He said he only had a minute but he wanted to tell me about . . . about . . ." She dissolved into tears again.

"About what?" Stan asked urgently. "Did he mention Seamus?"

"No!" Char wailed. "But he said something about someone named Kelly."

"Kelly?" Stan froze. "Are you sure he said Kelly?"

"Like I said, I couldn't really hear him well. But I'm pretty sure that's what he said." Char wiped her eyes with her sleeve, leaving a trail of black eyeliner. "So that's what this is all about, eh? I guess those nasty women who said he was off having a late-in-life midlife crisis were right."

"Char. I don't believe that. You must've heard wrong. Since you couldn't hear him well in the first place." Although Stan was fairly certain Ray had been trying to tell his wife about the Book of Kells. They'd been right after all.

Which meant Ray and Seamus were in big trouble.

Char shook her head. "No. I have to face facts, Stan. Ray's left me for a younger woman."

"Char!" Stan threw up her hands. "That's the most ridiculous thing I've ever heard. Ray loves you more than I've ever seen anyone love their spouse. Except for maybe my dad with my mother, which I couldn't really figure out. Anyway, I don't believe it. You need to sit tight and wait for him to call again."

"Oh, I'll sit tight alright," Char said grimly. "After I call my lawyer and file for divorce."

"You're not filing for divorce. Char, you can't tell anyone about this." Stan didn't want to tell her about the Book of Kells theory because she was afraid it would get Ray killed—but if the wrong people knew he was alive at all, that might have the same impact, depending on whatever was going on up in Boston. Or wherever they'd ended up.

Char frowned at her. "You're right. I guess I can't tell anyone. I'll be the laughingstock of Frog Ledge."

Stan knew she couldn't tell Char the real story. And Char wouldn't listen to any of her defenses of Ray. Char finally left in tears, careening down the street like a

NASCAR driver doing a qualifying lap. Betty had even tried to make her friend feel better, but Char wasn't buying into any of it. They watched her drive away.

"I'll go after her," Patricia said. "She usually listens to me. At least someone does." She winked to show she was teasing, then got in her car and headed to the B and B.

Betty looked at Stan. "Do you really think she's going to file for divorce?"

"Jeez, I hope not." Stan twisted her hair around her finger. "Do you think we could stop her somehow if she tried?"

"I have no idea." Betty thought. "I bet she'll call Marian LaRoche. She's a lawyer here in town. She handles a lot of divorces. I can give her a heads-up to stall Char."

"Good idea." At any other time, Stan would wonder about a town where people could poke their noses so far into someone else's business, but right now she was grateful. "I wish we could track the call. I need to tell Jessie."

"Have you heard from her? About this?" Betty waved a hand at the store, which looked a hundred times better than this morning.

"No. Lou responded to the call. I haven't talked to her. Look, Betty, I'm going to head out. Thank you so much for doing this for me. Truly. You guys made everything better."

"That's what friends are for." Betty kissed her cheek. "And Stan? Don't worry about the holiday-stroll planning. I've got it covered. You have enough on your plate."

Stan wanted to kiss her. "Thanks, Betty." She hurried outside before Betty could change her mind. Frank and his crew were finishing up with the window. "Will you lock up when you're done?" Stan asked him.

Frank nodded. "We won't be much longer."

"Thank you again. Really."

"Don't mention it."

Stan got in her car and pulled out her phone. She dialed Jessie. Voicemail. "Jessie. Ray called Char. Call me." When she hung up, she tried Cyril. No answer at his desk or on his cell. Ready to scream in frustration, she tried Tony. No answer there either.

"Where is everyone?" she muttered, pounding her fist on the steering wheel. If Char started telling people that Ray had called and the wrong people heard about it, it could cause major problems.

She didn't know what else to do, though, so she headed for home. When she got there, she got another surprise. Jake and Liam were out on the porch, stringing up colored Christmas lights. A wreath with a red ribbon hung on the front door.

Stan parked and walked up to the porch. "What are you doing home?" she asked Jake. "I thought you had to be at the pub."

Jake finished tacking up the string of lights in his hand, then turned to her. "I wanted to stick around here today. Figured it would make you feel better," he said. "And I knew you had a crew of people helping at the shop."

"Oh," was all she could manage, before she threw her arms around him and hugged him. "Thank you," she whispered.

He squeezed her back. "You don't have to thank me."

Once she had herself under control she turned to Liam on the ladder, shielding her eyes from the sun. "How are you doing? What happened last night?"

Liam grinned. "My cousin let me off the hook."

"She did? That's great news."

"Yeah. We had some words on the way to the station. I told her what that waste of skin had said about Izzy. Really, what my father said about Izzy and he was repeating. She gave me crap about being a knight in shining armor, but she actually said she was happy that we were together."

"Wow. She's getting soft. Did she say anything about how she brought Izzy down to the station?"

"I did. I told her to knock it off. That if she tried to arrest her she'd have to go through me." He winked. "I don't think she was that impressed, but I do think she's crossed her off the list."

"Does she have another suspect? Did she get more information?"

Liam lifted his palms. "She didn't confide in me on any of that." He climbed down the ladder and plugged the lights in, nodding when everything lit up as planned. "Nice. We good for out here?" he asked Jake.

Stan turned to Jake, who'd been quietly listening to the exchange. "It looks great," she offered.

Jake smiled. "Good. That's what I was going for. You should see your sister's house, though. I think her neighbors are jealous."

"Oh boy. That good, huh? We didn't even get to decorate our tree yet." She slipped her arm around his waist. "Come on. I'll make you guys some hot chocolate. Liam? Coming?" Grabbing Jake's hand, she tugged him inside. "Are you still hosting the party at the pub for the winners?"

He nodded. "So it's kind of good timing. Everything happens during the holiday stroll. And the party will be at night after you close the shop, so you won't have to miss it."

She blew out a breath. "Yeah. I'm not sure I'm doing the grand opening, Jake."

"What? Why not? Didn't Frank finish the window today?" He'd already pulled out his cell phone. "I told him he had to. He needs to get back over there—"

"Jake. He's done. They did a great job. Thank you for getting him so quickly." She took off her coat and grabbed the cashew milk out of the refrigerator. "I just . . . I'm not in the mood."

"Now wait a second," Liam cut in. "You can't just not do it. Look at all the planning you've done. Twice."

"Exactly," Jake said. "We're getting the place up and running again, no? You can't let them win, Stan." He came over and grasped her arms, causing her to abandon her hot chocolate–making. "I won't let you give in."

She locked eyes with him, grateful they'd made it back to each other. "Thank you for getting everyone to help. And Lester, with the tree." She reached up and touched his cheek. "It meant everything that you did that." She kissed him.

Behind them, Liam cleared his throat. "Hey. I thought I was getting hot chocolate?" he asked.

Chapter Forty-seven

Once Liam left to go to Izzy's, Stan told Jake about the phone call. "She couldn't hear him and thought he was confessing to an affair with someone named Kelly," she said, dropping her forehead into her palm. "What a disaster. And I couldn't tell her differently. She'd tell the whole world."

"My God," Jake said. "So what now?"

"I don't know. I called your sister, but she didn't call me back."

"Were they still in Boston?"

"No idea. The connection sounded bad."

"Well, at least we know he's alive," Jake said. "That's a good thing."

"Yeah," Stan agreed. *But for how long?*

Since Jake had taken the day off from the pub, he had to go in and help out for the night. Stan went to the town hall alone for the zoning board meeting. The public comment section on Kyle's restaurant proposal was at the end, but she decided to go for the whole thing anyway.

She grabbed a coffee at Izzy's on the way; otherwise she was sure she'd fall asleep. Town zoning board meetings weren't known for their excitement.

When she arrived, Victoria and Miss Viv were already there. Kyle and Caitlyn were too. The pairs were each sitting as far from each other as they could manage.

Oh boy. This could get ugly. She waved awkwardly at the sisters and sat down with Caitlyn and Kyle. They both looked nervous.

"I hate this," Kyle whispered.

"You'll be fine," Caitlyn said, squeezing his hand. "Right, Stan?"

"Of course," Stan said, trying to avoid Victoria's glare. "They'll come around."

A couple of other people filed in soon after. Stan recognized them as town meeting regulars—the types who loved to offer opinions on anything.

After a coma-inducing session about a permit for a new fence around an existing farm and some updates on projects in progress, the head zoning official finally opened up the floor on the restaurant matter, letting Kyle speak first.

"I'm Kyle McLeod, and I recently moved to town with my lovely fiancée, Caitlyn."

Caitlyn waved. Stan wanted to cover her eyes.

"I'm a chef, and I'm looking to bring a vegan offering to town." Kyle went on to explain his vision for the restaurant, how it would benefit the town, the new people he hoped to bring in. "And this is the perfect location for it," he said. "It's near a main road, there's development already in the works, and plenty of new people will be moving in. I hope you'll support this venture." He sat back down, nervously twisting his hat in his hands.

The zoning official looked unimpressed. "Anyone have anything to add?"

One of the regulars, an old farmer, stood. "This is a

farming community," he said. "We don't need a vegan restaurant here." He spat the word *vegan* as if it were synonymous with Satan. "You'll put the farmers out of business!"

Before Kyle could stand to defend himself, Victoria rose. "The board should consider how something like this could disrupt the residents' quality of life," she said. "Especially the residents who've lived there for a long time. It's bad enough we have condos and all these young people to deal with. Now we're going to add drunken revelers and people who eat tofu to that list?"

She sat down in a huff. Stan hid a smile. People who ate tofu were right up there with thieves and rapists, apparently.

Kyle stood again. "We're not looking to upset the farming community," he said. "We want to be good partners, and we're planning to source all our vegetables locally. We just want to give people another food option."

The conversation went on for another ten minutes, with Victoria getting increasingly more agitated. Miss Viv said nothing, just stared off into space, even when her sister nudged her to try to get her to chime in. Then, abruptly, Miss Viv got up and walked out as Caitlyn was speaking.

Caitlyn trailed off. They all stared after her. The zoning official cleared his throat. "Please continue," he said.

Stan stole a glance at Victoria, who looked like she was about to blow her stack. But she refocused on the matter at hand and continued rebutting everything Kyle and Caitlyn had to say. The two of them looked exhausted from the effort of keeping up with her.

When the meeting ended, Stan went over to Kyle. "You did a good job," she said. "Don't worry. This is just to check a box." She lowered her voice. "They have no good reason to block you."

"I know. It's just nerve-wracking." Kyle took Caitlyn's

hand. "Hey, want to come over and see the house? We're all done decorating."

Decorating. Shoot. She and Jake still hadn't made time to do their tree. "Sure. Give me a few though, okay?" She waited until they filed out before she turned to Victoria, who still sat stiffly in her chair. "Can I sit for a second?" Stan asked.

Victoria shrugged as if to say *makes no difference to me*. Stan sat. "I understand your concerns about the land," she said. "I feel terrible for you that your family's land had to be sold. But my sister and her fiancé don't want to disrupt your life any further. They just love it here and want to make a living."

Victoria glared at her. "You don't understand," she said. "You have no idea what it's like to lose everything. My parents—our parents—were so proud of that land. If they knew what had happened, they'd roll over in their graves." She stared down at her lap, her eyes filling with tears. "And to be left with the house in such a condition, well, it's overwhelming. I'll have to sell that too when my sister leaves me. I'll have to move into one of those awful condos." Her last words caught on a sob.

Stan's heart ached for her. Victoria was right. She didn't know what that was like, to lose everything. Especially in her seventies, which is probably where Victoria was. It must feel terrible.

Her cell rang. It was Jake. "Excuse me," she muttered and turned away to answer.

"Stan. You better come down to the pub. Char's here and she's pretty drunk. She's asking for you. Miss Viv's here too, and they're sort of brawling."

Chapter Forty-eight

Abrawl between two late-middle-aged women was not exactly what Frog Ledge needed right now. Stan turned to Victoria.

"I'm sorry. I know this isn't the best time, but your sister is at McSwigg's. She's . . . having words with Char. Can you come help me talk sense into them?"

Victoria brushed at a tear. "Leave it to my sister to make me forget one set of woes for another," she said ruefully.

When they arrived at the pub, a small crowd was gathered around Char and Miss Viv. Stan noticed Seamus's friends in the fray, watching with amusement. Char was falling off her shoes as she shook a finger at Miss Viv. Miss Viv's tiny hands were clenched into fists.

"Good Lord in heaven," Victoria said, and marched over to her sister. "What is going on here? And why did you leave me alone at the meeting?"

"Oh, sissy, I'm sorry," Miss Viv said, clasping her hands together. "But it was terribly boring. I came over to see if Seamus's friends were here, and Char started . . .

yelling at me." She looked at Char reproachfully. "Saying Seamus led Ray astray. She's just mad at me because she can't control her husband."

Stan grabbed Char's arm before she could clock Miss Viv. "Okay, ladies. Let's take it easy," she said. "Char, why don't you come with me?"

Victoria was dragging Miss Viv the other way, toward the door. She protested the entire time, but Victoria won and dragged her outside. Disappointed, everyone went back to their beers.

Char wrenched her arm free from Stan. "Shoulda let me hit her."

"Char. This is not the way to behave," Stan said. "Char!" But her friend had spotted Cyril and made a bee-line for him.

"Thank goodness!" she slurred. "I need to take out a personal ad."

"A *what*?" Cyril looked at Stan, astonished.

"Don't humor her," Stan muttered, but unfortunately Char heard her.

"Humor what? There's nothing to humor," Char huffed. "I'm getting divorced, and I need to get on the dating scene as soon as possible. Y'all know I'm not getting any younger, although I'm still a dish." She fluffed her hair.

"How much has she had to drink?" Cyril asked Stan.

"Jake said a lot," Stan confirmed. "I need to talk to you. But I have to get Char home."

"I'll help you." Cyril pocketed his notebook and stood. "Char," he said loudly, "let's go. We're going to take you home."

Char sent him a dirty look. "I'm drunk, honey, not deaf. Stan, why is he here?"

"I don't know, Char, probably to get a drink. Which now he's not getting. Come on. Let's go." She grabbed her friend's arm.

"Oh, I know. My personal ad." Char got up, swaying slightly. "I need to tell Cyril here all about that dirty skunk Raymond and what he's been up to."

"Char." Stan looked at Cyril and shook her head. "What happened to not talking about this, like I asked?"

Char frowned at her. "Don't tell me what to do, missy. I have nothing to be ashamed of."

"Well, if that's true," Cyril said, raising his eyebrows at Stan, "it's his loss. But remember, Char. I only run personal ads once a month. You'll have to wait for the next round to get on the schedule." He winked at Stan. She flashed him a thumbs-up.

"Let's go," Stan said, taking a firmer grasp of Char's arm to pull her along.

Cyril took Char's other arm. Stan waved to Jake, who watched from behind the bar, shaking his head. They went outside.

"How did you get here?" Stan asked.

"I drove."

"Well, we'll have to get your car tomorrow. Come on." They loaded her into Stan's car and drove to the B and B. Once Stan had put her to bed, she went down to where Cyril waited at the front door. They got back in Stan's car.

"What was *that* all about?" Cyril asked. "She's not really divorcing Ray, is she?"

Stan groaned. "You won't believe this." She told him about the phone call. "I think he was trying to tell her about the Book of Kells. She heard Kelly and thinks he was telling her he ran off with someone."

"Well. That's a mess," Cyril said.

"No kidding, crack reporter," Stan said.

"Hey, you don't have to get personal."

"One thing's bothering me about this whole mess, though," Stan said. "Did Jessie ever say what type of poison was used?"

Cyril shook his head. "Not to me. I asked. She deflected."

"Regardless. Poison seems like a lot of work for a gangster. Why wouldn't they just shoot Seamus?"

Cyril thought about it. "That's a good point."

"I mean, I still think the Book of Kells is the key, but that's tripping me up. I wish I could get someone like Kevin to really talk."

He smiled. "I may have a lead, actually."

"You do? What is it?"

"I can't tell you until I know if it pans out." He leaned closer. "But it may involve one of these so-called friends."

Stan frowned. "Who? Kevin?"

"Sit tight," Cyril said. "If all goes well, I'll tell you tomorrow."

Chapter Forty-nine

Stan tried the whole ride back to the pub to get him to tell her, but he refused to budge. She dropped him off, annoyed but grudgingly admiring of his dedication to his sources. She'd just gotten back to the house when her cell rang again.

"Hey," Izzy said. "Liam and I just went by your shop and there were lights on, but I didn't see your car. Wanted to make sure everything was kosher."

"Lights on?" Stan's heart started to pound. "I'm not there, and I know I didn't leave the lights on. Was there a car outside? Is Brenna there?"

"I didn't see anything. Want us to go back?"

"No," Stan said. "I don't know what's going on and I don't want you surprising someone who's not supposed to be there. I'll call Jessie. Thanks, Izzy."

She hung up and dialed Jessie's number. She answered on the first ring.

"Did you get my voicemail earlier?" Stan asked.

"I did. Was going to call you back. What's up?"

"I'll tell you that later. I have a new problem now. I

need you to meet me at my shop. Izzy just saw lights on over there, and no one's supposed to be there."

"Did the alarm go off?"

"Not that I know of."

"Did you call 911?"

"No, I called you," Stan snapped. "Can you go or not?"

Jessie muttered a curse. "Fine. I'll meet you there in ten."

Stan hung up and grabbed her coat. On second thought, she called Jake. "Can you meet me at the shop? Izzy saw lights on. Jessie's on her way too."

"On my way," Jake said. "Let me just ask Brenna if she can close up on her own. And Stan? Don't go inside until Jessie or I get there."

She didn't have to worry about it—by the time she drove up, Jessie was already there. There were no lights on now, and the store looked like it was in perfect order. Jessie had her flashlight in one hand, her gun in the other as she approached the front door. She shined the light around. No smashed windows, Stan noted with a flood of relief.

Jessie tried the door. It was locked. She turned to Stan. "You're sure no one who has a key came in to get something? Your mother, maybe?"

Stan shook her head. "I don't know why she would. The only people who are in here regularly are me, Brenna, and my sister sometimes."

"Did you talk to your sister?"

"I didn't. But—"

"Unlock the door."

Stan obeyed. Jessie stepped past her, pushing it open and continuing to shine her light over everything. Nothing seemed out of place. Nothing smashed. The new Christmas tree stood in its spot, blinking happily. Caitlyn had come in at some point and replaced the decorations.

Maybe she'd been doing that when Izzy saw the lights on. Shoot. Had they all overreacted?

"I'll call my sister," she said. "Maybe it was her."

Jake pushed open the front door and came in. "Everything okay?"

"Seems so," Jessie said. "Stan thinks maybe Caitlyn came in to put the decorations up. I'm going to finish taking a look around." She moved down toward the back, flicking on lights, shining her flashlight into the bathrooms and the storage closet as she made her way to the kitchen.

Stan dialed her sister's number. Jake went over to the alarm panel. "Is this supposed to be blinking?" he asked.

Her sister's phone went to voicemail. Stan left her a quick message to call, then came over and surveyed the alarm. "I don't think so," she said. "Why is it saying low battery?"

Jake moved behind the counter and picked up her cordless phone. He pressed the talk button and waited. No dial tone. "Your lines are down."

Down the hall, Jessie swore. They looked at each other, then hurried in her direction.

"What is it?" Jake asked, rushing into the kitchen, Stan on his heels. Jessie stood in the back doorway, blocking their view into the back parking area. "Jess, what—oh crap." Jake pulled up short next to his sister.

Stan could see the back floodlight—another security measure her mother had insisted on, given that they'd be using the back entrance often—shining brightly over the parking lot. But she couldn't see anything else.

"What?" she demanded, pushing past them. Then she stopped dead in her tracks, eyes widening in horror. A man lay in the parking lot directly behind her door. Unmoving. A plaid cap lay a few feet away. A cap that looked exactly like the one Kevin had worn the first night he'd shown up at the pub.

Chapter Fifty

Stan made a move to rush outside, but Jessie blocked her way. She pulled out her radio and called for backup and an ambulance. "Get back inside," she told them both. Jake pulled Stan inside the door, watching as his sister checked around and inside the dumpster—the only hiding place in the lot.

"Is that . . . is he . . ." Stan trailed off.

"It's not Kevin," Jake said. "But I think it's one of the guys who was staying at Char's."

Stan gasped. "No!" Please don't let it be Redhead, she prayed. Liam might find himself in the clink if it was. "Can you tell what happened to him?" She watched as Jessie circled the body once, twice, then leaned down and felt for a pulse. She must not have found anything, because she then pulled out her phone and started taking pictures.

Jake shook his head grimly. "But I didn't take a close look, Stan."

Another crime scene. This time, in her parking lot. Behind her new shop, which had just been vandalized last night. Had this person been on his way inside to do more damage? Why? And who had killed him on the way? And why was everything happening at her store?

Jake's cell rang. She could tell he thought about ignoring it, then changed his mind when he glanced at the caller ID. "It's Brenna. I told her I had to run over here, so she's going to want to know what's going on." He answered the call. And Stan watched his whole body go on alert. "What's wrong?"

Outside, they could hear the sirens as the ambulance got closer.

Stan moved closer to the phone, trying to hear too. Jake pressed the speaker-phone button and motioned for Jessie to come inside. Brenna's voice filled the room. She sounded angry.

"He said they want Uncle Seamus within twenty-four hours. Or they're going to come after us. His family. Starting with the prettiest." She snorted. "I don't know who he meant by that, but it better have been me."

"*What?*" Jake stared at Stan, his face ashen. "Bren, are you okay? I'm coming over there. I never should've left you alone tonight."

Stan felt paralyzed. If something had happened to Brenna . . . "We should go," she said to Jake, grabbing her keys. "Let's go get her."

"Wait. What happened?" Jessie demanded. "I missed that."

"Some guy wearing a black mask grabbed me in the parking lot when I went to put the trash out. He said they want Uncle Seamus," Brenna answered.

Jessie's eyes darkened. "Are you hurt?"

"No."

"Are you sure he's gone? Where's Scott? Did you call 911?"

"Scott won't be back until later." Brenna took a deep breath. "They're gone. I saw the car take off."

"What kind of car?"

"Some sedan. Black."

Like the one that'd followed Stan and Kevin the other night. She looked at Jake, knowing he was thinking the same.

"Stay where you are. Don't move. And make sure the doors are locked. I'll send someone over. And Jake's coming. I can't leave here right now." She grabbed her radio and called it in.

"Why? What happened there?" Brenna wanted to know.

They all looked at each other. "There's a dead guy in the parking lot," Jessie said, pocketing her radio.

Brenna was silent on the other end. Then, "You're kidding."

"Don't I wish," Jessie said. "Then I'd be home in bed."

"How'd he die?" Stan asked.

"He was shot."

Chapter Fifty-one

After all the reports were taken, the body moved and statements given to the press (Cyril), it was nearly one in the morning. Stan had been sitting in her car for the last hour with Jake, after they'd gone to the pub to be with Brenna while she gave her statement and waited for Scott to return. They'd tried to insist Brenna come home with them, but she refused to be uprooted from her home. So they'd eventually left. And since Jessie wouldn't let them anywhere near her shop, she'd settled for cranking the heat in the car and huddling against Jake.

"This is crazy," he said.

"You're not kidding." Stan sighed. The dead guy had indeed been one of Seamus's friends, the blond one who hadn't spoken much that day Stan had met them. At least Char was drunk and sleeping it off right now; otherwise she'd be in hysterics.

Jessie rapped on the window. "You may as well go home. We're wrapping up here."

They drove home in silence. When they pulled into the driveway Stan said, "Kevin hasn't been back. I haven't seen him since we talked about the Book of Kells two nights ago."

"Yeah," Jake said. "I noticed."

"What do you think that means?"

"Either he's involved, or he's in trouble. Or," Jake said, "he got sick of the whole business and went home."

When Stan woke up in the morning, she rolled over and looked at Jake. He was awake too, staring at the ceiling. "Was that dead guy in my parking lot a dream?" she asked.

He shook his head. "'Fraid not."

"I didn't think so." She dropped back down and covered her face with the pillow. "Jake. Do you think that guy was killed because of your uncle? Like, they're looking for him and thought he knew where he was?"

"I don't know," Jake said. "I'm still trying to sort this all out in my mind. I mean, my uncle, stealing the Book of Kells? This is going to sound bad but . . . I didn't think he was that smart."

Stan nearly laughed out loud. "I'm sorry," she said, clamping a hand over her mouth. "None of this is funny."

"You know what I mean. You heard Arthur. It's not easy to pull that off. No one's ever done it before. For my uncle to be the one . . . that's like some bad joke on the criminal empire." He sat up and rubbed his hands over his face. "And we have to get up, go to work, and be festive tonight with all this going on."

"I feel like we've been doing that all week," Stan said.

They agreed to meet back at the house that night before Stan left for her Christmas decoration contest judging duties. Jake would then go back to the pub and get ready for the party.

* * *

Stan hid in the kitchen at the store most of the day, baking. It always felt better to have her fingers in some dough. As she worked, she felt herself relax enough to approach the problems differently. Caitlyn had come over to handle the counter. Brenna had taken the day off, more shaken up about last night than she'd admitted.

As she worked, she realized she'd never told Jessie about the call from Ray last night. They'd been too distracted by the dead guy in the parking lot. The dead guy who'd been shot, not poisoned. She washed her hands and called her. "Can you come by the shop? I need to tell you something."

Surprisingly, Jessie agreed without a fight. While Stan waited for her, she thought more about the weapon that had killed Harold. And it didn't fit with what she knew about gangsters. Those guys, especially ones with something like the Book of Kells at stake—wouldn't mess around with poison. Most of them, she guessed, wouldn't have the patience to figure out how to make that work. They just wanted to pull out a gun and shoot. So whoever might be looking for Seamus because of his involvement in the theft likely wouldn't try to kill him that way.

So who did that leave? Stan worked the dough harder. Half of his family, certainly. Maybe some of his friends. But the same would apply to his poker friends—poison might not be their method of choice.

So that left a few people. Abby, for one. Whatever business deal she'd been involved in with Seamus had left her bitter, and broke. She'd said to Miss Viv that she'd had to raise her store prices just to make ends meet. That had to be stressful. And then there was the usual suspect—the significant other. But Miss Viv loved Seamus. Had for fifty-odd years. Why would she try to kill him now? Unless . . .

When Jessie walked in a minute later, Stan was just

sliding a tray of cookies into the oven. She straightened and looked at Jessie.

"Your uncle was involved in the Book of Kells theft," she said.

Jessie's hands went to her hips. "You called me down here for that?"

"You knew?" Stan asked, surprised.

"I told you before, I did earn my badge. Now, it's not to say I believe he masterminded it, but I think he fell into it somehow. Probably someone promised him a boatload of money if he became the chump who had to get rid of the goods. Which, knowing my uncle, is probably exactly what happened. So yeah, you're right. He's in big trouble."

"But that's not why someone tried to poison him," Stan said.

Jessie paused. "I'm listening."

"I think that was personal," Stan said. "Someone who's carried a lot of animosity toward him for a long time and finally couldn't take it anymore. This other thing is just playing out in tandem."

Jessie crossed her arms over her chest. "Okay. So what's your theory?"

Stan began scooping dough onto her cookie sheet. "I wondered if it was Abby. She's got a mean streak, you know? And she seems awfully bitter about whatever this business deal is. But I don't know if she could've pulled this off without blabbing to someone. So I don't think it's her.

"And then I thought maybe Miss Viv," Stan continued. "Because eventually everyone gets tired of waiting around and dealing with nonsense, right? Even if you've been doing it for most of your life. But she just doesn't seem that calculating to me." She paused and grabbed another cookie sheet, began dropping dough on it. "On the other hand, her sister does."

Jessie frowned. "Victoria? She's too proper to be a killer."

"I don't know," Stan said. "She seems very despondent over losing their land. She's fighting Kyle on the restaurant even though she doesn't have a leg to stand on. She's sad that all they're left with is a falling-down house. She said to me that once Viv leaves, she'll be alone in that place."

Stan could see the wheels turning in Jessie's head. "Do you know what type of poison it was?"

"Liquid nicotine," Jessie said. "Which is a dime a dozen. You can buy it literally anywhere. It doesn't seem like the sort of thing Victoria would know about, though."

"No, but her sister does," Stan said. "She uses those e-cigarettes. She had one the day I bumped into her on the sidewalk."

Jessie's cell rang, interrupting them. She grabbed it off her belt and answered. "Yeah." Then her whole body tensed. "I'll be right there."

Chapter Fifty-two

"Where are you going?" Stan asked as Jessie headed for the door.

"There's a problem at the B and B."

"At Char's?" Stan dropped her empty bowl of batter into the sink. "I'm coming with you."

"You certainly aren't," Jessie snapped.

"Watch me." She ran out front and handed the timer to Caitlyn. "I'll be back. Don't let my cookies burn."

She hurried out back, grabbed her coat, and ran out the door, jumping into the passenger seat of Jessie's cruiser. Jessie swore. "Damn it. I don't have time for this. You're staying in the car."

"Who called? Char? Is she okay?"

"Cyril," Jessie said. She pulled out her cell and called someone. "Get some cars over to the B and B. And keep this off the radio." She disconnected.

"Cars, plural?" Stan asked, her heart pounding in her chest. "What's going on, Jessie?"

"I don't know for sure. Cyril was going over there to talk to my uncle's friends. But he said he thought there might be something going on inside because the door's locked and no one's answering." She paused. "And there's a black sedan parked a little ways down the street with no license plate."

"Oh my God." Stan felt the greasy knot of fear clench her stomach. "Do you think Char's hurt?"

Jessie responded by flooring the car. They sped past the green, Stan's house flashing past in a blur, and careened around the corner onto Char's street, stopping before they got to the driveway. Jessie pulled onto the curb where they had a good view of the house and the west side of the farm, and threw her door open.

"Wait," Stan said. "You shouldn't go in there with no backup."

Jessie paused. "Right now you're my backup. And I need you out here. Call 911 if something goes wrong. If you can't agree to that, I'm going to cuff you to the steering wheel. I probably should anyway."

"Fine," Stan muttered.

Jessie got out and headed for the house, slipping into the yard to come up on the back door.

Stan watched anxiously from the passenger seat. She saw no movement from the house. No sign of Cyril, or anyone for that matter. Where were all the guests?

She fidgeted in her seat, praying for the rest of the cops to arrive soon. Then a movement off to the side of the house caught her eye.

Someone was cutting through the farm and heading to the back door.

She leaned forward for a closer look.

It was Kevin.

Chapter Fifty-three

Stan froze. What was he doing here? He could be looking for the other guys, his alleged friends that she'd never actually seen him meet up with. But then he'd go through the front door like everyone else. No, there had to be another reason. And Stan didn't feel good about it.

Ignoring Jessie's warning, she slipped out of the car, crouching down so she wasn't in full view of the windows in case someone was looking out. Keeping her eye on Kevin, she raced to Char's yard, arriving just as he reached for the door.

"What are you doing?" she demanded.

He spun around, his eyes wide with surprise. Stan's gaze landed on the gun in his hand. She opened her mouth to scream but he shook his head frantically, grabbing her and covering her mouth with his hand. She bucked and kicked, fighting him the whole way.

"Stop," he commanded, his grip like a vise. "I'm not here to hurt you. I'm here to save your friends."

Stan paused just as she was about to deliver a well-positioned knee strike, wondering if she should trust him.

If he wanted to shoot her, he could've done it already. She motioned him to let go of her mouth.

He looked wary about letting her go, but lifted his hand just slightly.

"What do you mean? The cops are coming, Kevin. One's already here. It's over."

"If you don't let me get in there, lass, it's going to be over and not in a good way. There are some bad men in there. Worse than me. Now. Get back in that car and wait for the police."

"Why don't you wait for them?" she asked suspiciously.

He smiled. "Because I'm a bad guy too. Just a different kind." He gave her a shove out of the way. "Now go."

And with that, he leapt back onto the porch. With one smooth flick of his elbow, he busted the window pane, reached in and unlocked the back door. Then Stan heard the gunshots, followed by screams.

Chapter Fifty-four

Stan dove around the side of the house and hit the ground, throwing her hands over her head. Who was shooting? Was Jessie okay? Char? Her heart felt like it was about to beat out of her chest and fly away. She fumbled for her cell phone and dialed 911.

"We need police. Lots of them. There's gunshots. I think someone's hurt." She rattled off Char's address and hung up despite the operator's attempts to keep her on the phone. She lay there, listening, but the shots had stopped. There was only silence from inside. A different kind of bad guy, Kevin said. What the heck did that even mean? Had she had a gangster staying at her house?

Then everything seemed to happen at once. Jessie shouting. Sirens blaring as the first round of cavalry arrived. Pounding footsteps as someone took off running.

Then Jessie burst out of the house, gun drawn, and ran halfway down the back yard. She paused, scanning the landscape, then turned and came back to the house. "What are you doing?" she demanded when Stan ran toward her. "I thought you were going to stay in the car!"

"Did you see him? Kevin?" Stan asked breathlessly. "He was here!"

"I saw him, alright. He shot the two guys who had Char, Cyril, and Seamus's crazy friends tied up. He took off out the back door."

"Tied up?" Stan shook her head. "Who are the guys? What did they want? Is Char okay? Cyril?" She took a step toward the house.

Jessie blocked her. "We'll figure out who they are when we do their autopsies. As for what they wanted, you were right. They were after my uncle, because they believed he had something they wanted. Now get back in the car. You'll see Char and Cyril soon."

Jessie headed to the front of the house, where Lou and five other cops converged, guns drawn. Stan followed, ignoring the directive to get back in the car. Two of the cops went inside to deal with whatever mess was in there, which Stan shuddered to think about. Char would be devastated that two gangsters had been shot in her beloved house.

"We have people in there who need to be brought out," Jessie called to them before turning to Lou. "Spread out and check the surrounding woods. White male, about six feet, brownish-blond hair."

"He had on a black jacket and jeans," Stan added.

"I think he's gone, but there might be others. Are there cars looking too?" Jessie asked.

Lou nodded. "We've got cars patrolling a three-mile radius around here. I'll call the description in. If he's on foot, we'll find him."

Stan wasn't so sure about that. Kevin had been stealthy as a cat when he'd shown up. And the way he busted in the door before even she realized what was happening. He didn't seem to be the type who operated on a team.

Another car careened up to the B and B and pulled into the driveway. Three men got out. One of them, the driver,

Stan had never seen before. The man who got out of the passenger seat was Ray Mackey. And the third man, who climbed out of the back seat, was Seamus McGee. He saw them and waved, as if he'd simply been down the street getting milk at the store.

"Holy . . . do you see who's here?" she asked, grabbing Jessie's arm.

"I do," Jessie said. "I got word they were coming. Someone else must've too."

"Hello there!" Seamus called, coming over to his niece. "It's good to be home!"

He looked like he was about to hug her, but Jessie bared her teeth at him. He pivoted and turned to Stan instead. She accepted the hug because she wasn't sure what else to do.

"Go wait in my car," Jessie snapped at him, handing him the keys and pointing. He did as he was told without argument.

Ray started toward the house, but one of the cops held him back. They promptly started arguing.

"Ray! Hold on a second. Char's fine. She's coming out shortly," Jessie called. "You can't go in there. It's a crime scene."

Ray looked like he was about to faint. The cop led him away from the porch as the ambulances screamed to the curb. People were starting to come out of their houses now and stood on the sidewalk, watching the action.

The driver walked over and shook Jessie's hand. "Joe Stanford. Special agent."

"Sergeant Pasquale. Thanks for bringing them down."

"Not a problem. My other agents here?"

"Special agent?" Stan asked. "Like, FBI?"

He nodded and glanced at Jessie. "Who's she?"

"Nancy Drew," Jessie said. "Did you recover the goods?"

"Yes. Seamus turned everything over to us in exchange for immunity. He claims he didn't know what was on the shipment he was supposed to collect. He just had instructions to meet the ship, pick up the car, and make the transfer to someone else. Then all hell broke loose. But turns out the shipment was actually in another car. We have the book back safe and sound, thanks to Seamus." Joe Stanford nodded admiringly. "There were a lot of people involved in this thing. They almost managed to pull it off."

Jessie opened her mouth to ask something else as another car pulled into the driveway. This place was starting to resemble Grand Central Station. Three more guys got out. Stan recognized them from the library event Cyril had held on the Book of Kells.

"Nice of you guys to show up after the action," Joe Stanford said to his men.

"Sorry," one of them said sheepishly. "We got held up by the lady at the general store."

"You guys are all FBI?" Stan asked, incredulous.

Joe nodded. "We tracked the activity here. Looks like there were a few people involved in this mess. Beginning with Kevin O'Malley, who works for a major crime figure in Ireland. He was the one who stole the Book in the first place. He commissioned someone else to sell it for him. That middle party is where your uncle came in," he said to Jessie. "The guy who hired him thought he'd outsmart the big guy by trying to sell it out from under him. But your uncle, ah, seemed to have panicked when things didn't go his way. Decided better broke than dead and called his old FBI pal and copped to the whole thing. Didn't work out too well, as those two inside will attest," he said with a grimace. "Both dead?"

Jessie nodded.

"O'Malley?"

"Gone like the wind."

"Doesn't surprise me. We'll never find him." Joe sighed. "He's good. He's pulled off a lot of heists in his time."

"So he . . . is a major criminal?" Stan asked, clearing her throat.

"Kevin O'Malley is one of the baddest guys to come out of Ireland," Stanford said. "I've been tracking his crew for a while. They have some Boston ties."

And he'd been living in her house. Sleeping on her couch. And yet, he'd let her live. Stan thought she might pass out.

Jessie grabbed her arm. "You okay?"

"I guess. Did you know . . ."

"Of course not! You think I'd let a mobster stay at your house?" Jessie shook her head. "Joe and I just put two and two together this morning when Seamus started telling the whole story. We were working on the best way to corner him, but the other bad guys jumped the gun."

"You're the lady whose shop was vandalized?" Joe Stanford asked Stan.

She nodded. "And had a dead guy left in my parking lot."

"Yeah. The two guys in there"—he jerked a finger toward the house—"must've thought you and O'Malley were in cahoots. That's why they targeted your shop. As for the dead guy, he was nobody."

"One of Seamus's friends," Jessie said. "Likely sticking his nose where it didn't belong, and it didn't end well."

"I like O'Malley for that too," Joe said. "He must've thought the guy was going to do more damage to your shop." He cast a sidelong look at Stan. "That's his other MO. He takes a shine to certain ladies. Looks like you were on his good side."

Stan tried to process that, but she couldn't. Instead she focused on Seamus and Ray. "So where have they been all this time?"

"Staying with Seamus's friend, the former FBI agent. This guy didn't loop us in until last night. Thought he was protecting Seamus and Ray by keeping them holed up with no contact, but he could've gotten a lot of people killed."

"Raymond!"

They all turned. Char had barreled out the door of the B and B, almost knocking the cop aside to get to her husband. She threw her arms around him and hugged him so tight Stan feared she'd break his back—he was half the size of her. Still, it was amazing to see them back together.

"I tried to call you so many times," he told her. "But I was hiding in a basement with no signal so I could never get through. Until that last time. I tried to tell you what was happening."

"I guess they won't be getting divorced," Jessie said, but she was smiling.

"I guess that's what all the calls we thought were pranks were about," Stan said.

Another cop, followed by Cyril, came out of the house next. Despite whatever harrowing experience he'd lived through inside, Cyril had his notebook out and dogged the officer all the way back to his car. Finally he turned and came over to where Stan stood with Jessie.

"Can you imagine what a story this will be? A first-hand account of being held hostage by people who may have actually touched the Book of Kells! My dad will be so proud. And we'll get to interview one of the peripheral thieves." He beamed. "It's a good day to be a journalist."

Chapter Fifty-five

The next day, Stan stood in the doorway of her shop watching the train of pets come through to get their pictures taken with Santa. Seamus had recovered enough from his ordeal to happily don his Santa suit. He played the role to the hilt, making up for lost time. Tyler Hoffman shot photos for the paper as Miss Viv watched from a café table.

"You think she's doing okay?" Jake asked Stan, coming up next to her.

"I don't know. How can she be? Her sister tried to kill her boyfriend." The whole thing was terribly sad. After the excitement at the B and B had been sorted out yesterday, Jessie had gone to talk to Victoria. Stan's theory had been right. It didn't feel good to be right, in this case. But Victoria had confessed without incident. "She told Jessie she didn't want to be alone."

Jake shook his head. "So sad. For everyone involved. And poor Harold. Collateral damage in all this."

"Yeah. I have no idea how we're being festive today. And, man, I can't wrap my head around this Kevin thing."

"Don't even talk about it," Jake said. "I can't believe . . ." He trailed off.

"Never mind that, what does it say about my gut?" Stan asked. "I swore he was okay. But maybe in a way he was. In a weird way, he was looking out for me. The FBI guy said so."

"Yeah, well, I can look out for you. You don't need a gangster to do it. Jeez. Hey, listen to this, though. Seamus said this morning that he and Miss Viv might stay here in Frog Ledge. He wants to live here full time."

Stan's mouth dropped. "Here? Why?"

"Viv wants to be near her sister, whatever happens to her," Jake said. "And sounds like she's fine with giving up the island life. I guess Seamus is ready to come back to the States full time. I think this thing really shook him up."

"What about Izzy though?" Stan asked. "That's going to make her life hard."

"I don't think he'll be giving her any more trouble," Jake said, his eyes twinkling. "My dad laid down the law. I expect Izzy and Liam will be getting a heartfelt apology in the coming days."

"Wow. Just like that?"

"I think Seamus, despite his carefree attitude, had a moment where he thought this time he may have pushed his life to the limit," Jake said. "My guess is he'll be looking for a more low-key existence going forward." He nodded to where Caitlyn and Brenna worked the counter. "Your sister looks happy."

"They won the house-decorating contest. She's over the moon," Stan said. "And while they feel terrible about Victoria, I think this means Kyle's restaurant won't be blocked anymore. Which is a huge relief to them."

"So after one of the craziest weeks in Frog Ledge history, I hesitate to say it ended well, but better than it could've," Jake said.

Stan nodded. "Absolutely."

"Although there's one thing that could make it better."

"Yeah? What's that?" Stan asked, watching one of the dogs lick Seamus's beard. When Jake didn't answer right away, she turned her attention back to him.

And gasped. He held a small ring box in his hand, and he was smiling.

"Stan Connor, will you marry me?"

Recipes

Chicken Ginger Biscuits

Ingredients:
2 cups whole wheat flour
½ cup wheat germ
1 tablespoon ground ginger
½ cup chicken broth
1 egg
¼ cup vegetable oil

Directions:
Preheat oven to 375° F.
Combine all ingredients in a large bowl and mix until well blended.
On a lightly floured surface, knead the dough and roll out to 1/4 inch thickness. Using cookie cutters, cut into desired shapes.
Repeat rolling and cutting until all dough is used.
Place biscuits on a greased baking sheet and bake for 25 minutes.
Let cool and serve!

Sweet Potato Treats

Ingredients:
1 large sweet potato
¼ cup vegetable oil
⅛ cup honey
1 egg
1 cup unbleached white flour

Directions:

Preheat oven to 350° F.

Bake sweet potato in oven for about 30 minutes. Cool, peel, and cut potato into small pieces.

In mixing bowl, combine oil and honey. Add egg and potato and mix thoroughly. Add flour and finish mixing.

Drop spoonfuls of mixture onto a lightly greased cookie sheet.

Bake for 20 minutes.

Cool and serve!

Fish Food Treat

Ingredients:

3 cups unbleached white flour
½ cup cornmeal
½ cup wheat germ
1 cup water
½ cup vegetable oil
1 can tuna in water, drained

Directions:

Preheat oven to 350° F.

In large bowl, combine all ingredients.

On a lightly floured surface, knead the dough until firm.

Roll the dough out to ½ inch thickness. Use a fish-shaped cookie cutter to cut cookies.

Transfer to a baking sheet and bake for 30 minutes.

Let cool and serve!

Treats can be dehydrated to last longer.

Honeydew Ice

Ingredients:
2 pounds honeydew melon
¼ cup water
3 tablespoons honey
1 tablespoon fresh lemon juice

Directions:
Cut the honeydew into 1-inch chunks.
Combine the melon, water, honey and lemon juice in a blender and purée the mixture.
Pour the mixture into ice-cube trays. Freeze until solid.
Serve as a whole ice cube for a dog to lick away at, or place a few ice cubes in a small ziplock bag and crush to serve in a dish.

Simple Doggie Fro-yo

Ingredients:
32 ounces of nonfat plain Greek yogurt
Choose 1-½ cups of peanut butter, blueberries, or strawberries as your flavor

Directions:
Combine all yogurt and your flavoring of choice in a blender until well mixed.
Pour into 3-ounce Dixie cups and freeze.
To serve, unwrap Dixie cup from fro-yo once fully frozen and place in a doggie dish!

Acknowledgments

I always say this, but it's never been more true than this time—writing a book is not a solitary process. There are certain people without whom this book might never have made it to the shelf, and I owe them many thanks.

Jessie Crockett and Sherry Harris, two of my fellow Wicked Cozy Authors, thank you for all the plotting brainstorming and crack editing you provided under the gun to help me make this a readable story. I am so grateful for you both being there when I needed you the most. You guys rock.

Thank you to John Talbot, my awesome agent, for guiding me through this sometimes crazy process and always providing a voice of reason when I most need it. You've been an amazing partner for many years now, and I'm grateful for you.

Also super grateful for John Scognamiglio, my editor at Kensington, for keeping Stan alive. And for the whole Kensington team for making the finished product fabulous, from cover art to blurb to promotion. I'm very lucky to be part of this publishing house.

And the rest of my Wicked Cozy sisters—Barbara Ross, Julie Hennrikus and Edith Maxwell—you guys know how much you mean to me. Thank you all for being so supportive, in both the book world and personal world. Again, so grateful.

A huge shout out to the loyal readers of the Pawsitively Organic Mysteries—there would be no books without you on the other end. The animals and I are so grateful to you all for supporting Stan and her adventures. And to all the librarians and booksellers who help connect us writers with the readers, thank you. It's so gratifying to have a forum where we can all meet in person.

And finally, Gareth Moss. Thank you for lending your expertise in everything Irish to the plot of this book. But most of all, thank you for coming into my life at the perfect time. You've changed everything. X